The viscount remained silent until Jackson p— a halt before Number Thirty Green Street. Suddenly he chuckled aloud and squeezed her hand in an oddly affecting way. "You may presume what you like, Adele. Only do not expect me to apologize for kissing you."

"But why?" she demanded as he threw open the door and let down the step. Her heart was pounding so hard she thought he must surely be able to hear it. But if he did, he made no sign as he assisted her out of the coach and to her entrance, then removed the key from her trembling fingers and unlocked the front door. Adele passed over the threshold before he entered, and returned the key to her.

He raised his golden eyebrows as though condemning himself for a fool. *"Why* should I apologize?"

"No, my lord, that isn't what I meant," she said, placing her hand on his sleeve. "I . . . why did you kiss me?" She felt very foolish and was about to remove her hand, but he covered her fingers and held them gently, but firmly.

"Did you not like it?" he asked.

Stunned, she raised her face to meet his unwavering gaze and said, "Too well. Perhaps I should beg *your* pardon, for being too forward or too—"

To her complete surprise, he stole another kiss before saying, "Now you must send me away. But I shall return in a week's time, hoping you will remember your promise."

"I shall do my best," she whispered. And she let his arm slip out of her fingers, saying, "Take care of yourself on the way."

ZEBRA'S REGENCY ROMANCES
DAZZLE AND DELIGHT

A BEGUILING INTRIGUE (4441, $3.99)
by Olivia Sumner

Pretty as a picture Justine Riggs cared nothing for propriety. She dressed as a boy, sat on her horse like a jockey, and pondered the stars like a scientist. But when she tried to best the handsome Quenton Fletcher, Marquess of Devon, by proving that she was the better equestrian, he would try to prove Justine's antics were pure folly. The game he had in mind was seduction — never imagining that he might lose his heart in the process!

AN INCONVENIENT ENGAGEMENT (4442, $3.99)
by Joy Reed

Rebecca Wentworth was furious when she saw her betrothed waltzing with another. So she decides to make him jealous by flirting with the handsomest man at the ball, John Collinwood, Earl of Stanford. The "wicked" nobleman knew exactly what the enticing miss was up to — and he was only too happy to play along. But as Rebecca gazed into his magnificent eyes, her errant fiancé was soon utterly forgotten!

SCANDAL'S LADY (4472, $3.99)
by Mary Kingsley

Cassandra was shocked to learn that the new Earl of Lynton was her childhood friend, Nicholas St. John. After years at sea and mixed feelings Nicholas had come home to take the family title. And although Cassandra knew her place as a governess, she could not help the thrill that went through her each time he was near. Nicholas was pleased to find that his old friend Cassandra was his new next door neighbor, but after being near her, he wondered if mere friendship would be enough . . .

HIS LORDSHIP'S REWARD (4473, $3.99)
by Carola Dunn

As the daughter of a seasoned soldier, Fanny Ingram was accustomed to the vagaries of military life and cared not a whit about matters of rank and social standing. So she certainly never foresaw her *tendre* for handsome Viscount Roworth of Kent with whom she was forced to share lodgings, while he carried out his clandestine activities on behalf of the British Army. And though good sense told Roworth to keep his distance, he couldn't stop from taking Fanny in his arms for a kiss that made all hearts equal!

Available wherever paperbacks are sold, or order direct from the Publisher. Send cover price plus 50¢ per copy for mailing and handling to Penguin USA, P.O. Box 999, c/o Dept. 17109, Bergenfield, NJ 07621. Residents of New York and Tennessee must include sales tax. DO NOT SEND CASH.

The Fashionable Miss Fonteyne

Cynthia Richey

ZEBRA BOOKS
KENSINGTON PUBLISHING CORP.

*For Betty and John Crump, with love. Thanks for
Accentuating the Positive, Mom and Dad.*

ZEBRA BOOKS are published by

Kensington Publishing Corp.
850 Third Avenue
New York, NY 10022

Zebra and the Z logo Reg. U.S. Pat. & TM Off.

First Printing: November, 1994

Printed in the United States of America

One

It could not truly be said that Dysart Carter, Viscount Windhaven, marched into Miss Adele Fonteyne's saloon, for his movements were more languid than precise, and his bearing more relaxed than soldierly. In his impeccably tailored blue coat—enhanced by his golden hair, arranged *a là Titus,* and his angelic smile—straw-coloured breeches and top-boots he wore the uniform of the Bow-window set, in whose exalted company he travelled. And, like his associates, he was known as one who rarely stirred himself on another's account, or risked wrinkling his trousers, tearing his elegant coat or spoiling his neck-cloth for anything but sport.

Despite his top-lofty appearance and reputation, Adele could not help but regard him in an heroic light. Rising from the piano where she had been practicing Mozart to entertain her cousin who was recovering from influenza, she moved gracefully towards the viscount.

"Look, Elvira," she said to her cousin, a teasing lilt masking the genuine delight she felt at seeing her visitor. "See, the conquering hero returneth."

"If you mean to tax me over my accidental heroics at Waterloo," Windhaven said, his tone waxing on irritated boredom, "I shall go home at once." But he took the hand she stretched towards him and bussed her cheek in the familiar manner of good friends.

His lips brushing her soft cheek set her pulse aflutter, but disciplining herself, she said, "Welcome back to London, my lord."

"You will never convince Adele you did not mean to save the duke," Elvira said in a voice that sounded as if her shoes pinched her toes.

Windhaven flushed momentarily, before he regained his customary care-for-nothing manner. "I was merely in a position to do my commander a service," he said. "Anyone would have done as well."

Elvira sniffed into a handkerchief then said, "I do not know why you scorn noble deeds."

"Do you not?" Windhaven asked in mild, but challenging, tones. "To lower expectations, Miss Willoughby." He directed a curt bow towards Miss Fonteyne's older cousin, then turned an amused smile on his hostess.

"Really?" Adele asked as she twinkled at him. "Then your reputation is safe with us, for I hold no expectation of you."

"Ah," he said on a long, pensive breath. Gently squeezing Adele's hand, he teased, "May I hope you missed me?"

Gentle, becoming color infused Adele's cheeks, but she replied in a light tone, "I will say only that town life was rather flat in your absence."

He chuckled. "If you recall, the duchess said you ought to join her, but you *would* remain in town."

To confess she had chosen to remain in town to nurse Elvira through a bout of the influenza would have been unfashionable in the extreme. Rather than allow Windhaven to praise her noble sacrifice when he deprecated his own, Adele airily replied, "I had better things to do than wait in smoky halls for country gentlemen to return muddied from the hunt to loudly rehearse their glorious escapades."

"I imagine," he said, arching a satirical eyebrow in challenge, "that those Eligibles still remaining in town wasted no time in courting you."

"Don't be silly, Windhaven," Adele laughed. "Their only interest is courting my fortune. At least I am comfortable that you like me and not my gold."

"Good thing I do like you so well," he agreed, before chuckling, "Otherwise you might have punctured my colossal pride with your helpful suggestions concerning fashion."

His arch commentary stung Adele's feelings. Unaccustomed to being on the receiving end of his lofty censure, she said, "I assure you I remark oddities out of the noblest intentions."

"Of that I have no doubt," he agreed, tucking her arm within his and leading her towards the sofa. "Since I do not affect oddities, you can scarcely have spared a thought to me in the past month."

She could not suppress a chortle of laughter before exclaiming, "Would it make you happy to know how often I *did* think of you?"

Miss Willoughby sniffed audibly, as if to recall Adele to more modest demeanor. Windhaven, casting a dark glance towards the omnipresent chaperone, appeared to wish her gone. Then returning a carefully benign look upon Adele, he said, "I can say for certain that I occupied your thoughts only on two occasions."

Sinking onto the gold brocade of the sofa and offering him a place beside her, she allowed, "I did not write too many letters, thinking you might not like to be troubled to read them."

Spreading the tails of his coat, the viscount lounged at Adele's side, saying, "I delighted in both of them." He touched the left breast of the coat. Hearing the slight rustle of paper, Adele raised an enquiring look upon him and blushed when he said, "You brought the sparkle of town life into my dull country existence. I could not put your letters down."

He was gazing upon her with a steady sincerity so uncharacteristic as to lead her to believe he was taxing her for offering the simple diversion of correspondence. Unhappily, she removed her gaze from his and said, "Rural life did not seem to benefit you, my lord."

He regarded her silently before allowing, "You are the first to say so."

Without asking, she knew he was referring to the ladies who had been invited to fritter away the month with the Duchess of Redfern while the men gambled and hunted with the duke. Those returning early had been full of Windhaven's recent conquests.

Adele had no desire to hear about them from his lips. In as unaffected a tone as she could contrive, she said, "Pray do not bore me with an account of your latest flirtations, my lord. It takes very little effort to charm a country miss."

"But an exhaustive one to entertain her city cousin," he said, in self-deprecating tones. Then, affecting a stern facade, he growled, "If you are going to 'my lord' me to death, Adele, I shall return to the simple life."

Even though his eyes twinkled with mischief while he delivered his rebuke, Adele could not but feel he was serious. She pursed her lips to quell a mortified rejoinder, then sighed, "I hoped you might have missed London."

"I did," he confessed, leaning against the gold silk until his shoulder brushed hers. "But the roads were devilish bad, I couldn't travel for the mud. Looking back, I should never have gone."

"*I* told you not to go," said Miss Willoughby, in the tone of a martyr to whom no one pays attention.

"So you did," Windhaven recalled amiably. "But my period of rustication was not entirely wasted. I feel able to slay dragons now."

"Who wrought this miracle?" Adele enquired before she caught the corner of her lower lip between her teeth to suppress more anxious queries.

Laughing, Windhaven said, "If I said I have done it for you, you would only smack my hand with your fan and call me a tease. No, I am only well rested . . ."

"Now you sound like a doddering grey top," Adele said.

"Thank you," he replied. "Perhaps I shall need the sober disposition of an elder, for I have just been recalled to duty," he said with the cheerful anticipation of one who is about to take a plunge into icy water.

Stunned, Adele enquired, "Did you decide to marry one of the duchess's pretty guests?"

"That honor I was able to avoid," Windhaven allowed. He chuckled as if he had known she must misapprehend his meaning, then withdrew a letter from the inner pocket of his coat, saying, "This, I found I cannot decline as easily."

Before accepting the paper, Adele responded, "I do not see *why* you cannot. It has never been difficult for you to say no."

"Read the letter," he said, crossing his legs at the knee, which posture, Adele noticed with appreciation, did not in the least spoil the crease in his trousers. It was one of the least of the reasons she admired him, but one that never ceased to amaze her.

Removing her admiring gaze from his superb frame to pluck the parchment from his fingers, she quickly scanned the letter, which she deduced must have been written by a parson, from the references to "earthly travail," "unfortunate child," and "bosom of our Lord." She gathered that the viscount's late friend had made Windhaven his daughter's guardian. Regarding the viscount, she refolded the letter and said incredulously, "You do not mean to bring a little girl into your home?"

"That certainly was not my intention," he said. "What does a parson expect me to do with a child? I am a bachelor, and know nothing that would benefit a pretty little girl."

She returned the folded letter to him which he placed within his coat. Nodding sympathetically, she said, "Certainly it will entail a few sacrifices."

"More than a few," Windhaven began unfeelingly. Then, as if remembering a debt of honor, he said, "But her father was my closest friend. It is only to be expected that I should protect his daughter. But to bring her out . . ."

Miss Fonteyne knew that was a task to which Viscount Windhaven, for all his talents, was unequal. She would have no concerns as to his ability to guide Arthur

Gaines's son, had the unfortunate man been blessed with an heir, in the manners and conduct of a gentleman.

But like most men, Windhaven was insensible of a woman's feelings or her needs. A little girl would tax his patience beyond anything. He would need help.

Miss Fonteyne hoped he would turn to her for this badly needed support. Though she doubted her own ability to mold an impressionable child into a properly behaved young lady, she did know someone who was fit for the charge. Sliding a sidelong look at her companion who was obliviously stitching a border around a handkerchief, she said to Windhaven, "Go, fetch your ward; I shall discover one who can make your charge less burdensome."

An expression of pain clouded Windhaven's blue eyes as two dark furrows creased his fair brow. Adele wondered if he had suddenly been taken ill. He did not ease her concern when he was finally capable of speech, for he said in tones of extreme nausea, "I should prefer to place my ward in a seminary or day school."

"To be sure, I will make enquiries among the better schools in town," she replied, hesitantly. "However, I beg you to consider your ward's feelings."

His tone continuing rather afflicted, he

said, "You might consider mine." Folding his hands behind his back, he began to pace as he listed his objections to having a child in his establishment. "I live in bachelor's quarters. I entertain regularly, and my friends are not completely heedful of their language. It is entirely unsuitable to bringing up a little girl."

Adele meekly agreed that it was, adding, "But you could give Priscilla a home at Wind's Rest. You have been saying you wished to make the land profitable. It is the perfect time to begin."

He grimaced at her reminder of his neglected plans for his seat in Somerset, saying, "That would mean abandoning town at the beginning of the Season."

"I beg your pardon," Adele said.

"No, I have had quite enough of the country already," he said vehemently, flopping into a delicate bergere chair.

"Please, my lord," Adele said, as the chair creaked in protest. "It is not necessary to destroy my furniture to confirm my suspicions that you have not yet grown up."

He assumed a more dignified posture, as he said, "I beg your pardon?"

"I believe you understand me," she replied severely. "You are sulking, Windhaven."

He raised an eyebrow loftily. Tutting him,

she said, "You are, you know." She thought she detected his lip curling in a disdainful manner and scarcely managed to conceal a rueful smile behind her own hand. "Wretched man," she chided. "Do you think you are entitled to act the ogre because you have a cross to bear?"

"No, I beg your pardon," he replied. Then, his customary good humor restored by her gentle reproach, he enquired, "Are you still glad to see me?"

"A little less than I was," she replied, not willing to own the complete truth, that she would be glad to see him for any reason. Quickly reassuming a comfortably teasing manner, she said, "How lowering to discover your thoughts full of another lady. I must retire at once to recover my spirits."

Casting an appreciative eye over her slender, elegant form, Windhaven chuckled. "You needn't consider little Priscilla a rival. She cannot be more than eight or nine."

"I have not yet considered any lady a rival."

Miss Willoughby snorted derisively. When Adele favored her with a quelling stare, the other lady said in her tart manner, "You are too sure of yourself, Cousin. Unless a certain gentleman . . ." she slid a meaningful glance towards the viscount, but left her comment unfinished.

Immediately, Adele felt the warmth of embarrassment flood her cheeks. Though she willed herself not to look at Windhaven, she could not suppress a covert glance at him beneath her lashes. To her mortification, he was laughing.

Suppressing the flood of hot embarrassment with an effort of will, she said in an affable tone, "You are quite out, Elvira. Lord Windhaven and I would never suit."

"Indeed." He agreed rather too quickly to be pleasing, and continued in a manner rather too glib for Adele's satisfaction. "Miss Fonteyne is devoted to the Goddess of Fashion; I worship before the altar of the Almighty Neckcloth. We scarce spare a glance towards one another for admiring our own reflections in the glass."

Miss Willoughby sniffed behind her handkerchief and said, "You suit perfectly." Sniffing disdainfully, she added, "A fine pair you are to bring up a child. You will soon have her bowing and scraping to your false gods."

Miss Willoughby's uncivil assertion momentarily suspended her cousin's power of speech. Windhaven, however, did not waver before the dragon's disapproving stare. Snapping open an enamelled snuff box, he intoned, "How fortunate we are to prosper from your excellent understanding." While

Adele's companion preened before his sarcastic praise, he inhaled a pinch and replaced the container into his waistcoat pocket in an arrogantly dismissive manner that never failed to depress presumptive Nobodies.

Miss Willoughby arose, saying, "I detect a chill in the air, Cousin. I know a lady never feels the cold, but I fear the damp has invaded my bones. Shall I fetch your shawl too?"

"No, thank you," Adele replied. "But do see to your own comfort. Why do you not have the maid build up the fire in your room? I know how you enjoy your embroidery, and the light is so much better overlooking the garden."

"Yes, the southern exposure," agreed Miss Willoughby. "You are so kind, Cousin, but how can I leave you?" Unchaperoned, she did not say, but her suspicious glance at the viscount said it for her. "And what if you wished to play the piano? How can you practice without my help? I am forever turning your pages, and reminding you of your flats and sharps . . ."

"Yes," Adele laughed. "You are a great . . . help, my dear. Only you have just recovered from the influenza, and I shouldn't wish you to suffer a relapse."

Immediately Elvira gave over her arguments. "No, I shan't bother you any more," she said, gathering up her sewing basket and moving in fits and starts toward the door. "I am going, because you are so kind to think of me. But I shall return." Pausing at the door, she asked, "Are you sure I can do nothing for you?"

"Would you be so kind as to request tea?" Adele asked. "And don't forget to ask for your own favorite blend to be delivered to your room while you rest."

Stumbling on the threshold, Miss Willoughby said, "As you wish," in the familiar tone of the reluctant martyr.

A moment after she left, leaving the door ajar for propriety's sake, Windhaven propelled himself forwards and closed it. "Do you suppose she has gone for good, or will she return to make sure I don't take advantage of you?"

Adele sighed. "I cannot help but be sorry for Elvira. She feels her responsibility very keenly."

"Too keenly," he agreed mockingly. Rather than returning to his vacated chair, he crossed to the mantel, to gaze intently into the mirror.

Realizing the futility of wishing that he would bestow such a long, appreciative look upon her, Adele said, "No, she is only doing her duty," she allowed. "Only, I own it is difficult being the sole object of her concern."

"Don't put up with it," Windhaven said lazily as he adjusted his flawless cravat. "I should have turned her off long ago for being a meddlesome old maid."

"You don't mean it, Dy. Elvira has no where else to go." Arising from the settee, she glided across the floor, and placed a hand on his sleeve. Meeting his reflected gaze, she said, "She doesn't approve of us, you know."

"*I* don't need her approval," he replied, leaning an elbow on the mantel piece.

"You do," she said in a serious tone. "You will rely upon her when your ward is installed in London."

"She will have nothing to say about bringing up Priscilla," Windhaven declared as he pushed away from the warmth of the fireplace and strode across the room.

Adele turned and, with her gaze followed his progress to the far end of the salon and back.

When he returned, he still looked aggravated. But he suddenly grinned and said, "I do not want Elvira's help. But I do need yours."

"Oh, no," she said quickly. Lowering her gaze to the carpeted floor, she hesitated before she confessed, "I don't wish to meddle."

"No, of course you do not," he soothed in a voice that drew her attention as a magnet draws iron. As she raised her hazel-colored eyes to his twinkling blue ones, he possessed himself of her hand and said feelingly, "But I do need your help."

Strangely affected by his urgent manner, Adele called upon her worldly wisdom to control the erratic thumping of her heart. She was no green girl to wear her heart on her sleeve, especially for a dandy who exhibited too great an affection for his own reflection to bother courting a lady.

Such sentiments were far too volatile if she wished to count him her friend. Controlling her foolish romantical flutterings, she said in a remarkably steady voice, "I am wise to your cajoling ways, Lord Windhaven." As he closed one eye in a teasing wink, her heart thumped still harder. She was obliged to add in choked tones, "But I am not completely immune to them."

"I hoped you would confess one weakness," he teased.

"I hope it will not be my undoing," Adele replied, adding hesitantly, but with feeling, "But I shall do whatever is in my power to help you."

He bent over her hand as if he meant

to kiss it. In their sophisticated circle, the gesture was reserved for slightly eccentric ladies in their dotage. Suddenly and with startling clarity, Adele envisioned herself as the viscount must see her: not as the acknowledged leader of fashion among London ladies, but a pathetic ape leader. It was a vision guaranteed to fluster her.

Disengaging her fingers, she clasped them behind her back and said, "You have my word on it; pledged between friends."

"Yes, thank you," he agreed in a wry tone. "Now I can fetch Priscilla from Yorkshire at once."

Gone was Adele's joy in Windhaven's visit. However, she tried to answer brightly as she said, "You will scarcely make St. Albans before dark."

"Pea-goose." The viscount pinched her cheek gently. The teasing caress did nothing to make her feel less ancient or eccentric. "I did not mean to set out at this moment." He snapped his fingers as though recalling a prior commitment. "I cannot stay on; we are engaged with Lady Mathilda Castleton. And Lord Alvanley has invited me to dine with him."

"Very well," Adele said with an indulgent smile, "Since the arbiter of the school for scandal has called you to his groaning board, you are excused from my puny table."

"As a matter of fact, I refused his summons." Windhaven replied in an offhand manner. Placing the flat of his hand on the door panel as if he was loathe to leave, he added, "I accepted Lady Mathilda's invitation."

Remembering that lady's past dinner parties, Adele mused, "I fear the conversation at her table will fall sadly flat of that at Alvanley's."

"No doubt," he said, a curious grin curving his mouth as he met Adele's enquiring gaze. The look quickened her pulse, especially as she was caught between him and the closed door. He regarded her a long time before adding, "I was influenced more by the absence of beauty at Alvanley's table."

Rather breathlessly, Adele said, "I daresay you will take the shine out of all us ladies." She gave an unconscious toss of her head that caused an errant lock of hair to slide enticingly from its knot and caress the curve of her throat.

Removing his hand from the door to wind the curl around his finger, he said, "That is like the sun accusing the moon of casting her in the shade."

It was so unlike the Viscount Windhaven

to utter such an effusive compliment, that
Adele was startled into raising a hand to
his shoulder. But instead of resisting him,
she ran her fingers with pleasure over the
firm muscles that attested to regular bouts
at Jackson's Parlor. Beneath his high shirt
points and exquisitely tailored coat, he was
a powerful man who could take what he
desired by force. But instead, he was drawing her nearer, gently, by coiling her hair
about his finger.

Caught as she was, she could not help
but tilt her face invitingly upwards to meet
his steady gaze. Though her eyes widened
in awe, Adele knew no fear, for Windhaven
had always called her a friend. She closed
her eyes against a poignant, foolish longing
that he might look upon her with affection.

As her lashes shaded her eyes, his lips
gently covered hers. Her heart began an
erratic, agitated rhythm, inspiring her to
mold her slender form to his.

She was glad for the arm he had placed
gently around her waist. When at last he
broke away, she was surprised a simple kiss
could leave her trembling and so weak that
even raising her eyelashes was beyond her
ability.

But she was compelled to find the
strength. Of a sudden, he placed her on

her feet and strode off, muttering under his breath.

Retreating to cling to the back of a chair, Adele struggled to regain her composure. His kiss had delighted her; her quick response and his hasty withdrawal frightened her. She wanted him to kiss her again, yet suspected she had given him a revulsion of her manners in her impetuous response. Her confusion erupted in the shaken and trite reproach, "You forget yourself, my lord."

Turning to gaze upon her, he ceased his mutterings. "Have I?" he asked after a moment's deliberation. A wicked smile suddenly creased his face. "I own it is a new experience."

It was for Adele also, and she was not comfortable in it. Attempting to quell the fearful, exciting cadence still thrumming in her breast, she hid behind a mask of gentle reproach, "I think you have been too long out of polite company."

"You may be right," he agreed. He clasped his hands behind his back and strode towards her, lowering his golden head in a confidential manner. "Your radiance must have singed my wings. That is what comes of soaring too close to the sun."

Though his compliment elevated her, Adele disciplined herself not to encourage a dangerous flirtation. Windhaven was, some said, a hardened bachelor. They said he was no more likely to step into leg shackles than Beau Brummell. And if he did, Windhaven certainly could take his pick among the most beautiful, young ladies in London. Against such odds, Adele stood no chance.

The comparison brought her to earth with an unpleasant thud. "I know flattery when I hear it," she said. "You ought to forego Lady Mathilda's party, and sharpen your wit on Alvanley."

"My wit is not in the slightest need of repair," Windhaven declared, throwing open the door and striding into the hallway. "Do you go alone to the dinner?"

She followed him down the stairs. As they reached the bottom step, she remembered that Grosvenor Square lay between Green Street and St. James's. "It is very tempting to accept your escort," she teased, "But am I not rather out of your way?"

"You ask this of a man about to brave the wilds of the North Country to fetch a child sight unseen?" Windhaven enquired, his eyebrow raised in teasing challenge.

"I forgot you are about to try a new venture," she said in a distracted manner. "So I will not put you out. Elvira goes with me."

Shuddering, he shrugged into his greatcoat and said, "Then you are well chaperoned and don't need me." He winked and kissed her cheek, flustering her once more. "Until tonight." Then he was gone.

Two

Teacup in hand, Miss Willoughby awaited Adele in the gold salon. "I thought Windhaven meant to take tea with us."

Accepting the cup which her companion had poured out, Adele sat in the bergere chair on which was draped a shawl. "He could not stay."

"He might have said so at once," Miss Willoughby said raising her cup to her lips. Very promptly she lowered it, complaining, "Mrs. Murphy knows I don't like Gunpowder tea."

"Very likely, she prepared it for the viscount," Adele replied, setting her own cup on the spindle-legged side table and arranging the paisley gracefully about her shoulders. "You know how she dotes on him."

Miss Willoughby shuddered as if she knew all too well the housekeeper's fondness for Lord Windhaven. "Only because you encourage him to run tame in the house," she said with a moue of distaste. "It sets tongues a-wagging."

"The viscount is my friend, Elvira; there is nothing about him to cause scandal," Adele replied. A sly inward voice scolded that her response to his lovemaking was the essence of scandal. Aloud she said, "He is very discreet."

Her tone confidentially cutting, Elvira said, "He is a dandy, throwing good money after bad on things that moths will eat and rust will rot."

Bestowing a repentant look upon her companion, Adele said, "I take your point, Cousin."

"Oh, I did not mean to criticize *you,*" Elvira countered. "You are the soul of compassion. Only think how you cared for me while I lay near death with the influenza. Anyone else would have hired a nurse to—"

"Yes, well, don't paint me in saint's robes just yet," Adele said, sipping her tea absently as she tried not to recall Dy's kiss.

"Then why didn't you tell him to take his ward elsewhere?"

Adele shook her head, then said, "I couldn't, Ellie; any more than you could pack your bags and go somewhere else."

"That is different. I am needed here," Miss Willoughby began to enumerate the ways she was needed in this household, but Adele did not let her tick off the reasons.

"I am an adult, my dear, and have no need of a chaperone."

"But for the sake of propriety," Elvira gasped, truly alarmed. In an unaccustomed display of courage, she enquired, "Do you wish me gone?"

"No," Adele said after a moment's hesitation which she disguised behind her teacup. "You're my cousin. We do need one another."

"Oh, thank you," Miss Willoughby gushed.

"Nonsense, Elvira," Adele said, desperate to quell her cousin's fit of gratitude. "You have taken very good care of me over the years; how else can we deal together but as friends?"

"How else indeed?"

"And I am in need of a friend's help again," Adele said. "You know I have no idea how to go on with . . . children; however, you are quite good with them."

"Yes, I am," Elvira said, quite immodestly.

"I think you will like Windhaven's ward—Priscilla. Her vicar called her a pretty little girl. But I have no doubt she is very much in need of your settling influence."

"Yes, I shall be happy to be of use," Elvira said hesitantly. Then in a thoughtful aside, she said, "Lord Windhaven seems to have lost his way since Waterloo." She leaned forward, sipping the unwanted tea, then remarked, "Do you think him a fit guardian?"

"That is not for us to judge," Adele returned quellingly. "Lord Windhaven has not always been so reckless or vain. Perhaps this is what he needs."

"Is it?" Elvira asked. "Everyone knows he disdains noble sacrifice."

"Whatever *they* think, we must think of his ward," Adele said gently.

"*I* must think of you," Miss Willoughby said sternly. Her fringed shawl slipped from her black-clad shoulder as she confided, "That is why I say you must be careful. Lord Windhaven is a hardened bachelor."

Adele wondered if her cousin planned to say things to irritate her or whether they just innocently popped out of her mouth. But she did not give voice to such an uncivil query, only said, "And I am an independent lady. I can take care of myself and my household without expectation or fear."

Miss Willoughby only smiled and said, "I

am sure Eve thought she was equal to the serpent's wiles."

Unwilling to suffer through another of Elvira's improving lectures, Adele snapped, "Credit me with some sense; I cut my eye teeth years ago."

"Not so long past," Miss Willoughby reminded pettishly as she drew her troublesome wrap about her shoulders. "You are not yet thirty. I have the advantage of you by ten years."

Although she longed to remark that wisdom did not necessarily increase with age, Adele kept her tongue between her teeth, hoping her cousin would prove as forebearing.

"When you have been about as long as I, you will understand the wisdom of not trusting too much in the male sex," Miss Willoughby said, in the edifying tones Adele despised. "They are like bees, taking honey where they will."

Adele wondered how Elvira came by her knowledge. The speculation raised a modest blush to her cheeks and she felt compelled to ask in teasing tones, "How do you know so much?"

"It is a companion's business to know," Elvira replied, misreading Adele's becoming color as guilt. "You blush too much in Windhaven's company, dear Adele . . .

look, you are doing it now. It is not healthy, all that blood rushing to your head."

"I have never felt as well," Adele said, lowering her gaze to the tea in her cup. She could see her reflection staring back, and to her surprise, it did not give away her secrets. She was even able to say without a guilty increase in her becoming blush, "Lord Windhaven does not take advantage of our friendship, Elvira."

"He has done so, and shamefully," Miss Willoughby warned breathlessly, adding, "By asking you to sponsor an orphan under your roof."

Adele set her cup on the piecrust table at her elbow. Then, rising to the viscount's defense, she said, "Shame on you for thinking such evil thoughts. Dy is a good friend and deserves better from us."

Rather than reply to the mild rebuke, Elvira burst unaccountably into tears.

Accustomed to her cousin's histrionics, Adele allowed her the luxury of several moments of uninterrupted sobbing, then handed her a handkerchief and said, "If you insist upon being a watering pot, Elvira, pray make yourself useful." She indicated several plants which were leaning towards the wet windowpane as she added, "Your violets need a drink."

Behind the veil of Adele's handkerchief,

Miss Willoughby sniffed, "I forgive you. You are not yourself today."

Recognizing the truth of her companion's assertion in the wake of Dy's surprising kiss, Adele replied, "Indeed, I am not." She gave Elvira a comforting pat on the shoulder as she apologized, "I hope you will pardon my sharp tongue, Elvira . . . I am sorry."

Having elicited an apology, Miss Willoughby swept to her feet. She embraced her cousin, saying, "No wonder, my dear," in gracious tones that did not fool Adele. Elvira could afford to be amiable now that she thought she had made her cousin feel like a guilty child. "And who could blame you?" She went on, drawing Adele towards the stairs. "To have an unwanted child thrust into your lap. It is enough to give one the headache." She winced, as if the very mention occasioned agonizing pain in her temple.

Adele placed a supporting hand beneath her companion's arm as they mounted the stairs. "Do you mind, my dear," Elvira moaned, raising a shaking hand to the side of her head, "if I beg off Lady Mathilda's party?"

To say that she did mind would have been shabby and cruel. Elvira was often wracked by migraine headaches after any unpleasantness.

But it was inconvenient and vexing. Adele very much wished to attend Lady Mathilda's supper party, but the very strict conventions that compelled a single lady to engage the company of a responsible chaperone obliged her to forego the pleasure also.

Resigning herself to another solitary evening, Adele urged her cousin to rest in her darkened room, then sent a note round to Lady Mathilda's begging her to excuse them both from her assembly. That venerable lady returned a message excusing Elvira and her headache, but commanding Adele's appearance.

There was nothing to be done, except to obey the lady's rejoinder that Adele need not stand on ceremony among friends. Adele returned a short acceptance, then desiring Simone, her dresser, to make her shine, she was rewarded before her departure, when Elvira arose from her couch to wish her cousin a pleasant evening.

"How lovely you look," she said, touching her lips in a salute to Adele's cheek. "Ah, to be young again, and able to wear colorful silks and ribbons."

"I see no reason why you shouldn't wear more becoming colors," Adele said, betray-

ing some surprise in her companion's declaration. "You have been out of mourning
for years. Tomorrow, my dressmaker will fit
you out with a new, more becoming wardrobe."

"No," Elvira protested, shrinking from
her cousin as if she had suggested wearing
dampened muslins. "I couldn't put you to
such bother and expense."

"It is rather more bother to argue with
you, Ellie," Adele said, drawing on a pair
of white gloves. "And having you appear
with me in out-dated bombazine and rusty
crepe lowers my consequence in the
world." She shot a commanding, but affectionate look at her companion. "I know
you will say you care nothing for that or
that my vanity gives you the headache, but
I shall not be swayed from my purpose. Let
me dress you in pretty clothes, Cousin, to
make up for my sharp tongue and frivolous
manners."

"I suppose I have been selfish in denying
you the pleasure," Elvira said hesitantly, as
if anxious not to appear too eager, before
adding resolutely, "very well, then, Cousin.
Tomorrow I shall put myself in your
hands."

Laughing, Adele hugged her cousin and
bade her good night before sweeping down
stairs.

Alone once more, Elvira hugged herself. She could not resist peering at her pale reflection in the glass. An old lady, wearing a cap and a shapeless nightdress peeked cautiously back at her. It was enough to depress the most stolid hearted individual.

Wearing a dress of silver shot silk that shimmered like a rainbow as she entered Lady Mathilda's brilliantly lighted drawing room, Adele was unanimously held to be the diamond among diamonds at the evening's engagement. It was a reception which must satisfy the most demanding debutante, and did indeed raise her spirits. But though she sparkled as if issues no weightier than the *dernier cri* in fashion ever darkened her thoughts, her mind was in fact in turmoil. Viscount Windhaven had not yet made his appearance among the company, and though Adele made every effort to attend to the rampant speculations regarding Lord and Lady Byron's marital difficulties, her attention wandered towards the yawning portal.

When the viscount finally arrived, she was striving to attend to a debate between Lady Mathilda and a peer who was bitterly decrying wives who deserted their husbands. Looking at him through her quizzing glass, Lady Mathilda haughtily demanded, "Do you condone violence against wives, Lord Peverley?"

"Of course not," he blustered. "Only some women do not appreciate the place marriage gives them in society."

"All women understand that place," Adele replied. At that moment, she noticed Windhaven making his way through the company, greeting one or another of Lady Mathilda's guests, then moving toward her. He was grinning in a manner calculated to melt the most hardened heart. Her own began to flutter in confusion so that she was compelled to tear her gaze from his. Returning her wandering attention to Lord Peverley, she added, "Especially single ladies."

Peverley chuckled and inclined his head towards her in a familiar manner as he enquired, "Like yourself, eh?"

Adele bestowed a quelling gaze on him and replied, "It is kind in you to pity my spinsterhood, my lord, but your concern is misplaced."

"Eh, how is that?" he demanded stupidly, as though he did not recognize in an extremely courteous manner and quiet tone the unmistakable signs of an angry lady.

Smiling, she said, not quite truthfully, "I

am quite satisfied with my single state, my lord."

"Good girl," said Lady Mathilda.

"*Are* you?" Peverley was regarding them both in a doubtful manner which implied they did not know all the benefits to which a married lady was entitled.

His chilling gaze penetrated the filmy silk of her gown. Adele drew her shawl protectively about her shoulders. "Indeed," she replied, casting an appealing look towards Lady Mathilda, before she added in dulcet tones, "If Lord Byron and you are prime examples of husbands, I count myself fortunate I have escaped the bonds of marriage."

Her startling pronouncement had the welcome effect of silencing Lord Peverley until Windhaven succeeded in joining them. Then Peverley attempted to garner his support.

Windhaven listened thoughtfully as his lordship repeated his ill-considered opinions, then said amiably, "But of course a lady would have no reason to flee if her husband treated her half as well as he did his hunters."

Peverley's ruddy face darkened by degrees. It was common knowledge that his lordship spared no expense where it concerned his stable, but pinched pennies if their expenditure might benefit his long-suffering spouse. For a moment, his Adam's apple rose and fell as if it were a bellows that needed mending. It began to seem he might not find his voice. Then he blurted out, "Horses are more companionable than wives."

Desiring nothing more than to change the subject, Adele placed an appealing hand upon Dy's sleeve. He was chuckling as if enjoying a good joke. "You don't say," he said. Directing a conspiratorial wink towards her as if begging her indulgence for a moment, he folded his fingers around hers and tucked her arm within the crook of his left elbow. Feeling safe within his protective grasp, Adele allowed her taut nerves to relax.

"That's because you ain't bothered by the troublesome creatures," Peverley retorted. "Always weeping and complaining and having the vapors; they're enough to make you tear out your hair."

Since it was well known his lordship was bald, Adele found it difficult not to giggle. Even Lady Mathilda smiled in amusement. Windhaven grinned wickedly as he recalled, "So that explains it. I thought it was due to the jump you failed to take at the Chaseldon Hunt last fall."

Peverley's header was famous among the

ton by virtue of the fact that his ill-fitting brown wig had flown into a clump of bushes and had been torn apart by his own hounds as he tried to retrieve it. Windhaven's tongue-in-cheek recollection brought down the house as other guests began to recount their memories of Peverley's brush with mortality.

Adele had no wish to further damage Lord Peverley's pride, but the picture of a notable huntsman vying with his hounds for a ruined scrap of hair was too much to resist. Unable to restrain herself any longer, she began to giggle.

Peverley's face grew even more red. "You see what I mean?" he growled as though she was the cause of his embarrassment. "Why do we put up with 'em?"

"I suppose *you* do it for your nursery," said Windhaven, controlling his grin with an effort of will that was remarkable given the laughter convulsing the rest of the company. "By the way, I congratulate you on your son," he added, steering Adele towards the dining room.

But it seemed Peverley was not quite through, for he chuckled mirthlessly and said, "Does my soul good to see you ain't up to every rig, Windhaven."

The viscount drew up short and regarded his lordship as though he could see through him. Adele clung to his arm, scarcely daring to breathe. After a tense moment during which it seemed her fingers might be crushed in the convulsive fold of his arm, he relaxed his stance and said, "For all that you are credited with an abundance of horse sense, Peverley, you are a sad judge of character. I am up to *every* rig, including yours."

Peverley fidgeted, rather like a river rat caught in mid stream at flood tide. Then he stretched his thin lips into the semblance of a smile as he gloated, "Don't know your lady as well as you think."

"I have never pretended to understand a lady," Dy replied with a fond smile for Adele that did much to soothe her nerves.

Peverley chuckled, turning a coldly appraising look towards Adele. Then, turning his gaze from hers with a continuing chilling lack of cordiality, he said, "You're barking up the wrong tree, Windhaven, if you think she'll have you."

"Indeed," Dy said in tones that did not encourage rejoinder. He looked to Adele as if he deeply regretted his decision to forsake Alvanley's party.

"She's dead set against marriage," Peverley announced. "Dashed independent woman; I'd call her a man hater."

Dy was regarding her in a reassuring

manner that conveyed his belief that she was anything but a misanthrope. "Bad judge of character," he said, guiding Adele towards the comfort of the company crowding Lady Mathilda's dining hall as he tossed a parting shot to Peverley over his shoulder. "Pity you don't understand an independent woman is more companionable than a broken-spirited wife."

When the company had reassembled, the ladies having withdrawn after dinner to allow the gentlemen to sip brandy and blow clouds, Lady Mathilda announced an impromptu dancing party. Adele, who was across the room from Windhaven, smiled as he requested a dance with Lady Katherine Bermondey, a bran-faced young woman who had not taken last Season. She was clad in a gown of yellow silk which was particularly unbecoming with her brown hair and freckles.

To Lady Mathilda's sudden recollection that she had forgotten to engage musicians, Adele said, "If you can bear with my mistakes, I will gladly beat time." And so saying she stripped off her gloves and laid them alongside the branch of candles atop the pianoforte.

Windhaven, leading Lady Katherine towards the instrument, leaned down to speak to Adele. "If you think playing the piano will keep away fortune-hunters, think again. Someone will want to turn pages for you."

"I know how to turn aside unwelcome assistance," Adele laughed.

"Nevertheless I shall keep an eye on you," he warned in a voice that was not completely light in tone.

Adele turned a teasing, sideways glance upon him as she said, "Better to concentrate on your steps, so you don't tread on Lady Katherine's slippers."

She was delighted by his warmly appreciative smile. Giddy laughter bubbled forth as he defended himself, "I have never offended a dancing partner's toes. Come, Lady Katherine, let us show Miss Fonteyne how well we acquit ourselves."

Lady Katherine's amber-colored eyes flashed gratefully as she breathed, "Thank you, Miss Fonteyne."

Adele scanned the sheets of music to divert her mind from Dy's teasing grin. Lady Katherine's breathless sentiment arresting her concentration, she enquired, "Whatever for?"

"For giving us less fortunately endowed females an opportunity to shine."

Bestowing a chagrined look upon the young lady's earnest face, Adele remarked,

"Dear Lady Katherine, your sincerity puts me to shame."

The girl blushed to the roots of her tightly pinned brown hair and murmured a polite protest which Adele waved off.

What a shame, she thought, no one had considered ways to enhance Lady Katherine's unusual looks. She could become quite an Original if the right person took her in hand. Realizing she was the only lady in town who could work such a miracle, Adele said, "You must pay me a call one afternoon."

"I would love to." Lady Katherine looked at the floor as if mortified to be declining an offer to visit the most fashionable lady in town. "Only, Mama has filled my calendar this week . . ."

Adele patted the little freckled hand that rested on the edge of the keyboard. "Cruel calendar. Come whenever you can. I am sure if we put our heads together we would discover the way to make you shine in any company."

"Could you? I mean thank you!" Stunned, Lady Katherine whirled giddily away from the piano, right into the viscount's arms. Laughing, Windhaven caught her, but he spared an approving look towards Adele.

Warmed by his approbation, Adele returned his smile, thinking how much fun it would be to turn Lady Katherine into a Reigning Toast.

Immediately, she began to play a country dance. At its end, she was pleased that Lady Katherine suddenly seemed to have developed a cachet through Dy's endorsement. As partners were lining up for the second set, she accepted the offer of a shy young nobleman who was well known among the ton as "Dancing Fitzgomery." His soubriquet was not due to any gracefulness on his part; he considered himself to have no equal on the dance floor even though he kept his elbows moving all the time in discord with his feet.

As she performed a Scottish reel, Adele found the sight of Lady Katherine depending on the seemingly disembodied arm of Dancing Fitzgomery afforded a welcome diversion from the sight of Viscount Windhaven effortlessly leading a pert ingenue through the steps. He appeared thoroughly at ease with the wide-eyed girl on his hand. But every time the laughing couple passed into Adele's line of sight, her fingers stumbled over the keyboard. To her embarrassment, she began to strike more wrong than correct keys, giving the reel a recognizably discordant melody. When she finally completed the inelegant set, she clasped her hands together to stop them trembling.

"A waltz! A waltz!" cried the dancers.

"Oh, dear," Adele sighed. She leafed through the stack of music, stalling for time as she controlled a jealous wish not to see the viscount turning giddy circles around another lady. It was a petty and foolish desire, but she could not help it, and she felt more than a little ashamed of herself.

"You have performed long enough," Windhaven said sternly, startling her and drawing her attention from the instrument. "Someone else must play."

Adele looked stupidly on the hand he extended towards her and enquired, "Do you mean you have borne with my mistakes long enough?"

Lady Katherine gladly took her place at the keys. Several young men immediately offered to turn pages.

Drawing Adele away from the cluster of younger people, Windhaven replied in a significant tone that made her pulse dance in an erratic three-four pattern, "I mean I wish to dance with you. You will not embarrass me by counting the steps."

Laughing, Adele placed her hand on his shoulder as she turned to face him. "I don't know whether to thank you or take offense."

He pleased her by saying, "I did not mean to be impertinent." Placing his hand at her waist, he enquired, "Will you agree we are well-suited?"

Unprepared for the agitation that the warmth radiating from his fingers stirred up within her soul, Adele was compelled to acknowledge breathlessly that they did dance well together.

It was no idle boast. Their steps matched perfectly, and they could perform with grace the perpetual circles that had less competent couples lurching into other dancers.

As the music began, Adele raised her gaze to meet his. Of a sudden, the politely lingering gaze which perfectly suited them on the dance floor intensified until it seemed to her that her movements had become those of a mechanical doll. She could not feel her feet touching the floor, or even hear the music. She was aware only of Windhaven's supporting hand, his compelling, smiling gaze, and the continuous circles which transformed the drawing room into a whirling prism around them. As they moved in concentric orbits around one another, it occurred to her that for the first time in her adult life, she was not an independent woman.

Strange, for the first time in her life, the thought that she was not in control of her destiny did not frighten her in the least. Wherever the viscount led her, she would follow.

Shortly after the waltz concluded, and still dazed by the effect of whirling in his embrace, Adele called for her coach. Seeing the footman's hesitation, she described her livery. Still he made no move to call her carriage.

Overhearing, Dy told her, "I took the liberty of sending your coachman home."

Surprised, she enquired, "Did you?" She felt a glow warm her from within as he smiled down at her. She could not refrain from teasing him. "But why? I am an independent woman . . ."

"Spare me," he said before ordering his own coach brought round. Then, taking her wrap from the stoic footman who took himself discreetly away, he draped the fur-trimmed cloak about her and added, "Forgive my interference, Adele, but much as I respect your independence, I wish you will allow me to see you safely home."

Even though his hands were resting lightly upon her shoulders, Adele felt them as weights. His sudden concern for her safety suggested privilege of ownership, which excited a not unmixed pleasure within her heart.

She liked the viscount quite more than any gentleman with whom she was acquainted, probably because he had never seemed to expect more than friendship from her. Until today.

Suddenly Adele doubted she could be comfortable with him again. "I am perfectly able to take care of myself," she said in a maddeningly choked voice as the footman returned with Dy's coat and the announcement that Lord Windhaven's coach had arrived.

Donning his coat and hat, the viscount said, "I know it. But we are friends, and I want to see you safely home." He guided her into the chill night air and handed her into his coach. After climbing in beside her and tossing the fur rug over her lap, he added, "And I might not get another chance to speak privately with you."

Thinking he was commenting on the absence of her cousin, Adele protested, "I did not forbid Elvira the party to . . . force your hand."

"Calm yourself, Adele," he said, taking her fingers in one hand after he rapped on the roof. When his coachman had set his team in motion, he continued, "Small wonder you do not trust me; I did not treat you as a friend today."

"You are a true friend," she protested vehemently. "I did not mean to presume . . ." He was looking at her with a curious glint in his eye, as if he did not quite take her seriously. Not knowing what else to do, she fell quiet, and let her fingers rest within his warm grip during the short ride home. She found herself wishing the journey could go on forever.

The viscount remained silent until Jackson pulled to a halt before Number Thirty Green Street. Suddenly he chuckled aloud and squeezed her hand in an oddly affecting way. "You may presume what you like, Adele. Only do not expect me to apologize for kissing you."

"But why?" she demanded as he threw open the door and let down the step. Her heart was pounding so hard she thought he must surely be able to hear it. But if he did, he made no sign as he assisted her out of the coach and to her entrance, then removed the key from her trembling fingers and unlocked the front door. Adele passed over the threshold before he entered, and returned the key to her. He raised his golden eyebrows as though condemning himself for a fool before he queried, *"Why* should I apologize?"

"No, my lord, that isn't what I meant," she said, placing her hand on his sleeve. "I . . . why did you kiss me?" She felt very foolish and was about to remove her hand, but he covered her fingers and held them gently, but firmly.

"Did you not like it?" he asked.

Stunned, she raised her face to meet his unwavering gaze and said, "Too well. Perhaps I should beg *your* pardon, for being too forward or too—"

To her complete surprise, he stole another kiss, before saying, "Now you must send me away. But I shall return in a week's time, hoping you will remember your promise to take care of my little girl."

"I shall do my best," she whispered, hoping he wanted her to take care of him as well. But she let his arm slip out of her fingers, saying, "Take care of yourself on the way."

"Will you miss me?" he teased, his blue eyes twinkling mischievously in the candle-light.

"I shall be very busy," Adele retorted with a smile. "Buying toys for a pretty child. Will she like a doll, do you think?"

"How should I know?" Windhaven replied. "Buy her whatever you liked as a child."

Shaking her head as she laughed, Adele

said, "Then I shall buy her a huge dog, for Miss Willoughby tells me I ran wild with my pet all over my father's estate, when I wasn't riding the beast."

Laughing over the unladylike image Adele's memory conjured up, Windhaven agreed driving it must have been more fun than dressing up dolls. "But," he added, "it's a hard stretch of the imagination to envision you clinging to the back of a furry mongrel."

"Highly unfashionable," she giggled, arching her delicate brows in self-mockery. "And now I have given you a disgust of my manners, do you still wish me to turn your ward into a proper young lady?"

His eyes sparkled with good humor and affection as he said, "It will do as a beginning," before caressing her cheek in farewell. Then, bidding her to have a care for herself while he was gone, he took himself home.

Three

The yellow and black coach attracted considerable interest as it rattled over the cobbled streets of the quiet village of Osmotherley. The smart rig drew a following of noisy boys and barking dogs that pursued them to the gates of the parish church and school.

Letting down the step, and throwing open the door as one aggressive animal worried the toe of his boot, the coachman grumbled, "Here, lad! Take your beast off now, there's a good boy. Ow!" He clapped a hand to his head where a cabbage had taken off his hat.

Laughing at the joke they had dealt the complaining jehu, the boys hastily took themselves off down the street, their animals nipping in delight at their heels.

Windhaven descended, chuckling, from the coach.

Spying an ancient inn down the street, he placed several coins in his coachman's hand. "Have the horses rubbed down and fed while you wet your whistle, Jackson."

"Shall I bespeak a room for you, my lord?"

Windhaven's eyes narrowed as he calculated the likelihood of procuring clean linens or a good claret in the village hostelry. "I think not," he replied. "We shall take ourselves back to York before nightfall."

Jackson snapped the door closed and folded the step. "Very good, my lord," he said with a respectful nod before he climbed aboard the box and turned his team around on the street.

Windhaven paused before the gate, then pushed it open and strode through the neat church yard. When he entered the chapel, a thin, nervous-looking man came towards him, pushing a pair of spectacles up the bridge of his nose. From his sober dress, Windhaven presumed him to be a church man. "Have I the honor to be addressing Mr. Reeves?" he enquired.

"I am his curate," replied the reed-thin man. He wrung his hands. "Mr. Elliott. May I help you?"

Regarding the jittery Mr. Elliott, the viscount was hard-pressed not to succumb to laughter. "I am Windhaven, come from London at the request of Mr. Reeves."

"Oh, dear," sighed Mr. Elliott. He

cleared his throat and cast an uncertain glance towards the sacristy. "I shall see whether he is available."

"He will see me, Mr. Elliott; I shall not leave until I have received what I came to fetch." Windhaven swept off his many-caped travelling coat, dusted off a pew and lounged on it in a possessive manner. Mr. Elliott scurried into the vestry, from which soon emerged a person Dysart assumed must be the Reverend Mr. Ignatius Reeves. The man was walking with a cane and a marked limp, due to the fact that his right foot was thickly bandaged.

"Good afternoon, Lord Windhaven is it?" he said, leaning heavily upon his cane and putting out a hand as Dy came to his feet. "Pray forgive my curate; I am afraid my gout has made him cautious."

Dysart grinned amiably as he shook the clergyman's hand. "With good reason, sir. My father suffered from gout, and his family suffered from him. It is to be hoped you are following the physician's instructions."

"To the letter," said Mr. Reeves. "Pray come into the vestry, my lord, while we speak of your business here." Opening a door, he directed the viscount into a comfortably appointed room. "My predecessor preferred a view of the Cleveland Hills," he said, lowering himself into a chair by a window overlooking the churchyard and settling his bandaged foot on a padded stool. "However, this outlook," indicating the neat rows of gravestones and gnarled, barren trees, "keeps me in mind of my business." When Dysart made no comment, he seemed constrained to elucidate. "Saving souls, my lord."

"I hope you do not mean to enquire as to the health of my soul," Dy said affably. "That, sir, is between the Lord and myself."

"But you must admit, I have reason for concern. This dress," said the parson, indicating the viscount's coat of bottle green superfine and drab breeches, and the exquisitely rendered mailcoach neck-cloth, "Identifies you as a dandy, sir."

"Indeed?" Dy enquired with a lifted eyebrow. "Pray, what is that to our purpose?"

"I fear you will not render a settling influence upon Miss Gaines," said Mr. Reeves. "She is too enamored of dashing heroes."

"School girls do enjoy fairy tales, sir," Dy said gently. "However, I do not mean to feed such fantasy. She must learn how to behave in society so we may present her to her grandfather."

The parson harumphed, then folded his

fingers into a prayerful steeple. "I hope you do not tell her of that just yet, sir."

"I am well known for my discretion," Windhaven said.

"I hope you may be patient as well," replied Mr. Reeves.

"Tell me why I must be patient," Windhaven said.

"Knowing Mr. Gaines—that is Lieutenant Gaines—as you did, I assume you were aware of a family rift," Mr. Reeves said.

"Yes," Windhaven said. "His wife's family did not like the match. But Arthur was not bitter towards his father-in-law. He said I would know how to bring Lady Pamela back into his lordship's good graces."

"Only Lady Pamela remained bitter to her death," the vicar said. "But in the end, she entrusted me with the means of reconciling her daughter and her family."

"I don't know many families who would refuse to accept a grandchild," Windhaven allowed.

Mr. Reeves smiled enigmatically before saying, "Pray reserve judgment, my lord. You do not know the girl yet." At a knock on the study door, Mr. Reeves called out, "Send her in, Mr. Elliott." Regarding Windhaven intently, before the door was opened, he said, "I do not know you, but must rely on Lieutenant Gaines' confidence that you will do the right thing for his daughter."

"I shall do my best," Windhaven replied, hearing a soft footfall as Miss Gaines was ushered inside. He arose from his chair, and turned toward the door, expecting to see a miniature of Arthur Gaines: dark hair, laughing blue eyes, and angelic countenance. This was the sight he beheld; however, the girl crossing the room was no child. From her looks, Windhaven judged she must be nearly eighteen. He heard the parson's introduction, "Lord Windhaven, may I present Priscilla Gaines?" and nearly choked on his own retort, "Is this a jest?"

Priscilla's impish smile widened as she said, "Mr. Reeves, did you tell Lord Windhaven I was a pretty little girl?"

"Your show of vanity, child, is not in the least becoming," replied the parson somewhat severely. Then, he admitted his fault. "Indeed, my lord, I did place that mistaken notion in your head, did I not?"

Windhaven was so stunned by Priscilla's beauty that he could not reply for a moment. Not even the black woolen dress and sturdy walking boots which peeked out from beneath the hem of the starched white pinafore could disguise her looks, which were startling, both in beauty and in likeness to her father. However, where Arthur had been merely handsome, she was lovely.

Priscilla's beauty was likely to cast everyone in London in the shade. Brunette hair tumbled over her shoulders in charming disarray, despite the bandeau which attempted to restrain the stubborn curls. Her pink cheeks appeared to have been stained with the juice of strawberries, and her little bow-shaped lips, with raspberries.

In spite of the poorly chosen sobriquet given her age, Reeves had not misnamed her. Priscilla Gaines was a pretty, *petite* girl. And she knew it.

Dy dragged himself out from under the spell this fairy child was attempting to weave about him. She was posturing in a manner that gave him to understand he was expected to worship her. When he did not, Priscilla redoubled her efforts to charm.

"Have you come to take me to London?" she asked, gazing at him with wide blue eyes that seemed as innocent as an early spring morning. "Mama said I could be presented to the queen."

Looking at her as she stood with one brow raised in an arch challenge, he replied, "We may consider it, when you are out of black gloves," in a parental tone. "You must learn town manners first."

His stern rejoinder seemed not to diminish Priscilla's enthusiasm at all as she asked, "Of course, will you teach me?"

"Certainly not," he replied. "You will better learn those lessons from a lady."

"I . . ." She began on a defiant note, then seeing the parson's eyebrow raised, took a deep breath and said, "If you please, my lord, I wish *you* will tell me how to get on. I am too old to learn from a governess."

Mr. Reeves harumphed. "Really, miss, what will your guardian think of the lessons you learned here?"

She regarded the vicar dispassionately, then replied, "Indeed, I cannot imagine what Lord Windhaven will think. Only, I'm certain he knows rather better than you how to get on in the world, and . . ."

"Yes, you have often bespoken your wish to cut a dash," Mr. Reeves said in affectionate but mocking tones. "However, it is to be hoped your guardian can teach you to affect a more ladylike manner. It is too late to expect you to become accomplished."

Windhaven was gratified to see Priscilla press her lips together as if attempting to control another retort. "Be so good as to await without, Priscilla, before you explode," he said.

Her little mouth flew open, then snapped shut. "Very well, my lord," she said, executing a very soldierly about face and marching toward the door.

When she had departed, Mr. Reeves regarded him silently for several moments. Knowing his fitness as a parent was being weighed, Dysart returned a steady, but amiable gaze. At last, Mr. Reeves said, "I believe you will do for her what we could not."

"Indeed," Dysart said. "I make no promises as to presentation or brilliant match."

"I doubt either parent fostered such hopes for her. They're merely foolish fancies of an overimaginative mind. Just make her known to her illustrious grandfather. He will complete the work."

"Will this mysterious person not require proof that Priscilla Gaines is indeed his blood relation?"

The parson drew from his desk a wrapped package and a sealed letter. "Here. The letter and bundle contain everything that will identify Priscilla and prove the connection."

"Then I shall guard it well," Windhaven said, placing the package within the deep pocket of his garrick. "Does the girl truly know nothing of her family connections?"

Mr. Reeves shook his head. "She knows

only what her mother has chosen to reveal—that her own father disowned her and that she resented his continued rejection."

"No use raising her hopes beforehand then," agreed the viscount. "Her grandfather might remain stubbornly opposed to her."

"Only if his heart is made of stone," said Mr. Reeves fervently.

"There are many lovely girls in London, sir," Windhaven said quellingly. "Unless Miss Gaines is possessed of a quality more lasting than beauty or more attractive than wealth, they will put her in the shade."

"She has an education," defended Mr. Reeves.

"Which counts for nothing among the Ten Thousand. Other young ladies, although stupid, possess jealous mamas and generous dowries; distinct advantages in a town mad for family and fortune."

Mr. Reeves lifted a challenging eyebrow. "Are you implying the task is too difficult?"

A sly smile curved the viscount's lip upwards. "Nothing is too difficult for a Windhaven, sir. I was merely informing you of the odds against your pupil and my ward."

"I am sure *you* must think them formidable," replied the parson with something like a grin softening his lofty countenance. "However, I am hedging my bet, sir."

"You don't look like a sharp," Dysart said with dawning humor.

"Appearances are deceiving," replied the cleric with an answering grin. "I was a Colleger at Eton, and so was introduced at an early age to vice and excess."

"Yet you seem untouched by the experience," Windhaven mused.

"Hardly, sir. One cannot remain untouched by the depravities practiced by the residents of the Long Chamber." Reeves made two fists and struck a belligerent pose, though he did not arise from his chair. "Fortunately, I was good with my fives. After planting my first adversary a facer and knocking out two other bullies who rose to his defense, I was left alone. As were those I championed."

Windhaven saw that the parson's knuckles still bore the scars of those battles. "You must have been considered as highly as David," he marvelled.

"So it would seem." Mr. Reeves placed his open hands on the desk. Gazing upon them, he added, "The experience proved useful, sir. In the Lord's service, I have milled down even stronger men." He directed a menacing stare across the desk.

Although Windhaven felt the force of the glare, he compelled himself to meet the adamant look without blinking. "I am not about to challenge your assertion," he said. "On account of your gout, it would not be a fair fight."

"I assure you I should acquit myself admirably, sir."

"I don't doubt it," Windhaven said, grinning. "My father used to fight like a lion whenever his gout got the upper hand." Coming to his feet, he said, "Thank you for . . . warning me about my ward, Mr. Reeves. I see the sooner I get her home, the better."

"Mind you guard her," commanded the parson, half-starting to his feet before recalling his infirmity. Settling once more into his chair, he said, "She has been too sheltered from the World."

Grown tired of the religious tone the vicar seemed fond of affecting, Windhaven responded, "Nevertheless, the World is where she must live. She has to learn how to get on." Then upon hearing the cleric's concerned intake of breath, he said, "Don't worry, sir; I will make certain she observes the conventions and has every opportunity to meet her grandfather." His assertion seemed to allay the cleric's misgivings, and Windhaven said they would be going.

"I was hoping you might stay the night," said Mr. Reeves.

"Impossible," Windhaven replied, moving towards the door. There, he drew on his garrick. "I have business in town."

"Can you not postpone it?"

"Really, sir; if you knew me, you would not ask that."

"But that is exactly my point. I do not know you," protested Mr. Reeves. "How can I let you take Priscilla out of Osmotherly on such short acquaintance?"

"Because her parents trusted me." Windhaven threw open the door and, without acknowledging his ward, strode down the side aisle of the sanctuary.

Priscilla, sitting on a pew near the vestry door, sprang to her feet and ran after him. She caught hold of his arm and said, "I am ready to go, my lord."

Windhaven removed her fingers from the fine fabric of his coat. When she again reached for his sleeve, he commanded, "Pray do not cling. I am not about to abandon you."

"No?" she enquired. A tear slid down her rosy cheek. Windhaven had the impression that it was a performance, not a spontaneous display of emotion, and suppressed the urge to embrace the girl, even as she pouted, "Why should you not? Everyone else has. I do not even know you."

Handing her his monogrammed handkerchief, he declared, "My dear child, if you intend to be tiresome, I shall oblige you." Her blue eyes widened as she hiccupped into the linen square. Raising his own eyes upwards, Windhaven enquired, "How can Arthur have sired such a goose?"

She blew her nose, then returned the abused cloth to its owner. "I beg your pardon, my lord. Indeed, I do not mean to be so bird-witted. Only sometimes, I cannot help it."

Windhaven held his handkerchief distastefully by a corner, then, dismissing her performance as childish thoughtlessness, stuffed it into a pocket of his garrick. "You must make the effort." Seeing that she was draped in a shapeless black wool mantle, he grimaced and said, "Have you a trunk?"

Priscilla gestured to a small portmanteau. "This contains everything I own."

Windhaven suppressed a shudder. "We shall purchase a few items in York," he decided aloud.

"But I am perfectly content with what I have," she protested prettily.

"Perhaps *you* are," the viscount retorted. "I am rather thinking of my own comfort."

"Oh." Her pretty mouth curved up at the ends. "You mean I will not complement you."

Windhaven allowed a grin to soften his expression. "I mean precisely that." He was nearly floored by Priscilla's immediate and dazzling smile; however, he quelled his response, commanding Priscilla to hand over her paltry luggage and to follow him.

Dropping the scarred portmanteau with a clatter, the girl threw her arms about his neck and bestowed a grateful kiss upon the viscount's cheek. When he had extricated himself from her impulsive grasp, she said, "Thank you, my lord. I will be so good, you will never regret your kindness."

Retrieving the forgotten satchel from the stone floor, Windhaven nearly allowed that he already did regret his good turn. However, he stifled the uncharitable remark and indicated that she was to precede him outside. Priscilla skipped beside him as he moved down the street. "Pray consider how you look," he said, sensible to the stares which were following their progress towards the hostelry.

"I look happy," Priscilla replied, doing a graceful pirouette in the street.

"You give every appearance of being a Gypsy," he replied sternly.

"I should *like* to be a Gypsy," she said. "Then I should have romance and adventure."

"Nothing could be further from the truth," he answered, handing her into his coach and snapping the door closed. "You would be hounded out of town and forced to live the meanest sort of existence."

"Is that not the sort of life I have been living?" she enquired. "At least Gypsies wear bright colors."

Realizing she did not intend to give up her foolish, romantic notion, Windhaven exhaled an exasperated breath and gave the battered portmanteau to the footman who tossed it into the boot. "You know nothing about Gypsies except what you may have read in story books." As she was attempting to open the door to the coach, he affected his sternest scowl and commanded, "Stay where you are, miss. Or I shall sell you to the first Gypsies we encounter."

Evidently she thought he would do just that, for she released the latch and slid back against the thick leather cushion. "But I am hungry, my lord. Surely you could take me into that establishment for a cup of tea?"

"Most certainly I will not," he replied. Then before she could voice yet another absurd wish, he strode into the public room and claimed his coachman from the bar.

He also ordered a basket of potted meat sandwiches, cakes and a bottle of cold tea which his starving passenger could con-

sume while travelling. That would elimi-
nate for a time, he thought, any complaints
she might express about being forced to
ride within the closed vehicle alone.

Although Priscilla was tempted as he
strode into the inn to think her noble
guardian an ogre for locking her within
the coach like a prisoner, her opinion of
him underwent an immediate transformation when the basket of food and the precious tea were delivered into her hands.
She called herself the luckiest of girls to
have been blessed with a guardian of such
consideration.

"I believe you attribute too much kindness to me," Windhaven said, snapping the
door closed once more.

She looked up from an intense study of
the basket's contents. "Will you not share
this repast?"

"No," he replied, tugging on a pair of
yellow gloves. "I mean to drive."

Priscilla opened her sapphire blue eyes
wide. "Is there nothing you cannot do?"

"I think not," Windhaven said, smug in
his confidence. "You will not be sick?"

"Pray, do not waste a thought on me,"
she said, returning her eager gaze upon
the food. "I am never sick." And with the
unconcern of youth, she selected a sand-

wich of corned beef and began, hungrily, to eat.

She soon dispatched the luncheon and suffered no ill effects from the rhythmic motion of the well-sprung coach rolling over the hard-packed road. Another, more seasoned traveller, might have been tempted to nap after indulging in such a sumptuous feast. But as Priscilla Gaines had long wondered what adventure lay beyond the next hill, she tied back the curtains and leaned out the window so as not to miss her first sight of a highwayman or Gypsy.

As they turned southwards onto the main road towards Thirsk, she heaved a vocal sigh and inclined her head towards her hero wielding the reins of his team. "Could we not explore Mount Grace Priory?"

Without slowing their pace, Windhaven said, "Certainly not; I am not a travelling guide," with all the sternness of a professional jehu determined to keep his coach on schedule.

Disappointed, Priscilla sighed no less noisily and drew her head within the coach. Her mother had promised her time and again she would hire a donkey cart as soon as the weather permitted an excursion to the ruined monastery, and now, the romantic ramble was to be forever denied her. All because her guardian was so very strict.

For awhile, as she considered what losses she had already suffered during her short life, Priscilla allowed herself to think herself sorely abused by fate. That she had been rescued from a tedious existence in a remote village by a handsome nobleman who bore the unmistakable stamp of being, what Mama, before she became religious, might have called a prime one, she did not dwell upon.

Windhaven *said* he was taking her to London. But how was she to believe him? Despite what her mama had told her of the bonds of brotherly affection which had united her papa and her new guardian, Priscilla could not but regard Lord Windhaven as a dangerous stranger.

Not for the first time in her life, she allowed herself to be overset by an inventive mind. Her guardian was cast in the role of a wicked wizard spiriting her away from everyone she had ever loved.

The morbid thoughts which plagued her seemed of a piece with the ominous weather which loomed ahead. Lightning flashed from boiling black clouds and thunder echoed from amidst the dark, menacing hills which huddled on either side of the curving road. Realizing she was completely helpless to escape the fate towards which she was hurtling, she covered her face with both hands as if blotting out the sight might block all evil thoughts.

It was no use. Imagining she had been abandoned by everybody she loved, left without a friend to find her way in the world as best she could, she began to cry. Oh, how desperately she missed her mother! A hard knot of fear and loneliness beating against her breast, she curled beneath the heavy fur spread which had been folded on the forwards seat and cried herself to sleep.

"Poor bairn," said Jackson as Windhaven carried his sleeping ward up to the room he had hired for her at the Red Bear in York. "Y'ought to've ridden wi' her during the storm. Then someone would've closed the curtains."

"No," Windhaven replied, stopping to readjust his soggy burden at the foot of the stairs. *"You* ought to have ridden within. I was better occupied to keep the team on the road than to play nursery maid to a teary-eyed school girl." He indicated for the landlady who was lighting the way above stairs to proceed. When she had lit the lamp in the neat, but tiny chamber, and he had placed Priscilla on the narrow bed, he commanded the woman to find something dry for Miss Gaines in the battered portmanteau. The landlady scowled as he closed the door behind him on his way out.

He discovered his own travelling case had been delivered to the room in which he was to pass the night. After changing his shirt and neck-cloth, Windhaven returned to the public room where Jackson was partaking of a hot rum toddy. Seating himself at the table near the blazing fireplace which the tippling jehu had appropriated, the viscount said, "I'll have one of those myself," much to Jackson's apparent surprise, as he choked on a draught.

"You're not used to drinkin' wi' the likes o' me," Jackson reminded him as the landlord placed another steaming mug on the table.

Wrapping his hands around the warm tankard, Windhaven considered that he was initiating the first of many firsts in his life, but he did not share that philosophy with Jackson. Rather, he regarded his coachman with one golden eyebrow raised quizzically and, as Jackson raised the mug to his lips, enquired, "What, are you ashamed to drink with me?"

Once again the man nearly choked. Windhaven could not resist taxing him even more. "Did I overset us?" he enquired. "Run into a ditch? Lose a wheel?"

"No, my lord," came a humble reply as Jackson fingered the rim of his tankard.

"Then, I ask you, were we stuck fast in mud? Did I tangle the traces?"

"Ye know ye never did so in yer life," Jackson responded vehemently.

Windhaven humbly acknowledged his coachman's praise, then said, "But I must have fallen short in your sight in some way."

"No how," Jackson maintained. "Ye drive to an inch, my lord, and ye know I'm proud to drink wi' ye, any day o the week. Only what'll yer friends think, you drinking rum toddies?"

Windhaven sipped the warming drink thoughtfully. "I cannot be responsible for my friends' bias." Noticing Jackson's tankard was empty, he enquired, "Will you have another?"

"B'lieve I will, my lord," Jackson allowed. "Seein's I'm chilled to the bone."

The viscount obliged his coachman with another round, then excused himself to enquire of the landlady about his ward's state of health.

"She'll be fine, if she doesn't have weak

lungs," replied the stiff-backed woman. Handing Priscilla's wet cloak and gown to a serving maid with instructions to see that they be dried and pressed, she clasped one hand around her other wrist and demanded, "If ye'll pardon me askin', m'lord, what d'ye mean draggin' the poor child out in such weather?"

Windhaven bestowed an arrogant look upon her. "I presume, Mrs. Beaton," he said, "That you must prefer some other inn to have received my trade?"

"Well naturally, we are gradeful for yer bizness, my lord," she replied with a dip of her head. "But I can tell ye, the child c'n thank 'er stars, she's not been coddled til now."

"The girl is pluck to the backbone," he replied, fully believing his fabrication. "I expect she will be completely recovered by the time hunger wakens her."

Four

In fulfillment of her guardian's prophecy, Priscilla awoke with no ill effects from the afternoon's adventure. And she was ravenous.

But thoughts of satisfying her stomach's cravings were overshadowed by the discovery that she was clad only in a white flannel night dress and that her drab wool dress and cloak were missing from her other belongings which had been hung on pegs and set on a small chest of drawers.

Immediately her over active imagination embellished the dark adventure she had been conjuring ever since her guardian refused her first wish. Forgetting the confidence her parents had placed in Lord Windhaven and his initial kindness to her, she now was thoroughly convinced he was a black-hearted villain, and she his helpless captive. She was working herself up to cry once more, but just as the tears began to roll, realized the folly of resorting to hysterics when no one was here to behold how sensitive and alone and vulnerable she was. Sniffing back her tears, she decided she must save herself.

Bent on escape, she tossed off the covers and hurried to the mullioned window where she discovered she was on an upper storey within reach of a tree limb. She rejoiced that flight was not impossible, but merely impractical, as she learned upon the opening of the casement window. A cold rain falling in torrents blew through the narrow opening, wetting her sleeve thoroughly before she could latch the window closed. She watched water sliding down the leaded panes, fighting the irrational panic that was making her heart pound by chewing on a thumbnail.

A knock at the door sent her flying back into her bed. When she was huddled safely beneath the covers, she called out in a shaky voice, "Who is it?"

"It's Mrs. Beaton, dear. The innkeeper's wife," the woman added.

"What do you want?" she enquired as the door creaked open.

A smiling Mrs. Beaton peered round the half opened door. The merry apple cheeks and cherry shaped nose allayed Priscilla's fears a little. Her first words cheered the skittish girl even more. "I have your dress and petticoat, dear, cleaned and pressed. And your guardian was asking whether you might like your dinner now."

Completely deflated by Mrs. Beaton's mention of her guardian, Priscilla lied, "I'm not hungry."

"Not hungry, my dear? I never heard the like." Without waiting for an invitation to enter, Mrs. Beaton crossed into the room as if she owned it. Priscilla granted reluctantly she did of course own the room, but she could not like the familiar way the woman had of calling her "dear." "I'm sure yer belly's rubbin' yer backbone as Mr. Beaton is wont to say. Up wi' ye, now, dearie."

"I want to eat in my room," Priscilla said, shivering.

"Not to worry, yer gentleman 'as spoken a private parlor fer ye to take supper in. Now come here, an' get ye dressed."

"No!" Priscilla drew the covers more securely about her shoulders. "I mean, you don't understand. I . . . I . . . am afraid." Her eyes filled with tears.

Mrs. Beaton hung the heavy dress on a peg and clucked sympathetically. "Afraid? Of what?"

Priscilla heard the sounds of boots striding towards her room. She turned watery eyes away from the door. "I am afraid . . . of him," she said.

Mrs. Beaton waited until the footsteps passed before leaning forwards conspiratorially and whispering, "But ye needn't fear 'is lordship, child. He's yer guardian."

"I do not know him, ma'am." Suddenly believing the half truths she was telling, Priscilla sobbed, "My mama died, and I could not pay the school; and so they said I must go . . . with him."

"Who said you must?" Mrs. Beaton sounded quite sincerely concerned as she pulled up a chair beside Priscilla's bed.

Knowing the pretty picture she made when playing a distressed damsel, Priscilla allowed a few more tears to slide becomingly down her cheeks before telling the rest of her tale. During that time, the agreeable landlady clucked over her as if she fully believed the story Priscilla was creating. At last, she stammered, "Mr. Reeves, the vicar of St. Paul's church in Osmotherley said I must go with my guardian." She averted her eyes in such a manner that allowed her to observe her audience's reaction without being obvious. As she had hoped, Mrs. Beaton's full lips stiffened into a disapproving pout and she clasped her hands tightly in her ample lap.

"There is a school in Osmotherley," she was saying thoughtfully. Then, her countenance softened as she commiserated with

Priscilla. "Poor wee thing, all alone in the world. Never worry your pretty head, now, Mother Beaton will take care of everything."

Relieved to have someone else believe her tale of woe, Priscilla allowed the woman to give her a motherly hug, then obeyed as she was gently told to dress herself for dinner, when Mrs. Beaton concluded, "For if you wish to eat in bed, you'll get only bread pudding and milk." She added, when Priscilla meekly climbed out of bed and moved towards her dress hanging on its peg, "Pray be quick, now; I'll send my maid to direct ye to the dining parlor."

Priscilla stopped in mid-step. "But I . . ."

"Not another word," Mrs. Beaton declared with a finger to the side of her pursed lips. Then shaking the finger in a gently admonitory fashion, she urged, "Do as ye're told; there's a good girl."

What else was she to do, but obey?

As soon as Mrs. Beaton closed the door behind her, Priscilla donned her clothes. It was not difficult to tie the strings of her petticoat and button the dress up the front. Pulling on a fresh pair of itchy black wool stockings, Priscilla began to look forward to wearing silks and to having a maid to complete her toilette. But that, she realised with a guilty start, would only come to pass if she made peace with her guardian, who had no understanding of her fantastic wonderings. By the time she had stepped into the black slippers, she had forgotten her slanders against him and was in good charity with him.

The viscount, on the other hand, was not feeling at all in charity with his ward. In fact he was tempted to strangle the little chit. When the landlady, in the presence of her very large, frowning husband, revealed Priscilla's gross accusations against him, he took hold of his excellently folded neckcloth in order to relieve the constriction at his own throat. Finally, when he was capable of speech, he demanded, "She said *what?*"

"That ye had . . . er . . . abducted her," Mrs. Beaton said. Windhaven cast a stricken look in the direction of Mr. Beaton, who was standing at the door to the parlor, ham-sized hands folded belligerently across his barrel-shaped chest. In a suspicious tone, Mrs. Beaton enquired, "What, in fact, is yer relationship wi' the girl?"

Although nothing had been said about involving a magistrate in the affair, Windhaven knew that one would be summoned if he said the wrong thing. Weighing his words carefully, he replied, "The girl's father saved my life at Waterloo. He asked me, with his dying breath, to act as her guardian. Nothing on paper, but it was understood."

Mrs. Beaton's fingers drummed along the side of her arm as if calculating the odds that he was telling the truth. "Did ye send her to that school?"

"Certainly not," he said vigorously. "If I had paid for her education, she'd have gone to a fashionable school near London, not some seminary at the end of the earth." Both interrogators' countenances hardened at his disparagement of their neighborhood.

Then, Mr. Beaton uncrossed his arms, rubbed his chin and spoke. " 'E's a prime un, Meg. Above ur touch."

"He could be 'is royal 'ighness or the Duke of York for all I care," Mrs. Beaton shot back. "E's na gonna hurt that wee babe."

"Come noo," said Mr. Beaton in what Dy recognized must be his customary stolid fashion. He was scratching his head as if it aided the process of thinking. "Iffen'e came from Osmotherley, 'e's na takin' the girl t' the Border."

Windhaven began to think he might soon owe his life to the man.

"He might." The tightening of Mrs. Beaton's folded arms across her large bosom told Windhaven she was not convinced.

"Nah," disputed her mate as he opened the door. "He'd've got lost on the moors."

The viscount could not let such slander pass unremarked. "I have a very good map." And he produced a guidebook from his pocket.

"There, ye see, Mr. Beaton, 'e 'as a map," said the goodwife with a triumphant flourish of her hand.

Mr. Beaton perused it closely, then winked at his missus in a manner that reddened Dy's normally tanned face. "He'd still've got lost." Folding the map, he returned the guidebook to its owner.

Windhaven, his dignity as ruffled as his neck-cloth, received the book in silence, but said as he pocketed it, "Then I must consider myself fortunate in having come here rather than attempting such a perilous journey."

"It's the girl as is lucky in comin' here," said Mrs. Beaton with another waggle of her clubbed finger. "Ye'll na be leavin' the Red Bear until Mr. Reeves himself vouches fer ye."

"Come, Meg," said her lord and master. "Leave the Quality to their supper."

Staring daggers at their guest, Mrs. Beaton preceded her husband through the open door and below stairs where Windhaven entertained no doubts she would reason at length with him until the good man, growing tired of the tirade, resolved to retreat from her nagging and proceed directly to Osmotherley and Mr. Reeves.

Dy hoped Mr. Beaton might not get lost. He did not elect to spend the rest of his life in this uncomfortable lodging as Mrs. Beaton's unwanted guest.

A few minutes after he was left alone in the parlor, the door opened to admit his creative minded ward. "Good evening," he said amiably as she dipped the merest curtsey at him.

"Good evening, my lord," she replied, her voice as smooth and sweet as honey. She met his quizzical gaze with no down turned eyes and even smiled as if she had looked forward to their next meeting instead of having concocted this Canterbury tale about abductions.

Inwardly he marvelled that there was not a note of fear or guilt to mar the innocence of her manner. He decided she was either a child who lost herself in fantasy or an habitual liar. In either case, it would serve no purpose to expose his knowledge of her shameful revelations just yet. He doubted not that he would be subject to immediate tears or recriminations.

Once again, he recalled fondly the independent lady he had left behind to under-

take this folly. He felt an irrepressible longing to confide in the one he had no doubt
would sympathize with his frustrations.
The reverie strengthened his resolve to
hurry south where he could deliver his
troublesome ward into more capable
hands. Adele would know how to quell
Priscilla's fits and starts, just as she quelled
any forward young miss.

The expectation brightened his mood as
he enquired affably, "I trust you were re-
freshed by your nap?" He seated Priscilla
in one of the heavy black leather chairs at
the ancient pedestal table which was covered by a Brussels lace cloth.

"Oh yes, thank you," Priscilla said
brightly. "I can't think what made me so
sleepy, only it must have been the storm;
lightning frightens me so. When I am
afraid, I close my eyes and the next thing,
I fall into a dead sleep."

"I imagine setting off towards a new life
must be frightening."

"Well, yes, it might be," Priscilla agreed
thoughtfully as she coiled her unbound
black hair around one hand. Then, dropping the silken mass over one shoulder, she
added, "But I have longed for an adventure forever, and it must be dreadfully
poor spirited in me, if I *was* afraid."

He chuckled. "It sounds as if you are making an attempt to convince yourself."

"Well, I am," she replied. Catching her lower lip between her teeth, she confessed, "Mama was always praising Papa. She told me he was in heaven because he gave his life for a friend, for *you*. Whenever I do something chicken-hearted, I fear I am a disappointment to him."

"It is easier to tell oneself to be brave than actually to accomplish the feat," Windhaven said warily.

"Do you think so?" Priscilla was gazing at him with something akin to hero worship in her deep blue eyes. He made a point of pouring himself a glass of wine so as to remain unaffected by her adoring gaze.

"I know so," he replied as he fortified himself. She released a sigh and, arising from the hard chair, propelled herself across the room to look, he deduced, more closely at a picture. "Who is that?" she asked.

He followed her. Scrutinizing the smoke-dimmed portrait, he said, "Charles the Second, I think."

"He's much handsomer than . . ." Her gaze left the picture and settled on another more modern one.

Windhaven followed the path of her gaze

and discovered a portrait of King George III in his younger days. Covering a grin behind his tumbler, he said, "I hope you will refrain from voicing such sentiments to anyone else."

"Would I be charged with treason?" she enquired.

Unable to help himself, he laughed, "No, but you'd be thought very impolite." At that moment, a waiter appeared, bearing a large covered tray. "Come now," Windhaven said, offering his arm to guide her back to the table. "Let us eat."

"I'm so glad it isn't bread pudding," she said when the waiter placed a serving of veal cutlets and potatoes at her place.

Laughing, Windhaven agreed, but he was rather more glad that his companion was putting him in good humor.

Later, as she was retiring from the parlor, he said he thought they might take a tour around the walled city after completing that other business.

"Do you really mean to take me shopping?" she enquired, clapping her little hands together gleefully.

"Yes," he said with an arch smile. "Unless the magistrate claps me into jail for abducting you."

"Why should he do that?" she enquired,

tilting her head in a beguiling manner that nearly made Windhaven laugh.

"I'm sure I do not know why," he replied hiding a broad smile behind a hand. *"I* am the one who has been taken out of his way to champion a pretty little girl who possesses more hair than wit."

Her eyes danced towards a spotted mirror over the mantel. *"Am* I pretty?" she enquired, turning unmistakably coquettish eyes upon him.

"That is an impertinent question," he chided. Suddenly he recalled from memory an odd proverb. Entirely appropriate to his ward's circumstances, he recited it. "My old nurse used to tell me, 'Pretty is as pretty does.' "

She pulled a sour face and said, "I thought I was done with edifying platitudes. Don't gentlemen compliment ladies in London?"

Saying, "Only those ladies who are deserving," he steered her towards her door and deposited her within her room.

She stared at him with her little mouth wide open. Then, haughtily, she closed her lips, and affected a cool stare that Windhaven thought worthy of a peer. She seemed to hold his gaze until she was satisfied that her arrogance had impressed him, then with no lowering of her manner, said, "I pray you will teach me how to deserve a few tributes."

He pinched her cheek. "Don't seek them out, Priscilla, and they will fly to you. Good night." Then admonishing her to lock her door, he retired to his own chamber to read the letter that would reveal the secret of Priscilla's lineage.

The identity of Priscilla's grandfather daunted him. The noble gentleman was not among his circle of acquaintances, being by nature a recluse. But his sister entertained lavishly and often, and Windhaven had more than a passing acquaintance with her. If they could gain Lady Mathilda's sympathy, they might manage after all.

The sooner Priscilla was off his hands, the sooner he could get on with the real business of his life, which was doing whatever pleased him.

The next morning it began to seem as if he might never be rid of the troublesome chit. Mrs. Beaton threatened to send for a magistrate if they went to tour York before Mr. Beaton returned from Osmotherley with Mr. Reeves or his voucher. "For if I was to give ye leave t' wander aboot, what would keep ye from takin' the high road north?" she enquired with all the grace of a brood hen.

Priscilla's blue eyes opened as wide as

saucers in the face of this remark, and the viscount was convinced that her very next fantasy would take them straight to the Border. He was determined that it would not be with him that she flew to Gretna, in her daydreams or otherwise. "My good woman," he said tersely. "Can you actually believe I should wish myself to be leg-shackled to a goose-witted schoolgirl for the rest of my days?"

Mrs. Beaton's down-the-nose gaze told him that was exactly what she did think. Sheltering her abused chick with her large body, she said, "I only thank the good Lord this poor babe had the courage to speak of her fears before she had no choice but to pay the blacksmith."

"Bah," Windhaven said, turning on his heel to glare out the window. Unseasonable sunshine bathed the courtyard in heat and would soon dry up the puddles and mud holes that had made his progress north-wards such an agony.

Windhaven rubbed a frustrated hand over his golden head. Outside of truly ab-ducting his ward, he had no choice but to bide his time, trusting to Providence for their speedy deliverance.

And in good time, Mr. Beaton did re-turn, relieving Windhaven of his anxiety by proclaiming in his impassive fashion that the gentleman was in fact the girl's guardian, and in a rather more animated style that the parson had surprised him by laughing aloud at the good joke Miss Gaines had played on them all.

"Well he might laugh," Mrs. Beaton said tartly. "*He* was not obliged to lose sleep over an 'eedless prank." Turning her small eyes upon the viscount she declared, "What that child needs is a good spanking."

"For shame, Mrs. Beaton," Windhaven laughed, "That is hardly in keeping with your defense last night. Moreover, I do not think violence will mend my ward's opinion of me."

"I am not a child!" Priscilla maintained with a stamp of her foot.

Windhaven affected a scowl. "A fine manner you have of convincing me that you are a lady."

Immediately she was all contrition. "I beg your pardon, my lord," she said, tears brimming prettily on her lashes. "I did act like a baby." Then, in a worried tone, "Will you forget your promise to take me shopping today?"

"Certainly not," he replied, handing her up the stairs. "Go fetch your cloak. We shall do it now, before you can concoct another grievance against me."

As he expected, her tears dried instantly

and he was again praised as the kindest of men. As quickly as she skipped up stairs, Priscilla returned to the coffee room, full of excitement for their exercise.

But if she thought her guardian meant to escort her into every shop in York which catered to feminine fancies, she was sadly disappointed. Windhaven guided her into only one establishment and directed the proprietress to have a traveling cloak of dull gold broadcloth hemmed to fit his ward and sent before nightfall to the Red Bear. When she protested that the color would not suit such a pretty girl, he said, "Well you seem to have an eye for color. How soon can you have something ready for her?"

The shopkeeper proceeded to show them a carriage dress which had been ordered and never paid for. It was made of light blue cashmere. Priscilla squealed in delight. "Please my lord, may I have it?" she enquired, fingering the fabric as if she had never touched anything so soft.

"It might have been made for miss," said the self-assured modiste. "Except for the length, which is of no significance. The flounce can come off," she suggested, "And a rouleau substituted."

"I cannot wear this gold cloak . . ." Priscilla said with a sigh.

"I have a wonderful idea," said the

dressmaker. Placing the precious dress in her young client's arms, she hastened to her workroom, returning with a plaid woolen pelisse and highland bonnet. "If we add a matching plaid rouleau to the hemlines of your dress, just so . . ."

"Oh, yes! It is perfect," Priscilla agreed. Then, catching Windhaven's eye, she suppressed her enthusiasm with an effort that made him quirk a smile. "But it is really not for me to say. My guardian must decide."

"What, will you have me become the ogre once more?" he laughed. "You may have the dress *and* the pelisse if madame can deliver them to the inn before supper."

"It can be done," said the shrewd businesswoman, "But . . ."

Reaching within his coat, Windhaven extracted his wallet and tossed several sovereigns on the table. "That ought to take care of any objections," he said, noting the seamstress's evident satisfaction. "I shall leave you with madame, Priscilla." His ward clapped her hands together. He directed a final comment towards the dressmaker who was making an attempt not to grab the money. "Complete her ensemble with the necessary items."

"Shoes?" Priscilla interjected. "Gloves?"

"I have placed you in the hands of the

most excellent modiste in York," he replied
removing towards the door. "She will know
what you need, Priscilla. Just remember,
you are being outfitted for travel, not your
come out."

A trunk was set down at the Red Bear
just as Windhaven was escorting Priscilla
into their private parlor for supper. She was
wearing another new dress and blushed to
her eyes when he teased her over her purchase. "It seems you drive a harder bargain
than I was capable of," he said, approving
the ensemble of lilac twilled silk. Its chaste
neckline was filled with a pert white ruff
whose lace was repeated at the wrists and
hemline. "It seems this overworked seamstress can work miracles if she likes the
color of one's money."

At that moment, a maid announced that
a trunk had been delivered for Miss
Gaines. Priscilla, forgetting her resolution
to act the grown up, squeaked and began
a headlong dash toward the public room.

Windhaven caught her wrist, and subdu-
ing her impatience with a dark look, requested the maid to have the trunk sent to
Miss Gaines's room. "You may inspect madame's handiwork after we dine," he said,
seating his ward in her customary place at

the table as the maid scurried to do his bidding.

"But don't you wish to see what I . . ."

Affecting a yawn, he said, "As long as the style becomes your youth and does not offend convention, I shall have very little to say about what you wear. Now, will you have the chicken or beef pie?"

He thought she might be inclined to pout, as her lower lip was beginning to protrude sulkily. He shook his head ruefully, thinking if he had known this was what life with a schoolgirl was to be like, he would have sent a letter to Mr. Reeves on the return post declining the honor Arthur had done him. Deciding to put an end to Priscilla's fanciful grievances, he raised his eyebrow in a monitory fashion and said, "If you wish to accompany me to London, you will spare me the tantrum, Priscilla."

Heaving a great sigh, she exchanged her sullen look for one of worried innocence as she enquired, "When are we to go?"

"Early in the morning," he said, filling his plate. "If you decline supper, you might travel hungry."

She held out her plate. "I'll have the chicken, if you please."

Five

Left to her own devices in London, Adele could find no peace. What had he meant? What beginning did he have in mind?

They had been friends so long that she did not think they could begin on any other foot, though nothing else would please her as well. She cautioned herself not to be led by his very agreeable kisses to believe he had conceived a grand passion for her. That was a silly, romantic dream not worth indulging.

Adele had long ago given up romantic dreams, attributing them to dyspepsia. And since she still suffered from the effects of a stomach which contracted expectantly every time she remembered his kiss, she treated herself with peppermint and fennel until the memory might fade.

When after two days, the regimen had no effect on her involuntary reaction to him, she began to fret in earnest over what he had meant by the kisses. Her heart, longing to attribute it to affection, told her to trust the soaring feeling which the recollection of his ardent embrace occasioned. But her mind warned that a gentleman did not press kisses, however delightful, upon a lady until he had proposed. Her prudent self cringed at the memory of Miss Willoughby demanding to know in her roundabout manner whether Windhaven had declared his intentions. That he had not, that he had indeed made a jest of the matter persuaded Adele that matrimony was the furthermost thing from his mind.

Her cheeks flamed with chagrin even as her traitorous heart pulsed with the rhythm of his name: Dysart, Dysart.

How could she have been so foolish as to trust her heart in such a matter? For all her sophistication in matters of fashion, she simply was no match for a man of sophisticated tastes.

Had she shown too much partiality towards him, thus encouraging over familiar conduct?

To turn her mind from such lowering thoughts, Adele set about transforming Lady Katherine Bermondey from a shy wallflower into a blushing rose. The self-effacing heiress quickly benefitted from Adele's patronage and gentle beauty treat-

ments that, though they did not fade the
despised freckles, made her gold flecked
complexion shine with good health and anticipation. Before week's end, she was allowed to appear at select evening affairs in
shimmering gowns of mauve and Mexican
blue, and once in the Park at the fashionable hour of five o'clock wearing a becoming white cashmere walking dress and
pelisse of brick-colored merino, which
Adele had given her from her own closet.

Topping shining brown hair cut daringly
a la mode, Lady Katherine wore a Caledo-
nian cap that became her new self-pos-
sessed, but still demure manner. To say she
was a triumph in the Park would be to have
uttered faint praise as she was besieged on
every hand by handsome young bucks anxious to make her acquaintance, only to cry
out in wonder at the beauty she had hid-
den for two prior Seasons.

Lady Katherine's newfound popularity
served in no small manner to soothe
Adele's sudden loss of regard for her own
style. But Adele could not admit to others
what so appalled herself: that she could
not muster any but the most polite interest
in Fashion excepting as it enhanced other's
amour propre.

However, her interest in others offered
another unexpected advantage in Miss Wil-

loughby's more becoming appearance. As the week progressed, her cousin found less to criticize and more to smile about, thus making her a more amiable companion.

As the week ended at an early ball, Adele noticed with an almost parental satisfaction the expanded court of bachelors vying to dance with the young lady. Even Elvira was seen to tread the boards with a gentleman or two. Perhaps, Adele thought, as she sat among the chaperones, it was not too late for that lady to find happiness in her own home.

Adele's newfound modesty did not go unnoticed. Seating herself beside Adele, Lady Mathilda sent a footman off to fetch glasses of lemonade, then commented, "I see your companion has finally succumbed to your example."

"I hope you don't mean to tell me she is now an unsuitable companion for me," Adele said in what she hoped were laughing tones, as one matron had indeed spitefully suggested that very thing. "Elvira is much easier on the eyes in her brighter plumage than ever she was in raven's weeds."

"Yes; only I thought you preferred the contrast," said the lady, her tone mildly reproachful as she looked over Adele's gown of Scotch plaid silk. Turning to admire Elvira's gown of shot lavender silk as that lady turned a figure of the dance, she said, "Not every lady would like having a shadow who rivalled her in looks, would she?"

The footman returning with their refreshment, Adele refrained from replying until he had dispatched his duty, but her heart was not easy. Feeling as if she must sink under the weight of the gentle lady's disapproval, she said, "I do not begrudge my cousin's good looks. One cannot shine at all in the shadow of a black cloud."

"I suppose not," the lady returned absently, fanning herself. Adele took the opportunity of the lull in conversation to savor her hostess's lemonade.

As they sipped glasses of tepid lemonade, the kindhearted women suddenly ventured, "You seem of a sudden full of good works, Adele. I could scarce believe my ears when Phillipa told me you'd taken her daughter under your wing."

Adele turned a startled eye upon her friend and enquired in dismay, "Am I accounted so unfeeling?"

Lady Mathilda fluttered her feathered fan desultorily as she nodded a forbidding acknowledgement to several passersby who abruptly turned aside. "Have you turned over a new leaf?" she demanded with a steel edge to her normally soft spoken voice.

Adele was uncomfortably aware that the most popular of Society's dragons did not approve of her. "I hardly think enhancing Lady Katherine's and Elvira's looks signifies I have become a different person."

Lady Mathilda's gaze settled in a considering manner upon her, as if she was experiencing difficulty believing Adele capable of such generous behavior. "There can be no doubt of it," she said at last, tempering her pronouncement with a gentle smile. "The *former* Miss Fonteyne would have thought nothing of making a mockery of Lady Katherine's unfashionable debut or of ridiculing Miss Willoughby's old gowns. What can have changed you, I wonder?" She released Adele's uncertain gaze to sweep the assembly hall with a searching look before enquiring with a raised eyebrow, "Or, ought I to ask, for *whom* have you changed?"

Adele directed a cursory glance around the ballroom before lifting her honey-colored eyebrows and confessing in all honesty, "No one here could have the least effect on my character, my lady."

Lady Mathilda chuckled as if enjoying Adele's parry. "Then I must assume he is not among the company tonight, my dear.

Pity. I should like to congratulate him on your very gratifying transformation."

"Nonsense," Adele replied, affecting an amused tone despite the embarrassment she felt. She sipped again from her glass, hoping to cool her self-consciousness.

It was not so much that Lady Mathilda suspected her heart was vulnerable to a certain gentleman's influence. That event was only to be applauded. Rather, Adele felt real chagrin that her past selfishness had given rise to public astonishment that she could turn her hand to doing good for others. Extricating herself from the perceptive lady's measuring presence as the dance ended with the excuse that she had ignored Miss Willoughby for too long, she allowed privately, and not quite truthfully, that not even Windhaven's kisses had given her as much satisfaction as transforming Lady Katherine and her own cousin.

She began to look forward to the day Windhaven would bring his young ward into her home, so she could devote herself to molding Priscilla into a perfect lady. One who was as charitable as she was fashionable.

The majority of the journey southward passed uneventfully, though not peacefully.

Windhaven's ward was either in raptures over the countryside or at daggers with him because he refused repeatedly to detour towards an interesting ruin. The fact that he spent more time on the box driving than riding within was undoubtedly the reason neither actually drew blood during their brief but pointed disagreements.

The weather continued fine for the first day and only concern for his ward, despite all her protestations that travelling did not affect her ill, induced him to pull into the Angel at Grantham. He could not have made a more agreeable choice as far as Priscilla was concerned. The thirteenth century inn more than satisfied her hungry imagination. Said to have been founded by the Knights Templar, the inn was reputed to have served Richard III as he signed the death warrant of the Duke of Buckingham in 1485. Priscilla was in alt. "Can I see the room?" she enquired of the maid who had so kindly revealed this fascinating information.

"Well, miss, ye're sleepin' in one of 'em," said the somewhat doltish female. Windhaven, passing by his ward's chamber at that moment, leaned in his head and sternly reminded the maid to be about her business. When Priscilla excitedly asked if he thought the hunchbacked king might actually have slept in her room, he glanced around its confines and told her in un-equivocal tones that he doubted it. He had no intention of feeding her overactive imagination when he knew very well if he did, she was likely to pass an anxious, sleepless night.

Upon her joining him the next day, he was confirmed in his suspicions. Her eyelids were heavy smudged with dark circles and she jumped at the least out of the ordinary sound. "Did you see King Richard?" he en-quired as he poured out a cup of chocolate for her. She shrugged her tired shoulders and said, "No, but I thought I heard his unequal shuffle going down the hall." She bristled when he laughed.

"Goose," he chuckled. "That was a late arrival's trunk being brought up." When she opened her mouth to make a retort, he urged, "Hurry up, we still have a long way to go," satisfied that the implied threat would bring down her defenses and hasten them on their way.

Clouds began to pile up in the afternoon and before nightfall, a cold rain forced them to call a halt to their travels at the Lion Inn in Buckden. When Windhaven let his shivering ward down, she enquired wea-rily, "How much farther to London?"

"What? are you worn out already?" he

said, ordering hot chocolate to be sent to her room.

"Perhaps I should not be, if I were used to it," she said dully.

"Where has the romance gone?" he asked. She shot a dagger look at him.

"I have had quite enough of romance," she said. "Will you stop taxing me and answer my question?"

"We shall be there tomorrow," he said handing her over to the landlady who clucked over her like a mother hen. When he adjured her not to tell his ward of the romantic history of the establishment, she tutted him for a fool. "I keep a respectable inn, see if I don't," she said, bustling Priscilla to her room and promising her a hot bath and a comfortable bed. "An' I don't hold wi' romance."

Windhaven was tempted to bless the woman, but knew she would think it an impertinence, so he kept his tongue between his teeth. When she returned to the public room, she told him respectfully, but firmly, that miss was already in bed, and, as she'd decided to take supper there, he did not need to speak a private parlor for his supper. Furthermore, she informed him that he could take potluck with the rest of her guests as she had more to do than to cater to the tastes of Quality folk.

Laughing at his hostess's abrupt manner, the viscount gratefully accepted her kind invitation, and just as eagerly after a plentiful but plain supper, took himself to his own bed where the sound of the rain drumming on the gable lulled him to a sound sleep and dreams of the sensitive lady awaiting him in London.

He awoke the next morning with a splitting head and the beginnings of a cold. Jackson, mistaking his master's malaise for a hangover, hauled him into the coach with Miss Gaines. "You'll na be drivin' us into a ditch today, my lord," he said apologetically. "There'd be no gettin' us out, that's for certain."

"Is he unwell?" enquired Priscilla. Jackson raised his hand as if downing a glass of spirits. "Oh," she said.

"I know what you think," Windhaven growled, wincing as Jackson latched the door. "And you're wrong, you old flycatcher. Though you're both enough to drive one to drink."

"'E'll be all right and tight an he sleeps it off, miss," Jackson assured. "Just pull on the checkstring, if ye needs me."

"Yes, I will," Priscilla said nervously. Behind closed eyelids, Windhaven could feel her eyes boring a hole in his forehead. He thought uncharitably that she ought to give him the forward facing seat as he was under the weather. However, there was nothing for it but to endure until he made it home.

It seemed like hours later that they turned off the main road and drove down a deucedly bumpy lane. Opening his eyes, Windhaven discovered his ward had disappeared, and was half-inclined to think he had dreamed the entire journey as a nightmare induced by his headache, when he heard her giggling somewhere above his head. "I wish you will let me drive them now," she was saying. The viscount sat upright, saying in his most commanding voice, "Jackson if you let her take the reins, I shall let you go immediately!"

He heard Jackson say, "There you have it, miss; m'master says I must not," but he was not completely easy in his mind. It sounded as if the man were winking at him.

They were travelling next to a river, which due to the rains was running high. But for some strange reason, probably owing to his cold, Windhaven felt as if the coach was actually travelling down the middle of the stream. The wheels were kicking up streams of water and occasionally, he was struck with the dizzying sensation that the entire vehicle was floating. He might have been satisfied with attributing the unsettling feeling to his illness, except that at the same time Priscilla emitted one of her ear-shattering shrieks and began to giggle on a rather hysterical note.

Windhaven sat up, placing his feet in the foot well with a splash. "What the deuce?" he demanded, leaning outside the window to see the River Ouse running alongside him at a great rate and themselves seemingly in the midst of it. "What is the meaning of this?" he demanded.

"Oh, I knew he wouldn't like it," Priscilla said. "There's not an adventurous bone in his dried up old body."

Despite her unflattering assessment, Windhaven was far from dry-boned. He stood in water nearly up to his knees and was distinctly aware of the cold, muddy water that was spilling over the tops of his Hessians. Out of all patience with romantical schoolgirls and their scheming champions, he asked, "Who is responsible for this infernal detour across the River Styx?"

"Hah!" exclaimed Priscilla. "A fat lot you know; this is the Ouse!"

Cursing beneath his breath, he shouted above the rush of the water, "I know *where* we are, you demon-child." He sneezed violently, throwing his broad-brimmed beaver from his head into the watery well. "I want to know *why!*"

The coach began to shift towards the off side and its submerged hazards of ditch and stone wall. As it lurched, Windhaven lost his balance and sat down, up to his chest in cold water. For a few moments, he gasped wordlessly in shock, then when he had regained his voice, demanded, "Damn, Jackson; do you wish me to drown?"

"Devil a bit," responded the jehu, taking the reins into his own capable hands. "Hey up! you miserable nags." He cracked his whip over the heads of the recalcitrant team they had acquired at the Falcon in Huntingdon urging them towards dry land at a pace which threatened to overset them.

Then, at a critical moment when the coach was listing heavily to port, Jackson brought them on an even keel, allowing the four wheels again to turn in unison. Windhaven perceived the more regular slip-slop of iron-shod hooves striking muddy ground rather than the watery sound of an ark plowing its way through the flood. He expected every moment that Jackson would pull up and set him upon dry ground, but his coachman proceeded apace until they achieved yet higher ground.

"*You* may be high and dry," Windhaven said through clenched teeth which were beginning to chatter nonsensically. "But *I* am still up to my waist in high water. Set me down immediately!"

The haste with which Jackson complied with his command threw Windhaven's hat, which was still bobbing about on the receding tide, onto the forward seat. Windhaven heard his ward saying in awful, hushed tones, "Pray, do not let him out; he might kill you."

Jackson climbed down from his perch, causing the coach to lurch and its watery contents to wash from side to side. "Do ye wish to let 'im out yersel, miss?" he enquired with a chuckle. "Dinna think so." Without further ado, he unlatched the door and for his trouble received a frigid foot bath. "Beggin' yer pardon, my lord," he said, letting down the step.

Despite his soggy attire, Windhaven descended from his coach with as much dignity as if he were being set down before Carlton House. "I do not hold you responsible, Jackson; you were merely following the misguided instructions of my ward."

"She was sayin's how she wished for some fun, my lord," Jackson said, quite subdued by his master's restrained manner.

"She has been plaguing me for some fun ever since it was my misfortune to pick her up in Osmotherley," the viscount growled. "And you see where it landed me . . ."

"Aye my lord," Jackson said, his head lowered contritely.

Windhaven wished the coachman would not stare at his boots, hideously stained as they must be. Regardless of his own passion to peel off the waterlogged footwear, he forced himself to maintain an unaffected posture as he concluded, "You will kindly refrain from indulging her whims in the future." His dignified set down concluded with another potent sneeze which quite destroyed his elegant manner.

"Would you like a drink, my lord?" Jackson said, assisting him into the coach. Windhaven did not deign to reply, but gratefully accepted the flask of Irish whiskey which Jackson proffered. When he climbed atop the coach, Windhaven thought to hurry them towards an inn. But a moment later, his coachman returned and wrapped a blanket around his shoulders.

Throwing off the dry cover, Windhaven protested, "I do not need . . . ah . . . ah . . . choo" and sneezing again, allowed his coachman to fold the warm wool around his shoulders.

"Ye've caught yer death," Jackson said, backing out of the coach.

"That ought to make by ward happy," Windhaven said miserably as he leaned his aching head against the cushion. To his surprise, Priscilla, who was standing beside his coachman, burst into abashed tears.

She was contrition itself the remainder of the journey. While Jackson attended his master at the George in St. Neots, she, installed in a private parlor, wrung her hands and wept over her guardian's desperate condition.

The landlady, enquiring as to the nature of the gentleman's attack, added an uncertain, "I hope it's not catching."

"No," Priscilla assured her. "Only I have drowned him. And if he dies, it must be my fault." Then she dissolved into inconsolable, but beautiful tears.

The flood receded only when Jackson appeared to assure her that Lord Windhaven's life was not in the balance after all. "Are ye certain ye aren't wet through yersel, miss?" he enquired.

"No, thank you," she replied, relief shining in her stricken face as if the sun had broken through the clouds. "Your great coat kept me as dry as toast." Clasping one of the coachman's knotty hands in both of hers she pleaded, "Will you tell my guardian I will try to be good from now on?"

Jackson squeezed her hand in a fatherly manner. "That he will be happy to hear."

Very soon after, the viscount himself appeared in the parlor. His aristocratic nose was red, his eyes were puffy, and Priscilla thought he looked as if he had been crying. But she refrained from saying so with a restraint that Windhaven, if he had known of it, would have deemed extraordinary.

Furthermore, she did not throw her arms about his neck in a fit of grateful praise when he announced rather thickly that Jackson was speaking them a post chaise with which to complete their journey. "For I mean to sleep in my own bed tonight," he added as if neither hell nor high water could delay him any longer.

Six

Reaching London that evening, the viscount placed his ward in his butler's care before he took himself directly to Miss Fonteyne's home. He was let in immediately, the footman informing him he was just in time for evening tea.

Setting aside her needlework, Adele arose from the chair and glided towards him, her hands outstretched in genuine welcome. But she saw more in his appearance to concern than delight her. His handsome face was pinched and flushed, and his normally well-groomed blond hair was uncharacteristically tousled. Worried by his haggard looks, she took his arm and placed him in a comfortable chair, enquiring in alarm, "My lord, have you taken ill?"

"The trip was," he said, brushing a hand over his disheveled locks, "rather wearing. However, I shall not burden you with the details, only say I have arrived with Priscilla in tow."

"Oh, is she here?" Adele enquired, soothing the fabric of his sleeve unconsciously. "Why did you not bring her up?"

"Rather than subject you to her at once, I left her at my home," Windhaven said. "She can be . . . somewhat of a handful."

"Yes, well," Adele responded, attempting to soothe the viscount's agitation, "it was to be expected; you, unused to children's tantrums, and her, cast without warning, into the keeping of a stranger. How did she weather the journey?" Adele enquired.

"Far better than I," he replied, sneezing involuntarily into his handkerchief. "The girl exhausted me."

"I can see that. When she is more settled in your home, I expect she will be less burdensome."

"I beg your pardon," he said, blowing his nose inelegantly, "for exposing you to this cold. I would not have done so, were I not in need of your assistance. Priscilla . . ."

In a teasing voice Adele said, "I imagine you two are quite attached by now."

He rolled his eyes towards the ceiling. "She thinks of me alternately as the hero and the ogre of a fairy tale."

"And she is your little princess?" Adele prompted.

"Hardly. She is a thorn in my side."

"Well, after all, Dy, she is but a child."
Adele could not like herself for breathing
a sigh of relief. "You must be patient until
she acquires some grace."

"Must I?" he demanded, punctuating his
query with a dubious arch of his brow.
"Fortunately, I may depend on you to deal
with her," he asserted.

"Of course, I said I would help . . ."
she began.

"And she is not a child, her very words,"
he said.

"They will always have it so," she agreed.

"For once, she has the right of it," he
said. "She is seventeen."

Adele could not quite discipline her features from betraying her dismay. "Heavens!
She is a young lady!"

He shook his head. "Believe me, Priscilla
is no lady, despite her noble relative."

"She has family?" Adele enquired in a
rather choked tone. "Why then was she
given over into your care?"

"Suffice it to say, her mother was considered to have married poorly and conse-
quently was disowned for her choice. I
need you to turn my country miss into a
worthy young lady before a *rapprochement*
can be devised."

Adele uneasily fingered the amethyst
brooch at her throat. Suddenly, everything

about the situation seemed wrong. "Of course, I shall do whatever I can to help," she said. "Even though I believe I am not the proper person to effect this transformation."

"Nonsense," he said, arising from his chair to stroll to the mantel where he gave his appearance a disdainful inspection. Then, turning to regard her, he grinned. "You are the most proper person for this charge."

She closed her eyes in a quick gesture of resignation and said, "All I can do is turn her into the latest fashionable toast. Do you wish your ward to become as frivolous as I?"

He strode towards her, covering her hand with his. "I like you very well," he said his voice husky with his cold, "And would be very pleased if Priscilla turned out half as well."

He spoke so fiercely, that Adele was compelled to wonder whether the chit had melted his heart. He was bound to fall in love some time, she knew. She did not think that his unexpected fervor for a girl just out of school should distress her. But it did.

It was difficult to convince herself that she was merely disappointed in his appreciation of superficial appearances, and so said, "It pains me to admit it, Windhaven, but it was driven home to me while you were on your errand. Lady Mathilda does not approve of me at all."

"Does she not?" Windhaven enquired. "I can scarcely believe she would speak an unkind word to anyone."

"She did not," Adele said. "Only, she expressed surprise that I should turn my hand to doing good works."

"Have you? Then I shall depend upon you to work a miracle with my ward."

She was about to pose an extremely impertinent query to him, when Miss Willoughby returned followed by a footman with the tea tray, providing a welcome opportunity for Adele to form her features into a more cordial expression. "After your breakneck journey," Elvira said as she eyed his *deshabille* with undisguised horror, "I suppose you would like a cup of tea also."

Dysart accepted the cup with a sidelong glance toward Adele. What he would like was a few more uninterrupted moments with her. But he did not confess such impolite sentiments, only reconciled himself to Miss Willoughby's inevitable interference and cautiously sipped his tea as she chattered on.

Ten minutes into a long-winded and unnecessary description of the lengths to which Adele had gone to refurbish her wardrobe and restore her forgotten sense of style, Elvira chirped, "The world looks so much brighter when one is done wearing black, my lord."

"I daresay," he agreed. "The view is much improved wherever one looks." To his surprise, the lady's cheeks flushed with a becoming tinge of pink.

"I know you for a sad tease," she gushed, ducking her lace-capped head over her teacup. "But I do not mind. In fact, I have been the object of several flirtations during the week."

"Have you, ma'am?" Dy asked, his voice menacing even though his eye gleamed mischievously. "You did not tell me your companion had become a shocking flirt, Adele."

"We have been occupied with vain pleasures," Adele said, sounding very much like her companion's guardian, except that she giggled at the last.

"Oh, do you think I have exceeded what is proper?" Elvira asked

"Scarcely," Adele gently assured her. "You are the soul of propriety, Elvira."

Before she could say anything further, Windhaven interjected, "I must have your reply, Adele. Will you . . ."

Setting her cup noisily in its saucer, Miss Willoughby bounced to her feet and scurried towards the door, prattling foolishly, "Pray, excuse me, do not ask until I have gone. Here, I am leaving. Do you wish me to close the door?" And to the startled couple's complete surprise, she did close the door.

"What is the matter with her do you think?" he enquired, looking from the door to his stunned companion. "I say, she is a strange bird. How can you stand to have her fluttering about your house?"

"In answer to your first question, I have no idea," Adele said, laughing over the rim of her teacup. "As to the second, Elvira amuses me. And so do you, Dy." Placing the cup on the table at her elbow, and arranging her skirts more becomingly, she pretended innocence and enquired, "Will I what?"

He smoothed his waistcoat then possessed himself of her hand and raised her from her seat. "Will you take Priscilla under your wing? Tonight?"

"She is your ward," Adele replied, withdrawing her hand from his fervent grasp and pressing it to her breast bone in an attempt to quiet her fluttering heartbeat. "Can she not stay with you for one night?"

"No!" he said vehemently. "You know how people will talk. Priscilla Gaines is an innocent child, and I will not allow a hint of scandal to ruin her chances in society."

"What a doting father you have become," Adele said. "I suppose you will want me to procure a voucher for her at Almack's."

Removing an invisible particle of lint from the sleeve of his blue coat, he moved towards the hallway, saying, "Of course. It will help win the notice of her grandfather."

"Dy," Adele stopped him at the door with a hand on his sleeve as a sudden revelation flashed through her mind. "Are you in dun territory?"

"No," he said, covering the hesitant hand with his own. "I'm rich as a nabob. And I intend to use the ready to make my ward acceptable to her family and the world."

Adele's expectant gaze fell. Inasmuch as she knew he never expended funds to benefit another person except on a whim or for entertainment, his blunt declaration sounded very much to her like a confession of love. Swallowing her pride, she asked, "Are you in love with her then?"

"No," he said, giving her hand a squeeze. "Only, I promised to take care of her, and it's quite beyond my ken."

As much as Adele would like not to become involved, it was obvious that Miss

Gaines could not remain under her guardian's roof. For the sake of their friendship and Priscilla's good name, she must take the girl into her own home, even if it meant the end of her hopes. But she attempted once more to remind him of the world's opinion by saying, "What will people think of you for giving your ward into the hands of a lady not related to you?"

"Probably that I admire you above all other ladies," he ventured with a teasing grin. "And can think of no one else whose example I should like Priscilla to follow."

"That is extremely flattering," Adele said, blushing. "But I think my influence must be far from beneficial."

"You are the daughter of an earl," Windhaven reminded her. "With an impeccable lineage, and infallible taste which has finally benefitted your companion. Who better than you?"

"Elvira," Adele laughed. "Despite her improved looks, she would be the first to remind you that I am far too young to have a settling influence on a child."

"Oh no!" Dy retorted, dropping her hand and backing away in horror. "You do not mean to saddle me with that chatterbox. After an hour of listening to her worthy, but insipid commentary on the proper upbringing of delicate young ladies and

Priscilla's reciprocal complaints that Miss Elvira is stifling all her joy, I should likely strangle the both of them.

"I refuse to believe that," Adele laughed, although she herself had been tempted at times to resort to that tactic to silence her cousin. "You are the soul of compassion."

"Only where you are concerned," Windhaven replied. "No, my dear, since you won't take her, and I certainly can't keep her under my roof, there is only one thing to be done . . ."

Since he left the alternative dangling enticingly, Adele raised her gaze to his and enquired with a smile, "What might that be?"

In undeniable accents, Windhaven replied, "Marry."

"But I thought you didn't love her," Adele cried out, horrified that she had driven him to consider marrying a girl so lacking in grace as he seemed to find his ward.

"I don't," Windhaven replied with a shudder. Then he said in a dark challenging manner that made Adele's heart thud painfully against her ribs, "So, there it is. Will you . . ."

Once again, words failed him, but Adele knew what he meant. Would she groom Priscilla to be his bride. Despite misgivings and the disappointment of rejection, she bestowed a shaky smile upon him and said, "Yes, Dy; I will."

He surprised her by clasping her in a brief but crushing embrace that left them both breathless. "I won't go so far as to say you won't regret your decision," he laughed, accepting his cape and hat from a flustered servant who ran below stairs to relay the wonderful information that their mistress had accepted Viscount Windhaven without first ascertaining exactly what he had offered. Alone with Adele once more, he checked the impulse to kiss her, declaring with a moon-faced grin that made her heart trip over itself, "You have made me a happy man tonight."

Adele was far from happy, but reconciled herself to the task by allowing that she had never been able to say no to him. Waving him off with a smile that faded as soon as he crossed the threshold, she wondered how she could bring up a rival for the affections of the man she loved.

She had not solved her dilemma before the viscount returned with his pretty little girl in tow. Adele's heart sank even further as she compared the girl's rosy complexion and brunette looks with her own pale coloring and auburn hair. Priscilla was the complete foil for the Viscount Windhaven's golden perfection.

Realizing the war had been lost before the first battle had been joined, Adele decided to surrender with grace to the inevitable. She would do the best she could for Dy, and wish Miss Gaines happy.

Her first words did nothing to endear her to her reluctant sponsor. "But I want to stay with you," she said, clinging to her guardian in a manner that Adele could only describe as cringingly unfashionable.

"Miss Fonteyne will explain why you cannot," he said, disentangling himself from the girl's insistent grasp. "Really, Priscilla," he chided. "You will be much happier here."

"No, I won't," the girl sobbed. "You don't want me."

As she was ruining his elegant neck-cloth with her tears and clutching fingers, Dysart cried out, "Well, how could anyone want to deal with a whining chit who has more hair than wit?" as he directed a pleading look towards Adele.

Raising her eyebrows in full sympathy with his plight, she took charge of the distraught girl, saying stoically, "I daresay none of us will be happy for a while, Priscilla, but there is nothing for it, but to make the effort."

"I don't wish to," Priscilla stated, her lower lip jutting forward in a belligerent pout.

"That is perfectly clear," Adele said in gentle but firm tones. "However Lord Windhaven has asked you to, and since he has already gone to a great deal of trouble on your account, you must try to please him."

"I do not see why she must start now," Dysart said, going to the mirror to make an attempt to repair the effects of his ward's crushing grip. "It cannot bring about the least change in my opinion of her."

"You see," Priscilla sniffed from the comfort of Miss Fonteyne's arms. "He does not like me. Nobody does."

"Dy," Adele warned as she petted her charge's shaking shoulders reassuringly. "Do not be so provoking. The girl is frightened of you."

"No, she is not," he replied. Turning to face the allied females, he said, "Don't be taken in by her tragic air, Adele. Priscilla is fearless."

"There is some hope for her then," Adele said, offering the girl her own handkerchief with which to dry her eyes.

"But I," Windhaven interjected in dry tones, "being a helpless male, am terrified of her. She has concocted a Banbury tale with which I will not cooperate. You would do well to apply the proverbial grain of salt to everything she tells you."

Knowing the viscount to be a gentleman who was never rude except intentionally, Adele deduced that something must have caused the pair to quarrel. Suppressing the depression which the thought of his engaging in a lover's spat with anyone but herself, she suggested he ought to leave until they were all better rested.

"Nothing wrong with your logic," he said coming towards them. "That is why you are such a good friend."

Adele felt as if he was twisting a knife in her breast. But she compelled herself to reply in cordial tones, "How kind of you to say so."

"Well, I can scarcely speak anything warmer at the moment," he laughed, casting a meaningful glance towards his ward who was still crying woefully on Miss Fonteyne's spencer. Touching her averted cheek with a tenderness that made Adele heartsick, he adjured, "Do have the goodness to stop whining, Pris."

He might have saved his breath. Priscilla's tears fell unchecked, and his admonition earned him a startled rebuke from the lady upon whose shoulders all his hopes rested.

Seven

"I cannot believe my ears," Adele cried. Shielding Priscilla with her own body, as if she suddenly believed the viscount capable of doing violence to his ward, she said, "Take yourself home, my lord, until you have better control over your temper."

One eyebrow raising in counterpoint to the scowl that pulled down his lip, Dy stared at her while her frosty command sank into his fevered brain. Adele was looking at him as if she were Elizabeth defending her throne. It was plain by the wild look upon her usually serene face that she regarded him a dangerous foe. He felt an uncommon wrenching in the vicinity of his heart as he wondered what he had done that she should consider him in such an unfriendly light?

"Pray, forgive my outburst, fatigue must have rendered me temporarily insane," he said, ending his apology by sneezing miserably into his handkerchief. He took a moment behind the cloth to compose his countenance and his wounded vanity.

Peeking around the protection of Miss Fonteyne's slender shoulder, Priscilla hiccupped and said, "Think nothing of it." She added feelingly, "Nobody's perfect."

Although Adele praised his ward for her insight into human nature, Dysart inwardly groaned. *Look who's calling the kettle black.* However, he retained enough presence of mind not to speak the fatal words. Something warned him that Adele would only misconstrue anything else he might say against his ward.

Priscilla could be a charming little thing on first acquaintance, but he knew from harsh experience that she did not wear well. Longing to tell her just how far from the mark she herself fell, he said only, "That is no excuse; we are to make the attempt."

His warning did not appear to soften Adele's Amazonlike stance. Ringing the bell for a footman, she said, "That is all very well, but I am worn out with the effort. Good night, Dy." When her man appeared, she requested him to usher Lord Windhaven to the door, then take Miss Gaines's luggage to the guest room in the back of the house. "I think you will feel more at home overlooking the garden," she explained in a gentle voice. "It is quieter than—"

"Oh, I can sleep anywhere," Priscilla said in an animated tone that sent a chill up Windhaven's spine. The girl had the right of it; only *his* sleep had been disturbed. He felt as if he had been forced the last several days to take his rest on a bed of nails. But he had done his duty, seen Priscilla through hell and high water, and brought her to a protectress more formidable than the Virgin Queen. He could take himself home in good conscience, there to sleep off his cold.

A humourless grin creased his haggard face, evoking an enquiring and anxious look from the very lady whose sympathy he most craved. It was an encouraging beginning, and under normal circumstances he would be quick to share with Adele his misgivings about Priscilla's inconstant nature. But Adele must learn of her *protegee's* shortcomings the same way he had done— the hard way.

As the footman awaited him at the door, he bowed himself out, wishing the ladies a pleasant night's rest.

Suppressing the dismay she felt as he strode down the stairs after his stiffly formal *adieu*, Adele took Priscilla up stairs for a look at her room. "If it is not to your taste," she said, opening the door and standing aside to allow the girl to enter, "We shall have it done over."

She needn't have worried. Priscilla was enchanted by the twining ivy wallpaper and pink and green floral rug which warmed the floor. "Why, it brings the garden inside," she exclaimed, pirouetting in the center of the chamber before she skipped towards the window.

"I expect it must seem so," Adele replied, smiling as Priscilla fiddled with the latch. "But I shouldn't wish to bring the garden inside tonight; the damp, you know."

Giving over her attempt to open the window, Priscilla sighed, "Of course, how silly you must think me."

"Don't be so hard on yourself," Adele soothed, sitting upon a pink and green striped *chaise longue*. "As I recall, when I was seventeen, I expected everything to be just as I wished it might be."

"You, too?" Priscilla said on a note of relief that quite endeared her to Adele. "I was afraid I was the only one. Sometimes my imagination runs off with me . . ." Her bright smile faded as she crumpled at Miss Fonteyne's feet.

Alarmed by the girl's sudden breakdown, Adele lifted her to sit at her side. "There, my child, it is hardly an excuse for enacting a Cheltenham tragedy."

"Oh but it is. It is precisely why my—my guardian dislikes me," Priscilla confessed in a watery voice.

"I am of the opinion he rather thinks you do not like *him*," Adele said with a little sigh of self-pity.

"Yes, well, he does frighten me." Priscilla sniffed.

"That is to be expected," Adele replied, stroking the girl's silky hair. "The viscount has an elevated manner which intimidates everyone. That is what makes him so popular."

"I think it is odious." As the sniffing continued, Adele urged Priscilla to use her handkerchief. The girl applied it to her dainty nose and was soon twisting the slip of muslin and lace into an anxious knot.

"My dear, I hope you are made of sterner stuff than to shiver every time he growls. Lord Windhaven is no ogre."

"Sometimes he behaves as one," Priscilla said woefully.

Adele rose with a long-suffering sigh. "I can see why, if you pouted at him as you are now doing. He is not accustomed to a child's tantrums, Priscilla. For that matter, neither am I." Her eyebrows raised quellingly when Priscilla's met over her nose in a startled frown. "Pray, do not take offense, my dear," she said in conciliating tones. "I believe we both might benefit from an early night's rest."

Priscilla's tousled dark curls bobbed up and down slowly. Sensing the girl's fear that she was being banished from polite company for the rest of the evening, Adele added as she moved towards the door, "Would you like me to send up a supper tray?"

Priscilla's dark-lashed eyes flashed grateful relief. "Why, yes, thank you. I am just a little hungry."

Smiling indulgently, as she recalled what it meant at seventeen to be just a little hungry, Adele said, "I'm certain Mrs. Murphy is awaiting the chance to spoil you."

Tucking her chin within the modest lace ruff of her made-over pelisse of Bishop's blue so that her Oldenburg bonnet shadowed her face, Simone directed her gaze straight ahead—towards the opposite side of St. James Street. Though it was well before noon, it was still a dangerous place for an unescorted woman. No decent woman would ordinarily step foot on that section which the gentlemen's clubs— among them White's, Brooks's, Boodles'—

overlooked. But Simone was late returning from Mass, and decided to cut across Green Park rather than walk down busy Piccadilly. The shortcut would save her time. Besides, she felt the service she had just attended gave her an armor that rendered her invisible to the leering stares of any loungers who made St. James Street unsafe for others.

Stepping off the curbstone, she heard a low chuckle and a drunken, "Are you lost, little one?"

Attempting to ignore the query, Simone sidestepped the gentleman who placed himself in her path and pressed forward. But he took hold of her sleeve. Falling into step with her, he repeated, "Are you perhaps lost?"

"Non," she said, looking determinedly down St. James Place and the gates to Green Park. Shaking off the gentleman's hand, she said, "Pardon, Monsieur. I am late."

Tipping up her chin so he could leer into her face, he grinned, "You're not late, m'dear; you're right on time. Why don't you come wi' me, and we'll get better acquainted."

Backing away from the brandy fumes, Simone tried to escape her assailant's grip. He was drunk and unkempt after a hard night of play. "Thank you, no," she said, removing his fingers from her chin. "I mus' go, Monsieur."

"Wha's your hurry, *ma petite chou?*"

"My lady needs me," she said, though she knew she ought not talk with him, but just scurry away.

He nudged her and said, "Ain't Lord Peverley more to your liking?"

Avoiding the question, she said, "Pardon, Monsieur; I wish you will let me go. My mistress will worry if I am late."

"Tell you what. Send your mistress a letter and I'll make you *my* mistress. Won't that be fun?"

"Pardon," Simone said in frosty, frightened tones. "Your offer does not please."

"Doesn't please?" Peverley growled. "I'll show you what pleases." Whereupon he pressed a sloppy, sour kiss on her mouth.

Struggling against Peverley's superior strength, Simone did not hear the approach of another gentleman until he pulled his lordship off her and landed him a facer. "No way to treat a lady, my lord," said a large, handsome stranger, as he drew her protectively behind him.

Coming slowly to his feet, Peverley teetered a moment, then growled, "You bumpkin," while fumbling for a handkerchief to staunch the blood flowing from his nose.

"Be very careful what you say next, my lord. I don't want to hurt you again."

Peverley had the good sense to know when he was outmanned. Bowing stiffly, he said, "My apologies, Mademoiselle. I mistook you for someone else." Then, settling his hat atop his head, Lord Peverley strode towards his club.

"De rien," Simone said, in a distracted tone as the stranger turned to look on her. Her eyes were full of the handsome stranger who had come to her rescue. He was tall, and broad-shouldered. The fact that he was rather barrel-shaped seemed to escape her notice, for the tender, awestruck look on his ruddy face completely captivated her. Forgetting they were in the middle of the street, she held out her hand and said, *"Merci,* Monsieur . . . ?"

He bowed and took her fingers in a gentle grip. "Finch, Avery Finch at your service, Miss . . . ?"

"Simone," she sighed. "Simone Beaumaris. I must be going, Monsieur Finch."

"Will you accept my escort, Miss Beaumaris?" Mr. Finch asked, offering his arm. "St. James Street isn't safe for someone as lovely as you."

"Thank you," she said. "I would be pleased."

But they remained where they were, while

wagons lumbered slowly past them. Then Mr. Finch seemed to become awake to their location and drew her towards the flagway. "Where are we going, miss?"

"Green Street," Simone said without hesitation. "Number Thirty."

"Not hailing from town, I am not familiar with that address."

"I was going to go through Green Park. It's shorter and quieter," Simone said, blushing.

"Yes, but why are you out so early?" Mr. Finch asked. "Have you been to the market?"

"Non," Simone said. "I have been to church."

"Ah," he said with a thoughtful grin. "So, you are a churchgoer?"

Simone thought she had never seen such a handsome gentleman. True, he was not dressed in the first style of elegance, but that was not an indication of the inner man. No, his soul seemed to shimmer through his gaze. As he walked her home, the first gentleman who had ever walked her home, Simone fell deeply in love.

But she could not share her joy with her employer. Lady's maids were not supposed to fall in love. And so she went on as if nothing unusual had occurred that morning.

* * *

As a courtesy to her guest who was accustomed to country hours, Adele had awoken early. Before dismissing Simone so the dresser could attend mass, Adele dressed in one of her most becoming morning dresses, a wrapping dress of bronze-colored book muslin that seemed to reflect highlights of her own hair which she had fastened over her left ear with a golden clasp. She looked forward eagerly to the hours she and her *protegee* would be spending at her dressmaker's, imagining Priscilla's impatience to be about the business of becoming a fashionable young lady.

To her surprise, the girl was still travelling through the Land of Nod. And though her jet black hair had escaped its braid and her face was pressed against a pillow, Priscilla displayed none of the ravages of sleep that Adele was compelled to see increasingly in her own mirror.

With a start, Adele realized again that Priscilla was a very pretty girl. Quite pretty enough to have stolen Dy's heart, she acknowledged with another painful tug at her heartstrings.

Closing the door on her slumbering house guest, Adele went to the morning room, where the second housemaid was setting out a substantial breakfast. "Thank you, Emmeline, everything looks lovely."

After realigning a spoon alongside the teacups, the little maid curtseyed and departed below stairs. At the door, she emitted an uncharacteristic sigh of rapture.

Adele hadn't known that her maids depended so much on her approval. They had always performed their duties competently and quietly, just as she attended to hers without expectation of compliment. Still, a well-placed word of encouragement always served to buoy her spirits. Beginning today, she would make every attempt to encourage her staff in their work. Focussing on their feelings might distract her from her own cares.

At the moment, however, anxiety weighed heavily upon her shoulders. Sitting on the sofa, she leaned her head upon the rolled velvet cushion, and closed her eyes. A few minutes of uninterrupted peace would go a long way towards restoring her shattered peace of mind.

Blissfully unaware of her cousin's need for quiet repose, Elvira entered almost immediately. She had restrained her curiosity towards Miss Fonteyne's supposed engagement long enough, and was near to bursting with unanswered questions. "Is everything settled?" she enquired loudly.

Adele started from her drowsy state. Oblivious to the gossip making the rounds of her home, she nodded and said, "Yes, we're awaiting breakfast."

Miss Willoughby said haltingly as she glanced uncertainly about the room, "We? I beg your pardon?" Then, in a semblance of her usual forward manner she added, "I should think you'd be too overcome by emotion to eat, my dear. It isn't every day an event of such magnitude occurs in this house."

Adele felt as if she were paddling upstream with a teaspoon. What was her companion hinting at? Had everyone in the house gone mad? "Surprises happen more often than you would expect," she said carefully. "Who would have believed I should have developed an interest in fostering young ladies' fashionable debuts or have a care for my companion's looks?"

Laughing, Elvira preened as if she were sixteen. Her faded beauty no longer shaded in blacks and lavenders, she seemed once more to bloom as she said, "You are too hard on yourself, dear cousin. I always said you have a kind heart."

"As do you," Adele returned, pouring out two cups of coffee. Handing one to Elvira she said with a tantalizing smile,

"That is why I know you will not object that we must make room for one more."

Smiling as if she were the cat that had spilled the cream, Miss Willoughby accepted the cup as she seated herself beside the breakfast tray. Stirring cream into her coffee, she intoned, "I knew it, didn't I though," in a voice that could have melted butter. Adele bestowed an amused but perplexed smile upon her companion that, had she been attending, would have encouraged Elvira to explain what it was she knew.

Instead Elvira raised a triumphant gaze to her and enquired, "When can we expect this addition?"

Placing her cup and saucer on the edge of the table, Adele said, "Why, it has already occurred." Perhaps she ought to have consulted with her cousin before the fact. But Priscilla needed a place to stay immediately. "I . . . I thought you knew."

"You mean the viscount has already procured the license?" Miss Willoughby's hand flew alternately between her frizzed head and her heart, giving her the appearance of one who didn't know whether to laugh or cry. "Oh, how wonderful!" she sputtered, nearly spilling the coffee on her mauve-colored merino gown. Setting the bothersome cup aside, she demanded, "Why did you not let us in on your secret?

You ought to have invited us! Oh, how *could* he deprive us of the joy?" Of a sudden she clasped her hands together blissfully over her bosom and gushed, "He could not wait to make you his bride! How romantic!"

"And how mistaken," Adele said as Miss Willoughby's odd flutterings finally made sense. She knew Elvira had been deceived by Dysart's earnest enquiry during his earlier visit yesterday into thinking that he was about to make a proposal of marriage.

That it was her fondest wish only increased her own discomfiture. Admitting such an ambition was not ladylike in the least. Neither was admitting the lack of success in the endeavor.

She was compelled to look away from her baffled companion as humiliation inflamed her normally cool, pale cheeks. Her whole house must be under the wrongheaded notion that she was to marry Windhaven. No doubt his cook and valet would be congratulating him this very morning on his impending nuptials. What he might say to their very premature expressions she could only imagine, but conjecture shamed her.

"It is just like you, Elvira, to romanticize everything," Adele said between clenched teeth. "Or were you wondering how soon you might need to seek another position?"

"Oh my, that never crossed my mind," Miss Willoughby said nervously as the tables were turned upon her. She began to wring her hands. "But if you have already . . ."

"No time like the present," Adele said. An ironic smile up curved one corner of her mouth. "It just so happens I have made the acquaintance of a young lady who is in need of the settling influence of someone like you."

At that moment, Priscilla bounced into the salon. "I hope I am not too late," she cried, when both pairs of eyes turned to regard her. Miss Adele was smiling, making her feel at home. The other pair of eyes narrowed chillingly as if she considered her a usurper. Priscilla tugged the blue cashmere shawl more tightly around her shoulders to ward off the frigid stare.

The mantel clock chimed nine strokes.

"Not at all," Adele said approvingly. "Come sit next to me, my dear." As Priscilla hastened to comply with her hostess's invitation, Adele's benign gaze moved to the older woman. "Elvira, I wish you will welcome our house guest, Priscilla Gaines. Priscilla; Miss Willoughby, my companion."

"Good morning," said Miss Willoughby in a frosty tone.

Priscilla was vexed at the disturbing sensation that the woman perceived in her a threat. Unwilling to accept Miss Willoughby's cautious overture as a permanent dislike, she affixed a friendly smile upon her face, opening her eyes to their fullest as she reached forth a smooth hand and said, "I am most happy to make your acquaintance, ma'am."

At the respectful ma'am, the frown lines faded from Miss Willoughby's face, and she accepted the hand stretched towards her. But before she could respond, Adele interjected, "Priscilla is Lord Windhaven's ward. Isn't she lovely?"

"Yes." The corners of Elvira's lips uplifted in an uncertain guilty smile, as if recalling earlier imprecations against the girl. "Simply delightful," she allowed. "I suppose she is the young lady—"

"We have been waiting for," Adele finished neatly. She patted Priscilla's arm, then enquired, "Will you pour, Elvira, or shall I?"

"You pour, my dear," Elvira said. "Come, side by me, Miss Gaines. We shall become better acquainted. You have a look about you. . . ." she said, patting Priscilla's little hand affectionately. "No, don't tell me, I shall remark the resemblance soon enough."

"Here's your morning chocolate," Adele said, interrupting Elvira's reverie.

"Thank you," Priscilla said, accepting her cup. 'Mama said I favored my papa, but had something of the look of *her* mother. But she only said that when she was vexed with me."

"Frowns are so aging," Elvira said, raising her eyebrows in puzzled response to Adele's pointed stare. "You needn't stare so, Cousin," she chided. "I don't know how often you have cautioned me to smile more often."

"It was enough to set my back against *Grandmere*," Priscilla went on. "Even if she and Grandfather hadn't cast Mama out of their hearts for loving Papa."

"Oh," said Elvira before taking a nervous gulp of her coffee.

"Yes, oh," Adele agreed a little sternly. Then softening her rigid posture, she smiled upon Priscilla. "Miss Willoughby knows everyone in town and will introduce you around."

"Thank you, ma'am," Priscilla said, her eyes sparkling wetly. "But it will do no good to force me upon the marriage mart. I am convinced the polite world must consider me ineligible for any of their sons."

"I will not allow you to consider yourself

so harshly," Miss Willoughby said, setting her cup aside. "Your guardian—"

"Wishes only to be shut of me," Priscilla said, surprisingly without bitterness. "I would appreciate it if you would introduce me to several ladies in need of a governess or companion. I shall scarcely trouble you for more."

Adele could not have been more shocked had Priscilla announced she intended to take the veil and live a cloistered life. But she stifled the startled rejoinder which flew to her lips and said in the most maternal voice she could affect, "I am afraid you are quite mistaken as to your guardian's interest in your future. Lord Windhaven is quite dedicated to setting you up in society."

"But I don't know how to get on!" Priscilla cried out.

"That is where we can help," Elvira said, soothing the distraught girl. "If you will let us guide you, my dear, your future happiness is assured."

"Yes," Adele choked out, recalling that Priscilla's happiness must eclipse her own. Windhaven *had* decided to marry the girl, after all.

Stumbling to her feet, she said, "And we have much to do. Fittings, lessons . . ."

"You will not send me back to school?" Priscilla protested, popping to her feet.

"No, my dear," Elvira soothed, drawing her down beside her once more. "Adele is speaking of dancing masters and such. Oh, it will be such fun, acting the part of a fairy godmother! You will be just like Cinderella." Then, thinking better of her comparison, she added, "Only we shall not make you sit among the cinders or scrub pots. Your grandparents would not like to think you had been treated meanly."

Priscilla was on the brink of saying she thought it very likely they would not care, but the arrival of her guardian forestalled her.

"There you are," Windhaven said, seating himself alongside Adele and reaching for a muffin. "I hope you will forgive my calling at such an unfashionable hour, but I found my own breakfast table rather lonely this morning."

Flustered by Dysart's unannounced entrance, Adele strove to conceal her nervousness by pouring him a cup of coffee. Handing it to him but avoiding meeting his amused gaze, she stammered, "No, we are glad for your company, my lord."

"Are you?" he grinned, capturing her hand in his free one, forcing her to look at him. "I thought we were on a first name basis."

"I am sure that is improper," Adele said, tugging uselessly on her fingers. He only squeezed them gently, forcing them to lie obediently within his grasp. But Adele's gaze faltered as she protested, "Surely you agree we must present a good example to your ward."

"Priscilla, Miss Fonteyne and I are good friends of long standing," Windhaven chuckled. "We need not adhere to strictest rules in terms of address. But I should not like to hear you address any gentleman except by title or surname."

"Yes, sir," Priscilla said meekly, sipping from her cup. As her chocolate had grown cold, she set it aside and reached for a muffin.

Turning once more to Adele, Windhaven said, "We have not yet decided—"

"Come, Priscilla," Miss Willoughby said, arising abruptly and pulling her charge to her feet. Pushing her towards the door, she said, "Let us not intrude on a private conversation."

Adele began to tell her cousin and protegee they were in no way intruding; that Dy merely wished to discuss Priscilla's future. "Don't be silly, Elvira. Lord Windhaven has come on Priscilla's account; he must take it unkindly for you to take her away so soon after his arrival."

"No, I will not," Dy maintained. "For once, you are mistaken, Adele, if you think I came merely on that goose's account. She and I have had quite enough of one another, haven't we, my pet?" This last was uttered with such a glare directed towards his ward that Adele renewed her determination that he could not sacrifice himself on the altar of matrimony with that child. He would frighten her to death with killing looks and cutting words.

To her surprise, Priscilla did not dissolve into tears as she had done last night. Squaring her little shoulders she declared, "Oh, don't fear for me, Miss Fonteyne. Now I have had a good night's sleep and my breakfast, I am more than a match for my Lord Growler. He is never happy before he has had his coffee, you see." Skipping towards the door in Elvira's wake, she said, "I shall leave you to soothe the savage beast." And before Adele could respond, Priscilla was gone.

Staring after the cheerful child, Adele could scarcely believe this was the same girl she'd met last night. If this happy countenance was the more usual face Priscilla showed to the world, it was no wonder Dy was determined to marry her.

"Now," he said, breaking into Adele's unhappy thoughts. He possessed himself of one of her hands and stroked her wrist with his thumb as he continued, "We are alone, and can finally discuss the future."

The gentle, circular massage he was giving her felt so nice. She knew she ought to remove her hand from his grasp, but could not quite collect the resolve to do so. But she was not completely without scruples. He was talking about his future with Priscilla, of course, and that unhappy thought gave her the courage to snatch her fingers out of his. "Yes, I was hoping we might do so," she said, attempting to sound as officious as a stern duenna. "I am afraid the happy conclusion to your hopes must be postponed until your ward has been reunited with her family. And there is the mourning period, of course. Nothing can be done about your . . . plans until she is out of black gloves." Adele almost choked on the word proposal, before substituting plans.

Windhaven's eyes narrowed and his mouth tensed in what looked to Adele like an impatient frown. She was sorry for it, but knew her duty to Priscilla outweighed her affection for the viscount. "You must learn to quell your impatience, my lord," she said in what she hoped were sympathetic tones. "Priscilla's welfare must naturally prevail over your . . . wish for a hasty marriage."

"Yes, you are right, as always," he allowed, with no lightening of his frown. Adele was not certain he did not mean to elope, so grudging were his words. "I have a responsibility, and I will do it," he said, rubbing his hands together. Then, clasping them in a white-knuckled grip, he added, "So, we will talk no more of a wedding until she is in charity with her grandfather again."

As Adele thought it would be more useful to speak of the nuptials with Priscilla's grandfather when the time came, she did not speak her mind. No sense in hastening the day.

Eight

"How soon do you think we might effect a happy reunion between the girl and her relatives?" Dy asked in the tones of an anxious bridegroom.

"It will take at least a month," she said. "If you are willing to spend the blunt to outfit your ward quickly so she will not shame her family."

"I'll do whatever I can," he said, "to help you and Elvira introduce her to your acquaintances who can increase Priscilla's consequence."

Suppressing the jealousy that threatened to overpower her, Adele resolved once more to do her best for the girl. "I can begin by taking her to Lady Mathilda's musical afternoon tomorrow."

"Good!" Windhaven said in approving tones that had warmed Adele's heart on other occasions. "Lady Mathilda Castleton is just the person to profit our scheme."

"She knows everyone if Elvira does not,"

Adele agreed. "I must impress on Priscilla how important her friendship can be."

"Do that," he commanded. "The sooner they meet, the sooner our girl will be safely home."

Adele quietly allowed that the Marquess of Chaseldon's maiden sister was the perfect sponsor for Priscilla Gaines. Years ago, Lady Mathilda had bowed to her brother's wishes and turned down a proposal from a handsome bachelor whose only failing was that he was not the scion of a noble family. She had chosen to wear the willow for her rejected suitor all these years rather than marry dutifully, and could be depended on, Adele believed, to look on Priscilla Gaines as the daughter she might have had. And she ought to serve as Adele's ally in recommending the girl follow her heart's prudent counsel rather than accept an offer of marriage which satisfied the constraints of duty.

But Adele did not reveal any of her heart's uneasy musings, only saying, "Yes, and she is discreet, Dy. She will not allow Priscilla to simmer in a pot of scandal broth."

"I should say not," he agreed, taking her hands once more in his. "You are so good," he added as he raised her hands to his lips.

Adele found her gaze captured by his as

surely as her fingers were in his grasp. She could not tear her gaze from him as he bestowed a kiss on first one hand, then the other, setting her pulse aflutter. If only, she pined inwardly, ignoring his potent regard, he meant the kisses as a lover, not a friend.

He grinned when she did not pull out of his grip, and said, "I knew I could depend on you, dear Adele."

Dear Adele. Adele sighed as an inner, mocking voice amended the affectionate title. *Dear, dependable Adele*, became, *Dear, old Adele.* She snatched her fingers free and said in barely civil tones, "It is of no use to goad me, my lord. I said I would help you, and I shall."

"Yes, and I can see you are as eager," he began, still grinning in that irresistible, but mocking manner that endeared yet infuriated her. She longed to dam up his enthusiasm, but he went on relentlessly, "Just as eager as I am to bring this affair to its proper end."

"Proper ends take time," Adele stiffly maintained, wishing she were free to tell him what the only proper end of this affair could be, that he would marry, and his wife would require him to sacrifice his dear friend Adele to her domestic tyranny. "And very often," she added, wishing she need not speak at cross purposes, "require sacrifices."

Bestowing a look of befuddlement upon her, he asked, "Don't you want to get on with our lives?"

"I have done so," she said, risking a penitent glance at him. But she would not be swayed from her purpose. She was not the self-indulgent girl she had once been, who'd earned herself the sobriquet the fashionable Miss Fonteyne. She was older, and she hoped wiser. Moistening her lips she said, "Elvira and Lady Mathilda have convinced me of the futility of my former existence."

"You are too serious," he said, moving towards her.

Wondering whether he intended to relax her by pressing more very pleasant, but meaningless kisses on her, Adele stiffened her spine and faced him down until he halted his advance. "We cannot get on with our lives," she said, "as though others mean nothing to us."

"No, you are right," he agreed thoughtfully. Then, raising a wary eyebrow, he asked, "Have you become a Reformer?"

"No, Dy, I am no saint," she replied, folding her hands before her nervously.

"Then don't turn up all prim, my dear. I don't want to offend. I only thought you might like my company when you took Priscilla to the dressmaker's."

"Well, of course, you are welcome. But do you want to accompany us?"

"I do," he declared. "Depend on it, Adele, you will need me there."

"I have never yet needed a gentleman's help in purchasing a dress," she protested, as she wondered whether she had revealed in some way how very much she did need him.

"No, your taste is unquestionable. I was rather speaking of dealing with Priscilla."

"Oh," she said, "I daresay we shall deal together very well."

"I mean to ensure that you do," he said in quiet tones that did not reassure her, especially, when he added, "But I shan't trouble you when you pick out the wedding gown and trousseau."

"Good *heavens!* No," she cried, blushing against her best efforts. Coming to her feet, she moved across the room, making an attempt to compose herself. But it was beyond her ability.

He had promised not to speak of the wedding anymore, and she could not very well tell him the subject was most awkward without revealing her disappointment. Choosing instead to remind him of the constraints of tradition, she said, "That would be unlucky."

Grinning, Dy pursued her and grasped

her arms, increasing the heat that infused Adele's cheeks as he said in that provoking, teasing tone she liked so well, "I suppose we might disagree on the appropriate style for bride wear."

"I see no reason why we should," she said, in brisk, confident tones that in no way reflected her actual state of mind. "Our taste coincides in everything. It is one reason we are such good friends." Leaving him no chance to respond, she broke free of his improper, but oh, so agreeable, embrace to ring for a maid, keeping her distance until the girl had hurried above stairs to retrieve Priscilla and Elvira. When they were alone once more, she turned an amiable smile upon him, and was puzzled by the remarkable change in his countenance.

Dy's handsome face, at first drained of color, flushed, as with an angry fever. Adele wondered if he had been stricken ill. Anxious for his health, she moved to his side and took his arm in a gentle grip. But he drew away as if her sympathy offended him.

"Forgive me," he said, wiping his brow with a handkerchief before he brought whatever ailed him under his control. But his brow still furrowed menacingly over eyes that blanched from their usual inviting blue to the color of late winter ice. "I may have taken too much for granted."

"No lady likes being taken for granted," Adele said, seating herself so as to allow him to lower himself into a chair. Compelling herself not to touch him again, she asked, "Will you be all right?"

"I hope so," he said in abstracted tones that worried her. As if he sensed her uneasiness, he added in a state of more animation, "Yes, of course, I am fine; I must only accustom myself to new responsibilities."

"They are daunting," Adele agreed lightly, laying a hand unconsciously upon his sleeve. "But you are equal to any challenge, Dy."

To her surprise, he leaned over and touched her cheek with a quick kiss. "I hope you are right, my friend," he said, his jaw clenching on the final word. Then in more cordial tones, he added, "Tell Priscilla we shall go for an ice later this afternoon, if she is good."

"Yes, I will," Adele said, cupping her cheek in wonder and anxiety. How could a kiss he can only have meant as a brother stir such wanton longings in her? The sensual onslaught shamed her when she remembered whom Dy wanted to marry.

Priscilla.

The repeated realization that her own dream was not to be accomplished made Adele suddenly wish she could take to her bed with a migraine. However, she was made of sterner stuff than to abandon Dy to the whims of his ward. She had given her word. Dy was depending on her.

But Elvira had not pledged herself to turning Priscilla into a diamond of the first water. Adele was disturbed by the communication that her cousin had taken to her room with a blinding headache and was begging Adele's assistance. Excusing herself from the viscount with a distracted offer of coffee, she fled abovestairs.

"I'm so sorry," Elvira mumbled repeatedly as Adele tiptoed around her room, drawing heavy curtains to muffle the sounds of carriage traffic outside. "So much trouble. Please tell Priscilla she is not to blame herself," Elvira groaned. "Such a pretty girl; I cannot understand . . ."

"Don't fret, Ellie," Adele soothed, stroking lavender-scented water on her cousin's temples. "You're not yet well enough to chase after her." Sighing, she added, "I imagine you're worried about other things. But there is no need. Just rest now. I'll make sure you're not disturbed." After tying a scarf tightly around her companion's throbbing head, Adele sent for her housekeeper and directed her staff to go about the usual routine, working in the strictest silence.

"So Miss Willoughby is sick again," Mrs. Murphy said, looking suspiciously between her mistress and Lord Windhaven.

"It has been a hard winter for my cousin," Adele replied, hoping the housekeeper would not offer unsolicited felicitations to the viscount. "I imagine she is still suffering from the influenza." Hoping to distract her housekeeper, she presented Priscilla, who had just bounded down stairs. The girl obliged her elders by turning a dazzling smile upon the large woman, and saying "Poor Miss Willoughby," in the bracing tones of one who is never ill. "I shall go and comfort her." She hurried out of the room.

Adele gave Mrs. Murphy a few additional instructions when Priscilla ran back into the room. "Miss Willoughby has a scarf around her head like Gypsies," Priscilla added with a sparkle of mischief, earning a sharp glance from her guardian.

"*Not* like Gypsies," Adele corrected, sounding very much like a reproving governess. Quelling the guilty start that she was acting like a woman suffering from a disappointment in love, she said, "Miss

PRESENTING AN IRRESISTIBLE OFFERING
ON YOUR KIND OF ROMANCE.

*Receive 3 Zebra
Regency Romance
Novels (An $11.97 value)*
Free

Journey back to the romantic
Regent Era with the world's finest
romance authors. Zebra Regency
Romance novels place you
amongst the English *ton* of a
distant past with witty dialogue,
and stories of courtship so real,
you feel that you're living them!

Experience it all through 3 FREE Zebra Regency Romance novels...yours
just for the asking. When you join *the only book club dedicated to Regency
Romance readers,* additional Regency Romances can be yours to preview
FREE each month, with no obligation to buy anything, ever.

Regency Subscribers Get First-Class Savings.

After your initial package of 3 FREE books, you'll begin to receive monthl
shipments of new Zebra Regency titles. These all new novels will be delivere
direct to your home as soon as they are published...sometimes even before the
bookstores get them! Each monthly shipment of 3 books will be yours to
examine for 10 days. Then, if you decide to keep the books, you'll pay the pre
ferred subscriber's price of just $3.30 per title. That's $9.90 for all 3 books...a
savings of over $2 off the publisher's price! What's more, $9.90 is your <u>total</u>
price. (A nominal shipping and handling charge of $1.50 per shipment will be
added.)

No Minimum Purchase, and a Generous Return Privilege.

We're so sure that you'll appreciate the money-saving convenience of
home delivery that we <u>guarantee</u> your complete satisfaction. You may return
any shipment...for any reason...within 10 days and pay nothing that month.
And if you want us to stop sending books, just say the word. There is no mini
mum number of books you must buy.

*An $11.97
value.
FREE!
No obligation
to buy
anything, ever.*

ZEBRA HOME SUBSCRIPTION SERVICE, INC.

120 BRIGHTON ROAD

P.O. BOX 5214

CLIFTON, NEW JERSEY 07015-5214

Willoughby is a respectable lady, Priscilla; it is not your place to criticize her."

"I only meant . . ." Priscilla began, blushing unhappily. "I like Miss Willoughby, truly I do. *She* does not tell me what I ought to do at all times."

Not believing her for a moment, given her own experience with her cousin's loving but meddling ways, Adele warned, "Then I expect you to treat her as you wish to be treated, instead of teasing her." Then she said in a cajoling tone, "Lord Windhaven has kindly offered to take us shopping."

"Oh, I was so hoping he could!" Priscilla replied, clapping her hands in delight.

"Then hush," Adele said in a manner that commanded obedience. "And go get your bonnet."

"I'll see to the carriage, then," Dy said in tones of high amusement as he followed Priscilla.

Adele turned to Mrs. Murphy and smiled, but her expression lacked its usual warmth. "I particularly wish you not send Miss Willoughby her customary draught of elderberry wine."

"But, miss, she will be after me all day if I do not send up her medicine."

"If it were only one glass, I would not

deny her," Adele said absently. "Unfortunately—"

"She won't be happy about that, miss. What'll I tell her?"

"Tell her I have ordered you to send for the apothecary."

"The only thing that could make her happier would be if we had a wedding to celebrate." Mrs. Murphy seemed lost in thought, then added with a wink, "Come to think on it, that's the sort of news'd make us all a sight happier." She dabbed at the corner of an eye with her apron.

"You may put your wedding handkerchief away; I do not intend to make you happy," Adele said as she drew on her gloves.

"Oh, miss, never say you turned the viscount down," Mrs. Murphy persisted. She was wringing the corners of her starched apron in a manner that would soon send her to her chamber to don a fresh one.

Adele buried her face in her hands, sighing, *"Et tu, Brute?"*

Planting fists on either hip, Mrs. Murphy declared, "I don't know what the brute et, and don't care. I have enough trouble feeding this household. How I am to keep up with a gentleman and his—"

"Did you not hear me, Mrs. Murphy?" Adele said, miffed that no one seemed to be paying any attention to her. "I am not marrying *anyone*. I can take care of myself."

Mrs. Murphy sniffed her objection to her claim. "Well, pardon me for sayin' so, miss, but you're too independent for your own good."

"A single lady must of needs be independent," Adele replied.

"But it has grown into a nasty habit, miss."

"Like gossiping?" Adele enquired with an arched brow.

"I never," Mrs. Murphy sniffed. "Only, seein's how it concerned Claymore and Reynard, I may have let word of our happy news slip."

"And they will waste no time in congratulating a very surprised groom. If they have not already done so," Adele added on a note of horror. Was that the reason Dy wished to discuss wedding plans? Had he perhaps meant to disabuse her of the notion that he had asked for her hand?

Oh, she hoped he did not think she thought he had proposed to *her*. How foolish she would seem! How pathetic!

"Surely not, miss," Mrs. Murphy said. "Lord Windhaven's butler and valet are the souls of discretion."

"Are they?" Adele laughed, despite her vexation. "Then I would prefer my own staff keep their tongues between their teeth from now on."

"We did not tell anyone not directly affected," Mrs. Murphy defended herself. "Surely you could not wish us to keep secret such momentous news, when we must all learn to get on as one happy family."

"Your announcement was premature, I'm afraid," Adele said. "Lord Windhaven did not come here to make me his bride. He came to make me a mother."

For a change, Mrs. Murphy seemed incapable of speech. Her mouth flapped open and closed making her look very much, Adele thought, like a fish out of water. Then wondering if her untoward announcement might cause her staff to treat the viscount with a pronounced lack of respect or even hostility, she explained, "I meant by bringing us Priscilla, of course."

"That goes without saying, miss," Mrs. Murphy sputtered.

Hearing skipping footsteps, Adele turned to regard her protegee, dressed and cloaked for their outing in a sadly outmoded ensemble she came in. However, she was quick to perceive that, given the right wardrobe, the girl would dazzle the ton, and she was able to offer a safe compliment. "Ah, Priscilla, how pretty you look in blue."

The girl twirled a giddy circle, saying, "I have always thought so," with a remarkable lack of humility.

Adele smiled indulgently. Mrs. Murphy clucked her tongue against the roof of her mouth before she said, "How like you she is, miss."

"Oh?" Adele enquired, not at all pleased by the compliment. Smoothing the furrows that marred her forehead, she warned lightly, "Before you say she could be my daughter, I ask you to recall that I am not yet five-and-twenty; merely enough difference in age to be her elder sister. Now Priscilla, let us be off."

Priscilla skipped down the front steps and leapt into the carriage with very little assistance from her guardian. Adele followed more sedately, seating herself across from her protegee, knowing Dy preferred the forward facing seat. But it rankled, nevertheless, that he chose to sit next to his fidgety ward.

Adele whisked Priscilla to Grafton House on New Bond Street. Although they had reached the shop before eleven, they discovered the counter already thronged with other shoppers. They were compelled to wait a half hour before they could be attended to.

Seeing the crowd, Dy elected to remain

within the carriage with his morning paper. Inside the shop, Priscilla found much to distract her, and spent the entire time oohing and ahhing over elegant fabrics and admiring the fine ladies with whom she was rubbing elbows.

Her *protegee's* delighted response allayed much of the impatience which always assailed Miss Fonteyne on the occasions when she was crowded into a room the size of a shoe box. She imagined herself dodging a room full of Dancing Fitzgomerys, intent on attracting the notice of the belle of the ball, or in the case at hand, the shopkeeper's assistants. She was determined not to enter the fray, but by her customary detachment, drew attention to herself.

Finally her patience won over the clamor of noisier customers. Disengaging himself from the desperate clutches of a vulgar woman who was loudly insisting that she was next in line, the most senior assistant placed himself at Adele's disposal.

In very short order, she had selected several fabrics, all suitable for half-mourning—a muslin in white, a lavender colored jaconet, a dove grey zephyrine, and a delicate muslin striped in lavender and white, as well as material for spencers and pelisse in shades of lavender and grey—as well as three untrimmed bonnets and gloves and stockings. "Now, did I forget anything?" she mused aloud, pulling her own gloves thoughtfully through her hand.

"Ribbons!" Priscilla exclaimed, her eyes wide with the vivid choices that lay before her.

"Don't trouble your head, Priscilla. Mrs. Bell will know which trimmings to use," Miss Fonteyne remarked. She drew on her gloves, indicating their business here was at an end, then ushered her wide-eyed protegee into her waiting carriage.

Priscilla plopped down once more beside the viscount, startling him. " Are you awake?" she teased. "I don't know how anyone can sleep in this din."

"Do you not?" Dy asked, folding his newspaper as the footman gave Adele a hand into the carriage. "I thought *you* could sleep anywhere."

"But there is so much to *see,*" Priscilla persevered, adjusting her skirts so as to allow Adele more room on the backwards facing seat. "Why do you *want* to sleep?"

"Why indeed?" he chuckled, tucking Priscilla's fingers within the crook of his arm and turning an amused smile upon her. "Heaven help me if I wished to."

Adele could not help but see the affection in his gaze and felt the painful sting of loneliness and rejection. It was childish to do so, she told herself, when the viscount had made no formal declaration. Lowering her own gaze to the swatches of fabric she clutched tightly in her fingers, she compelled herself once more to silently relinquish any claim she felt she had upon him. Lord Windhaven was not hers, never had been, and now never would be. It was a difficult litany, but it was reality, and she must accept it. With a smile.

Nine

Reminding herself that Dy was too good a friend to alienate with a missish display of jealousy when she had no right to that possessive sentiment, she was at last able to accept the inevitable.

Dy broke into her reverie with another of his delightful chuckles that compelled her to look up from her contemplation of fabric samples. He grinned wider when she met his gaze, and Adele could not help smiling back to discover he was not laughing at his ward.

Priscilla was curled up, nose to the window like the child she was, staring at the traffic that rumbled past them, crying, "Oh, look! That wagoner just lost part of his load! Oh, stop! It is horrible." But Priscilla gave the lie to her words, giggling as barrels rolled erratically down Piccadilly, scattering passersby and scaring horses. Since no one was injured, it was all amusing.

"You see now why I couldn't sleep," Dy

laughed. "And why I should *not* have slept on the road south."

Caught in his twinkling gaze, Adele could only sympathize. "Yes, you have been sadly abused. But I believe you are safe in town, my lord. Gresham will not allow even *me* to drive his coach."

"You," Dy said, lowering his voice to a confidential growl that made Adele blush, "Can be trusted not to kick over the traces. And you are not without experience."

Adele covered a heated cheek with her fingers. Was he referring to their unfortunately impulsive embraces? If he was, she certainly did not want to be reminded of them now. In the frosty tones of a woman who wished to end a conversation, she said, "I have no idea what you mean."

"Why the dog cart," he said, with a provocative lift of an eyebrow. "Did you think I was referring to something else?"

"No, my lord," Adele replied, mortified that she had come to a mistaken conclusion, but unable to break his stare. "Only, I had . . . forgotten."

"One never forgets," he asserted. He stretched his leg across the footwell and leaned forward so as to create a private haven for them. "I certainly have not."

As he moved forward, Adele's wayward gaze suddenly dropped to his mouth, curved in an enticing grin that promised much and recalled everything.

She herself had forgotten neither his kisses nor the promise they seemed to imply. But now was not the time to make claims.

Priscilla was staring at them, her open, direct gaze increasing the now-guilty color that stained Adele's cheeks. She felt as if the girl could see into the darkest reaches of her being where jealousy had coiled itself around her heart.

Choosing to ignore that unpleasant vision and the very pleasant memories Dy was compelling her to recall, Adele said, "Driving a cart in the country is not at all the same thing as driving a pair in town. And don't forget, it was a long time ago."

"Not so long ago," he persisted, drawing her gaze from the distraction of their young chaperone towards his insistent stare. To her chagrin, he deliberately pursed his lips at the same time he dropped his gaze to her frustrated pout.

"Just a child," she protested, her nervous gaze darting towards Priscilla, hoping the girl would decry the appellation. Priscilla only arched her eyebrows, as if to say she would not rise to the argument, then turned back to the window and its passing view.

"No longer a child," Dy said in warm,

melting tones that threatened to overset Adele's careful reserve.

But at that moment, Priscilla groaned. "You two," she said in reproach, "are so silly. I hope I do not forget myself and act like two birds in love for all the world to see."

"I take it you are speaking from experience," Windhaven said, his response tinged with amusement.

"Not my own," Priscilla replied, nodding her head with the wisdom of ages. "But if Mama and Papa had been more . . . discreet, Grandfather might have objected less to their match."

"And how do you intend to make *your* match?" he persisted.

"I shall, of course, be led by your superior understanding," Priscilla said, smiling mischievously.

"When you look like that, I don't believe you for an instant," Dy protested.

"Then I shall follow Miss Fonteyne's example."

Adele was shocked into silence. Priscilla's incisive perception reminded her that the attraction she felt towards Windhaven was dangerous and completely ineligible. Dy's voice was a seductive purr that drew her like a moth to a flame. And though she knew it was wrong, dangerous, to flutter

too near, Adele knew she was helpless to
resist. She had unfortunately fallen in love
with the wrong man.

She devoutly hoped the girl would not
follow her example. But that not being a
subject she was inclined to address, she
only said, "You must do as you think best,
Priscilla."

Fortunately at that moment, the coachman drew up before Mrs. Bell's establishment, and Priscilla bounded to her feet,
calling out, "Please hurry, I am so excited
I am never going to wear an apron again!"

Resolving to school her emotions more
carefully, Adele followed her out of the carriage, accepting Dy's assistance with hardly
a flutter of her pulse. And as the younger
girl exclaimed over sketches and manne-
quins, hugging Windhaven and her with
artless affection, Adele could not help but
enter into the sentiments of joy and anticipation of which Priscilla was making no secret.

"Oh, look, Miss Fonteyne," she cried,
showing a sketch of a white silk ball gown.
"I shall break many hearts in this gown,
and I shall wear them on my sleeve."

"Don't you mean you will wear *your*
heart on your sleeve?" Dy asked, tweaking
the puff of fabric at her shoulder.

"Oh, no," Priscilla laughed. "It is too

easily snatched away. I meant to wear them as medals."

"What a cynic," he teased, crossing his arms and leaning against the back cushion of the dressmaker's settee until the ladies had concluded their business with Mrs. Bell.

Back at home, after eating ices at Gunter's Confectionery on the east side of Berkeley Square, Priscilla allowed, "So you see I cannot make my guardian happy, Miss Fonteyne." She shrugged. "Today he calls me a cynic. Last week he condemned my romanticism."

"Well, it does make a man dizzy," Dy said, sinking Adele's hopes completely despite placing himself at her side. "A man likes knowing where he stands. Friend," covering Adele's hand with his. To her embarrassment, he would not let go as he continued, "or foe. So much more comfortable, you know."

"I do see," Priscilla said, staring without expression at the clasped hands.

Mortified, Adele withdrew her fingers from Dy's grip. If he intended someday to make Priscilla Lady Windhaven, he must see how unkind it was to show partiality to any other lady. "Friends are well and good," she said, casting about for a suitable reminder, without speaking too openly. "But a lady needs a little romance, or she becomes discouraged."

"Does she?" Dy asked thoughtfully. Then, arching his brow, he asked ruefully, "I have not made gifts of flowers and bon bons, have I?"

"No." Adele said, inquiring of Priscilla, "Has he?"

"No flowers," Priscilla responded as she looked over a plate of pastries. "But I did receive peppermints."

"That is not romantic in the least," Adele interjected.

"I like peppermints," Priscilla allowed, eschewing the cucumber sandwiches for sweeter fare. Munching an apricot tartlet, she said, "So it must count for something." Then, excusing herself absently, she ran above stairs to entertain Miss Willoughby.

"Peppermints? Really, Dy," Adele chided.

"She likes them," he replied. Laying an arm across the back of the sofa, he looked fondly at Adele.

In other circumstances, Adele might have allowed herself to feel its warmth. It was a steady, direct gaze however, and not very lover-like, which caused Adele to wince. "However," he added as a slow smile warmed his regard, "I defer to your more excellent understanding. Since I have failed miserably to win my lady, what in your opinion, should I do?"

"I cannot speak for every lady," she hedged, pleating the fabric of her carriage dress with nervous fingers. How she wished it were proper to speak for herself.

Seeing her distress, Dy twined his fingers around hers. "I am not interested in courting every lady," he teased. "Only one. But, every lady of our acquaintance endorses your recommendations whole-heartedly. Even Miss Willoughby has adopted your style. So tell me, Adele, what could I do to win your affection?"

If only you wished to, Adele thought miserably. Then, wearied with pining over something she proved by her attitude she did not deserve, she said, "I like the usual round of activities, driving in the Park, dining al fresco, sailing . . ."

"Dancing?" he asked.

"Of course," she allowed, frowning that he had to ask. "You know I never sit out a set unless I choose otherwise."

"I had noticed," he said in almost peevish tones. "I congratulate you on your sacrifice at Lady Mathilda's last gathering. Do you regret making Lady Katherine into your shadow?"

"No," Adele said. He was confusing her,

talking in circles. "I mean to say, I was only too happy to help."

"Ah," he said, absently, as if he too were confused. "There is the thread. How would you help me, then?"

Wishing with all her heart he would stop bringing the conversation back to this sticking place she said, "I wish you would trust me. Priscilla will not disappoint."

He looked at her long and hard, then said in ironic tones, "That was not my concern, only that you will make me a happy man as soon as she is reunited with her family."

"Yes, you live for that day," she snapped. *Why must he be so obsessed with marrying that chit?*

Taken aback, he stared at her, then said in a voice that sounded as if his neckcloth was wound too tightly, "I want us to be together."

It was too much. Springing to her feet and propelling herself across the room, Adele protested, "Really, Dy, I do not think—"

"No?" Windhaven asked. "I thought we had agreed . . ." Stumbling to a halt, he tried again. "Come driving with me, Adele. Miss Willoughby may come, too, if you are worried I might not act the gentleman."

"No," Adele said, believing he no longer

wished to drive out alone with her. It was a blow to her confidence. Rather than make a scene, she offered a plausible excuse. "I shall be very busy . . . with Priscilla. Lessons, you understand. Fittings. And introducing her to our circle."

"Yes, well, I did ask you," he said grudgingly, arising from the sofa and moving towards the door. "But you will let me know how she's getting on."

"Yes, of course. But you're always welcome here, you know," Adele said, taken aback by his abrupt adieu.

"Then I don't mean to wear it out," he said grimly. Clasping her outstretched hand, he said, "No need to see me out, Adele. I've run tame in this house long enough to show myself the door."

"Do you mean to come to Lady Mathilde's afternoon gathering tomorrow?" she asked, holding him a moment longer, hoping he might meet her puzzled gaze once more.

"Don't think I will," he said. To her frustration, he looked at the chandelier hanging behind her. "Neglected too many other duties for this business as it is. Well," shrugging, "Don't need to after all. I have every confidence in you. Let me know how it goes." Then, without awaiting her reply, he nodded and took his leave.

* * *

"Makes a man dizzy," Windhaven said as he alighted from his curricle outside his lodgings on St. James.

"What's that, my lord?" enquired his tiger from his perch behind.

"Rub 'em down, Griffin," Windhaven said. "I shall walk. Need to think."

"Very good, my lord," Griffin said as imperturbable as if his master made a daily habit of engaging in such ungentlemanly activities as walking about town and thinking.

Without waiting to see that his orders were carried out, Windhaven set off past St. James Palace towards Green Park. The quiet, wooded preserve was the perfect place for him right now. No one would be there. He could mull over what went wrong and figure out a way to make it all right.

It was late afternoon, not quite five, and Hyde Park would soon be too crowded to consider anything but saving the toes of one's boots. Already, he could hear the rumble of carriages making their way to Hyde Park so their occupants could see and be seen by those whose opinion counted for something.

As he walked into the awakening verdure of Green Park, he was forced to acknowledge the fact that his proposal to Adele seemed to count for nothing.

Adele refused to talk about their wedding and acted as if she did not recall their kisses. These were not the usual responses of a happy bride-to-be.

Acquaintances told him their brides had bored them with constant referrals to the details pertinent to their impending nuptials—date, flowers, gowns, guests. And those lucky few who had contracted love matches sometimes hinted that their ladies' eagerness to be loved surpassed their own desire.

Rubbing his chin as he walked along a quiet, gravelled path, Windhaven admitted to himself that he wanted more than anything to claim Adele as his wife. So much, in fact, that he had been hard pressed not to embrace her upon first sight this morning. Though it had been a sore temptation at the time, he was glad now he had restrained himself. He would only have succeeded in making a fool of himself and alienating her more than he seemed to have done.

But the facts were undeniable, and he was a fool for ignoring them. Adele did not act like a woman in love. She had called him friend several times, even before he had driven away to fetch Priscilla, mak-

ing it clear she did not love him, at least
not in the way he . . . desired her.

No. To be honest with himself, he more
than desired Adele Fonteyne. But he would
not say he loved her. He must wait awhile.

As a man of action, Windhaven derived
little satisfaction in the decision to bide and
wait. It rubbed against the grain. He
wanted to be doing something.

That, he knew from experience, was not
always prudent. In hunting game, he had
learned to restrain his inclination to relentlessly pursue his quarry, but rather let the
prey come to him. In the service of his
country, he had learned not to make a
frontal attack against superior odds. Experience taught him when to take the field
in a flanking maneuver or stand firm in a
battle square.

As he came to an open meadow where
dairy cattle grazed contentedly, he sat on
the crest of a slight rise to watch the herd's
progress. They did not advance in line, but
meandered individually over the fields,
each animal selecting her own favorite
grasses and flowers from the tussocks that
carpeted the area. Occasionally, one would
raise her head and low insistently.

Though their progress appeared aimless
to a casual observer, Windhaven had the
presence of mind to notice the cattle would

not be distracted from their purpose, until a maid came to lead them towards a better thing—the cow-shed and milking time.

Windhaven watched as the last cow followed the dairy maid over the rise, then arose from his grassy seat and headed toward home himself.

How easy it had been for the girl to call the animals to heed and lead them into shelter, he thought, as he made himself ready for an early dinner at White's. Succeeding in arranging his neck cloth as if not a thought disturbed his mind, he continued his reflections.

If only it was as easy to get Adele to depend on him, to trust him, to love him. Forgetting his toilette momentarily, Windhaven ran his fingers through his hair, to stimulate his brain-box to find a way to compel her to love him.

Unfortunately, there was no reason why she should. She was a self-proclaimed independent woman, possessed of means and comforts no one else had to provide. She needed for nothing, it seemed, least of all, him.

Such a revelation might have thwarted a lesser man. But it only intensified his determination to make himself necessary to Adele's happiness. Brushing his hair into its more customary arrangement, he decided that if he could not advance his case with her directly, he would come at it from an unexpected angle.

He would be patient, act her friend as long as she allowed him. Certainly she could have no complaint in that at least while they had a common interest in re-uniting Priscilla with her family. He would not demand more than Adele could give, nor promise more than she would take.

The decision made, he felt lighter and more peaceful than he thought he could have done. Over his shirt and formal breeches, he donned his black evening coat, smoothing lapels and tugging on sleeves until just the right amount of snowy white linen projected from the cuff. Glancing at his reflection, he was pleased to see that he presented the unruffled appearance of an untroubled gentleman preparing for a night on the town. It was the image he always cultivated, the image which left him free from ordinary responsibilities, the image which had never troubled him much until lately.

He passed the evening at White's as he always did, relating humorous anecdotes, judging oddities of dress that would have been better left on the fitting room floor, and winning a couple rounds of piquet, so as not to arouse suspicion. It was best to go on as expected amongst one's cronies, so as not to disturb anyone's dinner. But though he went on as always, he found little to amuse him at his club. He very much longed to be at home—as he had begun thinking of the house at Number Thirty Green Street—with his little family surrounding him. But the best course, he believed, lay in remaining absent for a few days, when he hoped Adele would have realized how much she needed him.

Ten

Oblivious to Lord Windhaven's devious strategy, Adele returned the next morning with Priscilla and Elvira to Mrs. Bell's establishment to have one of her dresses, one Mrs. Bell had promised to have finished as quickly as possible, fitted. As Priscilla tried on the round gown of dove gray cashmere trimmed in black velvet, Adele nodded approval to the dressmaker, "My compliments, Mrs. Bell. It is perfect."

The dressmaker beamed, then clapped her hands, summoning a bevy of assistants carrying accessories to complement the gown. Without consulting Priscilla who was gazing suspiciously upon the expensive array of trimmed bonnets, gloves and shawls, Adele chose a gray silk cottage hat trimmed in black ribbon over a bonnet trimmed heavily in black flowers. "The black paisley shawl, I think," she said, turning towards Priscilla whose little face fell unconsciously. "No, on second thought, the one with the lavender pansy trim." Though it was a pretty alternative, she was distressed when Priscilla actually sniffed at her choice.

"I hoped I was to wear bright colors," Priscilla snapped, distastefully clutching the woolen scarf a maid obediently handed her. "Not black and gray. I'll look like a storm cloud."

"You know why you must appear for the time being in sober colors," Adele said. "It would not do for you to seem lacking in respect or modesty just now."

"I don't care," Priscilla stormed. "It isn't fair. You and Miss Willoughby are decked out in pretty colors, and you are both *old.*"

"It must seem so to you now, my dear," said Elvira in sympathetic reproach. "But it is not at all kind to remind us that we rival Methuselah in years. I hope you may be more considerate of your poor mother's memory from now on."

To Miss Willoughby's gentle reminder, Priscilla could say nothing that would not fly in the face of her mother's excellent example. She only hung her head penitently and submitted to the removal of her new gown, allowing the dressmaker's assistants to pin pattern pieces around her to form the shape of another dress, one with a high neck and tight, long sleeves. But she fell further from Adele's good graces by saying,

"No one will want to dance with me if you insist on dressing me as a dowd."

Adele turned towards her the quelling stare of which only she was capable. "You may depend on my judgment, Priscilla. The only dancing you will engage in for the time being is dancing lessons, for which a simple morning dress will suffice."

An ill-natured shadow settled over her *protegee's* countenance, and she turned a shoulder in a manner that spoke eloquently of displeasure and unwillingness to accept any more criticism. "I am nearly eighteen," she said, by way of defense, adding, "You needn't treat me as if I were a baby," when she stuck out her tongue.

Elvira gasped in dismay and cried out a gently monitory," "Priscilla, no!"

In all her life, no one had dared act in such a manner to Adele. Raising her glass to one eye, she stared Priscilla into red-faced silence when she said, "Ladies do not put out their tongues, my dear. And they endure necessary evils without complaining. Now we will say no more on this." Gathering up her gloves and reticule when the pattern was fitted to her satisfaction on Priscilla's sullen form, she arose from the cushioned chair. "I thank you for your trouble, Mrs. Bell. If you have finished taking measurements, we must go. Do you get dressed, Priscilla. We have much to do to properly turn you out."

Priscilla felt of a sudden childish and tongue-tied. But she was not so devoid of manners that she could not admit her error. "Pray excuse me. I suppose I am not so grown up as I could wish."

"We none of us are at times," Adele said, before she turned the subject towards the urgency of Priscilla's need. "You cannot deny she looks the country miss," she concluded as her *protegee* was buttoned into a provincial gown of an improper lilac stuff. The modiste concurred with regretful cluckings of her tongue.

Priscilla could not restrain stirrings of resentment. Her mother had always reassured her that she looked very well in her way, and Mr. Reeves had always called her pretty, a compliment which always buoyed her spirits, albeit given in an absent-minded, fatherly sort of manner. She decided her sponsor was using her very ill.

Although they left the shop with her new dress, hat, shoes, a dove gray spencer, and her shawl in hand and the promise that her wardrobe would be complete within the week, Priscilla could not shake the unhappy feelings that had suddenly, forcibly taken hold of her. Her mother ought to have had the privilege of ordering her first grown up wardrobe, not this stranger. And the dresses ought to have been gaily colored and brightly trimmed, not be elegant shadows of her gray school dresses. Moreover, it rankled that her sponsor had made all the decisions without once asking her opinion. Despite her aversion to the mourning colors, she could not even complain that the styles which Miss Fonteyne selected were too this or too that. Every dress, petticoat and other garment she was to have was of the nicest quality and in the latest mode and must forever put her in the lady's debt.

That she ought to be grateful did once occur to her, but when an assistant inadvertently stuck her with a pin as she was removing the pattern pieces, Priscilla suppressed such feelings as her conscience was eager to convict her.

Life was not at all fair, she thought, nursing sullen reflections all the way home.

Adele sat in the corner of her carriage, contemplating her silent charge who sat beside Elvira who said, "I thought the expedition went exceedingly well."

Hoping to open the flood gates of youthful exuberance, Adele agreed, adding, "It is a hopeful beginning, don't you think, Priscilla."

"If you say so," Priscilla pouted. Adele

noticed she was staring dully at the passing streets as if she didn't care whether or not she ever saw the new dresses.

Adele could not credit anyone suffering a fit of the dismals during an excursion whose very purpose was to make one acceptable to the polite world. She attributed her protegee's moodiness to exhaustion and removal from everything familiar, until she noted the almost contemptuous glances Priscilla was turning in her direction. Finally, she enquired, "Have I done something to offend you, my dear?"

"You wouldn't understand," Priscilla said still gazing upon the passing street.

"I dare say I do not understand why you did not offer an opinion of your new wardrobe."

"Do you not?" Priscilla enquired. "I do not recall being asked what I thought about *anything.*"

"Oh," Adele said, in a manner that conveyed her contrition. "I am sorry, Priscilla. No one has ever questioned my taste before. We must change whatever is not to your liking."

To this encouraging statement, Priscilla did not reply, but only directed another dark look toward Adele.

Shaken by the unfriendly stare, Adele

pressed her lips together and turned her thoughts inward.

As Gresham drew up before Number Thirty Green Street, she acknowledged guiltily, and not quite accurately, that Priscilla was treating her much in the same manner as she herself had always treated Miss Willoughby. Adele was ashamed to admit that until recently, she had behaved with an appalling lack of amiability towards her cousin. No wonder the poor woman retreated so often with a headache to her chamber. That she had done so again yesterday prompted Adele to think she may have expected too much of Elvira in regards to their young guest. How could she keep up with the whims and tempers of a seventeen-year-old, when she had come close to giving up on *her?*

Priscilla scarcely waited for the footman to let down the step before she erupted from the carriage and scurried above stairs.

"Pray, do not trouble Miss Willoughby," Adele called after her, when she realized Priscilla had headed straight to her cousin's room.

"She is no trouble, Adele," Elvira said, following the girl above stairs. "She is only a little disappointed that her new dresses are trimmed in black. I know I would be if I were her age."

"I suppose you are right," with a sigh, Adele handed her bonnet and gloves to her dresser who was already struggling under the weight of Priscilla's cloak and Elvira's pelisse "Thank you, Simone," she said wearily.

"You are not taking care of yourself," Simone said.

"But I have you to do that," Adele smiled.

"How can I, miss?" Simone complained, "When I am to feex Miss Willoughby's 'air. And who is to take care of your new improving project?"

"I have never doubted your ability to cope," Adele said. "But if it is too much, we shall need another—"

"Non, non!" Simone cried, resorting in her fear to her mother tongue. *"Moi tournez-pas, je vous en prie! Ou se trouve?"*

"I wouldn't dream of turning you out, Simone," Adele said. "Only meant to train a helper for you. Would you like that?"

A little appeased, Simone sniffed, *"Oui, mademoiselle.* P'rhaps one of the 'ousemaids."

Suspecting her dresser supposed a mere housemaid would allow her to rule undisputed, Adele only smiled again. "I shall find someone suitable."

With that she hastened off to rescue

Elvira from Priscilla's wearying exclamations. Finding them wreathed in smiles as they played a friendly game of cards, she only uttered a mild warning that Priscilla was not to tire Miss Willoughby, when both ladies giggled. "Oh, do not trouble yourself, Adele," Elvira said. "Miss Gaines is a breath of air. I am such a goose for allowing the headache to spoil our joy yesterday."

"Yes, well, don't overdo," Adele cautioned. "Do you join us at Lady Mathilda's for music this afternoon?"

"Oh, yes!" Elvira said, her eyes twinkling in delight. "I was hoping you might include me. Mathilda and I were bosom bows as girls, Priscilla. I know she will want you to succeed in society."

"I do not know why she should," Priscilla said, discarding an unwanted card. Elvira promptly scooped it up and placed her hand on the silk coverlet. "I win again, Priscilla. Really, my dear you must pay closer attention."

"No, you play too well for me," Priscilla laughed. "I only hope you do not suggest we play for stakes."

"Oh, no," Elvira tittered, gathering up the deck and beginning to shuffle again. "I have nothing to wager, Miss Gaines."

"Nor do I," Priscilla allowed with a little sigh as she picked up the cards she was

dealt. "So it is just as well we like to play."
And begging pardon for not including
Adele, who, Elvira said, detested cards,
they resumed the game.

Dismissed from play, Adele wandered
into her room for a rest. She felt she had
been rendered superfluous by Priscilla's
advent. Elvira no longer felt the need to
constantly monitor her needs, for which
she was grateful.

But Dy had not dropped in, as she
hoped he might.

Only Simone made her feel needed, and
only because she complained bitterly when
she was asked to help dress Priscilla and
Elvira before dressing Adele's hair. "You
do not want me," she protested. "How am
I to become a lady when I am chasing after
une eleve and *une vieille fille*—a schoolgirl
and an old maid?"

"You have elegant aspirations," Adele
said, looking shrewdly upon her dresser in
the reflection of her glass. "I hope you
may not fly too high."

"Non, miss," Simone replied around several hairpins, twisting a lock of auburn
hair around a finger and securing it ruth-
lessly. "As they say, the sky is the limit."

"Yes," Adele agreed, wondering how Simone intended to become this lady she
boasted of. The notion worried her. Maids,

even sophisticated ones, were too suscepti-
ble to silver tongued rakes whose promises
lured them out of secure homes and into
trouble. "But don't go chasing after pie in
the sky. It'll dissolve in your fingers."

"Oh, I shall come about, miss," Simone
maintained, weaving a ribbon within her
fiery curls. "See if I don't. Ah," she cooed,
cupping Adele's chin and scrutinizing her
coiffure, *"Vous etes belle."*

Handing her dresser a generous vail for
making the effort to turn out Elvira and
Priscilla despite her reluctance, Adele made
her way towards the salon where the ladies
were to meet prior to their engagement.

When they were assembled, Adele gazed
approvingly upon Priscilla. Attired in her
new gown, she appeared completely demure and modest as she proudly showed
off her elegant, but sober ensemble. Priscilla presented a charming picture.

Adele was forcibly struck by the thought
that when Dy saw Priscilla dressed *a la
mode* in the vulnerable shades of half-
mourning, he must surely fall in love with
her. But she compelled herself not to fall
into the dismals over the depressing
thought. The legendary appeal of young
ladies to older men often paled on acquaintance, on account of the girls' lack of
conversation or consideration. Though she

had no wish for Priscilla not to please, Adele fervently hoped someone else might recognize the girl's potential before she was leg shackled to a man whose standards of elegance intimidated even the Prince Regent. As much as she disliked admitting it given her admiration for Lord Windhaven, under his control, the unstable *amour propre* of a schoolgirl like Priscilla could only crumble. She might become a shadow, like Lady Peverley.

Telling herself Dy would never become as cruel as the overbearing Lord Peverley, Adele applied herself towards getting her party into the carriage.

As Adele hoped, Priscilla was welcomed graciously into the circle of acquaintances with only one or two busybodies asking her to make them known to her family. Fortunately, Lady Mathilda intervened seating Priscilla at her side.

Soon the musical part of the afternoon was over, and everyone turned to the more important reason for the gathering: gossip and set-downs.

Priscilla showed herself novice at the game. To the first lady who requested to know the name of Miss Gaines' mother, Priscilla ingenuously replied, "I'm sorry she cannot meet you. She died during the winter."

Several cups rattled in their saucers. Lady Bermondey peered at Priscilla through her glass and clucked like a disapproving hen, "And you not in deep mourning."

"Oh, dear," Elvira said uneasily.

"Dear Lady Bermondey," Adele said, smiling encouragement on her *protegee* as she defended her. "You must lay the blame at my feet. The girl has known too little joy in her life to be shut away just now when she needs the diversion friends can provide."

"It isn't proper," said Lady Bermondey.

"Perhaps not strictly so," Adele agreed in gently reproving tones. "But that is not for you to say."

"No, if you think it all right, then it must be so," Lady Bermondey said, flushing in a manner that ill became her gown of Capucine color.

"I for one am glad to see you, my girl," Mathilda said. "Your mother wouldn't have wished you to hide your light in a darkened room."

"No, she particularly forbade me to pine for her," Priscilla said. "Said her family would not like it. But I don't care. I do miss her."

Before Priscilla could say anything that might fan the flames of a scandal broth,

Adele said brightly, "Would you come here, my dear and meet Lady Katherine?"

As she hoped, the girls liked each other on first sight. Priscilla, who had been older than the other girls at the academy in Yorkshire and had been compelled in the last year to teach in her mother's stead, was only too glad to claim a new friend her own age. And Lady Katherine, who for all her friends, was never averse to adding one more to her list. With their heads together, she whispered, "Pray, don't mind Mama. She is feeling a little jealous of Miss Fonteyne's influence just now. She was kind enough to transform me from a plain Kate to whatever I now am."

"You are very pretty," Priscilla said, admiring Lady Katherine striking ensemble. "I could never wear gold to advantage."

"That I will never believe," said Lady Katherine, laughing. "You quite cast me in the shade, but I like you. One cannot snub prettier ladies, after all."

"Why not?" Priscilla asked.

"Why, gentlemen buzz around them like bees to flowers," Lady Katherine said, "And I might be fortunate enough to attract one of them by my proximity."

"Oh, you have a pretty soul, Lady Katherine," Priscilla said, hugging her. "Gentlemen must see it as well as I do."

Katherine sighed. "You are very kind," but she did not sound convinced.

As they said their good-byes, Lady Mathilda surprised them all by inviting Priscilla and Lady Katherine to join her during her afternoon drive in the Park. "It will do the girls good to be seen with me," she said, silencing anyone who might wonder aloud at the unexpected summons. "And it will do me good to be with them." Then, she dismissed the rest of her guests by asking Adele to remain behind a moment.

When they were alone, Lady Mathilda stared down her long nose at Adele as if waiting for her to fidget. Adele did not oblige the imperious lady, but only waited for her to speak. Finally, Lady Mathilda said, "I would like to entertain the girl; however, it is out of the question until the proper interval has passed."

"Quite," Adele agreed. "I hope you don't think it impertinent, Priscilla not appearing in deepest black."

"No, how depressing for her that would be," Lady Mathilda said, her voice thick with emotion. "The girl shows the proper feeling for her mama." Pressing a handkerchief to her long, straight nose, she added, "I scarce can believe it myself. Her mother was so full of life. I quite admired her when she stood with her young man against the world. All those years . . . a little, lost lamb. Yes, Miss Fonteyne, I will do what I can to bring Priscilla back into the fold."

"I knew we could depend upon you," Adele said, clasping the elderly woman's free hand in impulsive, but gentle fingers. "Priscilla believes herself to be all alone in the world."

"She feels herself abandoned?" Lady Mathilda's fingers clenched her walking stick in a manner that suggested she was suffering an arthritic spasm.

"Yes, but she is only seventeen, and prone to dramatics," Adele responded indulgently, not wishing to seem overly critical. "I am not certain she has any family living, although Dy—Lord Windhaven assures me she does."

"He is not mistaken," said Lady Mathilda, without elaborating. "You did right in bringing the girl to me. I can silence gossip as well as you can create a new fashion. And I will work with you to effect a happy ending."

"Thank you, Lady Mathilda," Adele said, blushing.

"Ah," said the lady. "There is more to this happy ending than you have told me. Does this Lord Windhaven figure into your plans?"

Adele attempted to make light of her unfortunate tendency to color. Shrugging, she enquired, "Wouldn't it be more apropos, Lady Mathilda, to ask whether I figure into *his* plans?"

"Yes, but to that query you prudently have no response." Lady Mathilda patted Adele's hand. Sighing, she added, "I doubt even you know what you feel for your . . . friend."

"He is a good friend," Adele said. "But I am reluctant to call him something closer—"

"Until he declares himself," Lady Mathilda completed the thought, then shook her head solemnly. "Gentlemen are often reluctant to declare themselves to ladies who seem too independent or reserved."

"Yes, perhaps you are right. Only he seemed to approve of my independence."

"Seemed to?" prompted the Lady with a spark of humor in her eye.

"Well, perhaps it is become a nasty habit," Adele allowed.

Lady Mathilda looked in a considering manner upon Adele and said, "Nasty habits are made to be broken, my dear."

"But will he not suspect if I become all at once a clinging vine? I should be a laughingstock. Worse, I should make him appear ridiculous."

"Heaven forbid," said the lady, tapping her cane on the floor in summons to a footman who silently entered the room, awaiting orders. "Believe that I have your *protegee's* best interests at heart. And yours. But I've no right to meddle, have I?"

"No, truly I thank you for your concern," Adele said, gathering up her gloves and arising from her seat. "I shall see Priscilla is ready to drive with you tomorrow."

"Good," the lady said, giving Adele's fingers one last gentle squeeze before letting her go.

Eleven

Ascending into Lady Mathilda's antique, but immaculate carriage the next day, Priscilla allowed herself to be engulfed in Lady Mathilda's embrace, faintly reminiscent of camphor and lemon. She felt as if she were suddenly recalling something from her infancy, but as soon as the pleasant but vague memory surfaced, it was submerged in the excitement of the present.

Indicating an elderly gentleman seated on the opposite corner who was dressed in a sober black frock coat, over a stark white shirt, gray waistcoat and breeches, Lady Mathilda said, "May I present—"when she was interrupted.

Taking Priscilla's hand in his, the gentleman said, "We agreed, no formality. Please call me Brush, my dear. Move over Mattie," he said, giving Lady Mathilda a gentle shove. "When I have the opportunity, I prefer sitting next to a pretty girl."

"How rude you are become in your dotage," Mathilda chided. But smiling, she moved to sit next to Lady Katherine. She went on, "I hope you may not have offended our other young guest, Milton."

"No, think nothing of it," Lady Katherine said, bestowing a forgiving smile on the elderly gentleman. "I quite understand, my lord."

"You see, Lady Kate does not hold a grudge," said the gentleman. "I hope I may learn that Miss Gaines don't either."

"I hope I do not," Priscilla said, sighing unhappily as she considered the long-lived bitterness that had deprived her mother and her of a family. Squeezing his hand in greeting, she added, "And if we are not to stand on ceremony, my lord; you must call me Priscilla."

"We shall get on very well," Brush said, patting her fingers. "In fact, I hope we may become fast friends."

His expression seemed so boyishly eager, that Priscilla returned his smile, saying, "Yes, I hope so, too," before she settled back to enjoy the drive through the Park. And though she was full of delight in her friends, on her return home she found it difficult to share her feelings with Adele. For some reason, as she returned that evening to Number Thirty Green Street, she felt she had abandoned her family to live among strangers.

This feeling persisted throughout the next week as shopping and fittings gave over to visitors and calls. She was very prettily behaved, especially to Lady Mathilda and Lord Brush with whom she felt so at ease. And her eagerness to sit quietly and listen to harmless social gossip endeared her even to such as Lady Bermondey who preferred that all debutantes be seen and not heard.

But her good manners were left upon the doorstep of Number Thirty Green Street. Not even Lady Katherine was immune to Priscilla's temper. As the two girls giggled one afternoon over a stack of *La Belle Assemblee,* several young gentlemen were announced. Priscilla looked up eagerly, expecting the men to flock to her side in fulfillment of Lady Katherine's prophesy. However, after introductions were made, they formed a circle around the plainer lady, each pleading for a dance at a ball, the pleasure of which Priscilla was denied, in deference to her grief.

Shut out of the joy of anticipation, Priscilla felt herself very ill used again. She felt that, knowing she was unable to attend the festive occasion, Lady Katherine ought to have declined all the entreaties and support her in her lonely vigil.

It wasn't fair for Kate to have all the fun, when *she* was a prisoner in a stranger's home. Clenching her fists within the folds of her new lavender and white striped gown to keep from crying out her resentment, Priscilla decided her friend was no friend at all.

When the gentlemen left, she thumped onto the cushion of a chair and said, "I ought to have denied them entry."

"Oh no, Priscilla, they were very polite," Lady Katherine said.

"To you, perhaps," Priscilla snapped, crossing her arms angrily. "But I might have been a flower on the wall for all they cared."

"Oh, that's right," Katherine said, sinking beside Priscilla on the settee. "We weren't very considerate." She shook her head. "Men are so single-minded, you know. But I dare say, next Season it will be different. They will all want to dance with you."

"Next Season, next year. I have heard that all my life," Priscilla cried. "I thought life would be different in London—bright clothes, brilliant parties, but no. I might still be in Osmotherly, dressed in my gray wool and apron, for all the fun I have."

Lady Katherine placed a gentle hand on Priscilla's shoulder. "But we have been to the menagerie, and the Strand and the British Museum."

"Oh yes, Lord Elgin's marbles and the stupid Rosetta Stone," Priscilla sneered, jerking her sleeve out of her friend's grasp. "Broken, moldy stones. Who cares for all that?"

"I'm sorry," Katherine said. "And I know it is difficult and sad for you."

"You know nothing." Priscilla sprang from the cushion and ran from the room, sobbing. "I hate you, and all your parties," she cried, leaving Lady Katherine alone and stunned.

Hearing the commotion, Adele followed Priscilla to her room. Entering even though the girl bid her to go away, Adele said, "It is difficult to watch others enjoying all the parties and dances which must be denied you."

Priscilla did not turn to regard her, but pulled her hairbrush through her hair. "What do you know of it?" she snapped. "You may go to any ball you like, wear whatever you like."

"Now I may," Adele allowed. "But when

I was nineteen, I was to have a Season in London."

"See how much good it did you," Priscilla remarked. "Still single."

"That is not to the point, my dear. I am single by choice, because I had the good fortune of being able to support myself and my servants. Not every young lady is as blessed."

"How nice for you," Priscilla said. "I suppose you cast everyone in the shade then."

"No, my mother and father caught typhus just as we were preparing to leave India. I did not get my season that year. So I know . . ."

"Don't tell me you know how I feel," Priscilla said, brittle-voiced. Hugging herself with one arm, she pressed a shaking hand to her mouth. "You can't know."

Despite Priscilla's vehemence, Adele remembered how abandoned, and all at sea she had felt after her parents died. Drawing aside a filmy, muslin curtain, she gazed off into the garden, where a bank of daffodils nodded in the breeze. Instead of budding branches and dripping statuary, she suddenly saw the arid garden of her childhood home in India. The crushing sadness rolled over her once more, leaving her with a clearer understanding of the rawness of Priscilla's grief.

Given the depth of her agony, Adele knew it was useless to argue or assure her that she would feel better someday. While it was true that the pain would subside gradually, Adele understood it was a sorry scrap of encouragement that discounted Priscilla's loss and her feelings.

Letting the curtain fall back in place, she turned to regard the girl, still brushing her thick, ebony hair. Gently, she removed the brush from her unresisting hand and ran it down the length of her tresses, her free hand following in a soothing motion. After a few brush strokes, she said, "I don't know how you feel now, but I can understand. It was the darkest time of my life. Because of the fear of infection, I was not allowed to see them or say good bye, not even attend the funeral. It all happened so quickly. One day they were well, the next sick, the next dead and buried."

"So you were orphaned overnight," Priscilla said. Some of the bitterness seemed to have dissipated under Adele's gentle handling, though she did add a resentful, "Poor, rich little orphan girl."

"Yes, small consolation, that," Adele said, still brushing Priscilla's hair in long, soothing strokes. "All my money could not buy back my parents' lives, and believe me,

I tried to bargain with God. 'If only You will bring them back, I'll . . . ' "

"I know," Priscilla sighed. "I even promised to devote myself to the poor, if only Mama could be spared."

"Well, your bargain was a bit more practical than mine," Adele said. "I suggested He take me instead of Mama and Papa. When they died, I felt that even He didn't want me."

"So?" Priscilla shrugged.

Despite the rather grudging query, Adele suspected Priscilla was concealing her own feelings behind a mask of indifference. "So," she said, tying a ribbon around Priscilla's hair, "I set out to be the kind of person He could not love—selfish, frivolous, judgmental, vain—in a word, fashionable."

"That is all very well for you," Priscilla said. "But I am a pauper. If I had a nabob's fortune, I could—"

"But you are not," Adele interrupted. " 'If onlys' are worse than useless. They make you a prisoner to the past, and keep you from adjusting to what is."

"I wish you will stop prosing on," Priscilla snapped, springing from her chair. "Why don't you go apologize to Lady Katherine?"

"It would be better if you would apologize," Adele said, setting the brush on the vanity. "But since you are unwilling, I shall make excuses for you."

Lady Katherine was all sympathy when Adele made her aware of Priscilla's continuing unhappiness. "I beg your pardon, and hers," Katherine said, her freckles shining gold through the blush of embarrassment. "How stupid I was."

"I understand," Adele said. "And Priscilla will next year, when she is able to attend balls and parties."

"Well, I scarcely know what to do," Katherine said, covering her flaming cheeks with her fingers. "She seemed so hungry for details, I guess I never thought she might not really want to hear them."

"I don't suppose hearing the details after the fact is as heart-wrenching as being excluded from the anticipation. It may seem as if one was actually there, if a friend shares her experience."

"Still, I cannot tell you how sorry I am to have caused Priscilla such pain. It doesn't seem quite fair to deny her the diversion of dancing after losing her mother."

"No, but that is the way of things," Adele said, ushering her towards the door. "Do not trouble yourself, my dear, that she will hold your exuberance against you forever."

As Lady Katherine left, promising that

she would remain patient with her friend, Adele admitted the possibility that she was being repaid for her sins of pride and self-ishness. How she wished she might consult with the viscount to discover, if it were possible, what she was doing wrong. However, he only sent a note to her saying that he had every confidence in her ability to deal with Priscilla's pets.

Without Windhaven's support, she was soon exhausted, and her suspicions increased that he would eventually declare for the girl. She could not refute the evidences of courtship—flowers, a fan, a parasol—that were delivered with his card, but no accompanying note, tucked in the box.

As yet another box was sent up to Priscilla's room, Elvira uttered a query that further drained Adele. "Are you quite sure the presents are proper for her?"

"Of course," Adele assured her. "Dy is her guardian, and may give her whatever he wishes." Nevertheless, she thought the colorful presents were odd things to give a girl in half-mourning.

But she retired to her room, to review the short note he'd sent round to her before the gifts began to arrive, reminding her of her promise to help him win his lady, and declaring his hopes that she would approve the presents which followed. Not having

been written in his customary careless but
affectionate style, it seemed to Adele more
a formal notice to a parent of one's intention of paying court than a friendly note or
a passionate *billet doux* to one's beloved.

The presents which followed were entirely inappropriate for a young girl in
mourning, but just what Adele would like.
A new fan of jonquille feathers and ivory
sticks came in a yellow silk box. Priscilla
fluttered it so inexpertly that Adele was
convinced the fluffy creation must molt.
Warning the girl to have a care that it be
fit for use later, when she was out of
mourning, Priscilla whined that no one
had given her a *proper* fan.

Adele presented one of her own very becoming fans of ebony and gray silk, but
the chit obstinately refused her cast off.
Nothing would do but that Simone accompany her to Schomberg House in Pall Mall
to purchase a more suitable fan.

That fan suffered an undignified demise
when Priscilla opened it for the first time.
Two sticks snapped and punctured the
transparent silk. Without regard to its cost,
Priscilla tossed it in the fireplace. Adele
watched it go up in flames and could only
be glad the same fate had not befallen Dy's
pretty gift which would have gone so well
with her new ballgown.

Then came a painted parasol which Priscilla insisted upon carrying even though the sun had yet, in the third week of April, to show signs of awakening from its winter hibernation.

During a brief carriage ride from Green Street to Curzon Street to show off her new present to her friend, Lady Mathilda, the heavens opened and the painted silk was wet through. Fortunately, Adele had brought a sturdier, black umbrella which saved their dresses.

Upon returning home, Adele scribbled a hasty note begging Dy to refrain from forwarding any more gifts to his ward until he was able to protect them.

Instead of penning a note in reply, Windhaven appeared on Adele's doorstep. As he entered the salon, he demanded to see Priscilla immediately.

Adele's delight in seeing him was instantly depressed as she realized he had come on his ward's account, not to see *her*. Wondering if he had even received her note, she said, "I cannot oblige you, my lord. Priscilla has gone with Elvira; paying calls, I believe."

"Just as well," he replied, placing himself next to Adele on the sofa without waiting for an invitation. Tugging off his gloves and tossing them into his hat, he added, "I have come for you."

Adele did not know how to respond to his announcement, since his grim countenance betrayed no pleasure in the visit. "I did not expect you to alter your schedule, my lord. As long as Priscilla is happy, we go along very well."

"That is not what your note implied," he said, glaring at her. "It seems she has been tyrannizing you."

"Oh, no," Adele countered. But Windhaven seemed unconvinced, if his unremitting gaze was to be relied upon. Disconcerted by the penetrating stare, she retreated into the habits of hospitality and offered him tea.

Dismissing her offer with a wave of his hand, he laid it along the back of the sofa, then demanded, "What do you mean giving my gifts to Priscilla?"

Adele said uncertainly, "I thought you wanted her to have them."

"No, Adele," he said, "I wanted *you* to have them."

Twelve

"Surely not," she laughed, covering her mouth in embarrassment. "You said I was to approve them, not keep them."

Propelling himself explosively to his feet, Dy strode the length of the salon and back, his hands clenched behind his back as if fighting to control his temper. "So you gave them to a child," he growled. "If you didn't like them, Adele, why did you not return the presents?"

"Oh, but I did like them. I still do," she vowed, wanting him to know how much. But he bestowed such a displeased look upon her, she could say nothing. She dropped her gaze from his angrily drawn together brows to consider the handkerchief she was plucking apart. Then she confessed what sounded to her petty and selfish, "I wanted to claim them for myself. But . . ." Ashamed, she fell silent.

Windhaven ceased pacing and stood quietly before her, then prompted gently, "Go on." Adele looked up from her embarrassed contemplation and met an encouraging, if wary, smile. "Why did you give them to Priscilla?"

"Oh dear," she said, avoiding his query by cataloging his many kindnesses. "You have done so much for the girl. Given her a new life; a home; hope for a family and friends. So noble, so heroic."

"Don't attribute any noble qualities to me, Adele. The only reason I took her in was out of respect for her father."

"I thought so at first," Adele allowed, "But once I met her, I suspected you protested too much. Anyone might attempt to fly to the moon on her behalf."

"Not I," Dy said in heartless tones. "I rarely go out of my way."

"That is why I feared you must have . . . cared for her more than you let on," Adele said, determined now to have her concerns in the open.

Windhaven withdrew a snuff box from his waistcoat pocket and considered the enamelled hunt scene depicted on the lid before replacing it in his pocket. "I never wished to care for a little girl; still don't. But I gave my word to Arthur, and there you are." He shrugged, as if attending to duty was scarcely worth mentioning. "Nothing to be done, but must be done."

"Yes," Adele sighed. "But is there no other way? Must you . . . marry her, Dy?" Hurrying on, giving him no opportunity to respond, she began to explain herself, "I mean, I know I have no right to say anything, but your decision seems so . . . hasty and . . . though I do not want to criticize you in any way, well . . . rather Gothic."

"Is this a polite way of calling me a villain?" Windhaven asked, his manner stiffening in offense. Unconsciously, he rubbed a hand over his head as he was wont to do when upset. Recognizing his distress, Adele hastened to his side, but he held her off, saying, "What do you take me for, Adele? A cradle robber?"

"No, I beg your pardon," she said, taking hold of his sleeve despite his seeming aversion to her touch. "But she is so pretty, how could anyone blame you? And she is not a child."

"She is to *me*," Windhaven insisted, pacing once more in agitation. When Adele made to speak, he waved her silent. "No, I begin to understand. You thought I proposed to *her;* how could you? There were times on the road I'd have gladly left her, bag and baggage."

"You don't mean that," Adele said.

"Don't go telling me what I mean and don't mean," he snapped. Just then a maid came in. Shushing him, Adele heard the girl's explanation that Mrs. Murphy had sent her to inquire if she was to prepare refreshments, and sent her away.

When the maid left Dy renewed his attack. "I want to know why you think I wanted to marry the girl."

"You said it yourself," Adele whispered in reply, clasping her fingers together to keep from clinging to him. "For respectability."

Windhaven could say nothing, but only stare at her for a long time as if trying to make sense of her argument. "Poor Adele," he said, smiling at last. "All this worry because you believed I intended to sacrifice myself with Priscilla on the altar of respectability." His gaze softened as he smiled, his eyes darkening invitingly. "Don't you know I care nothing for what other people say about me?"

Adele did not know at first how to respond to his provocative declaration, due to the agitation his forgiving blue stare caused her. Even had she been able to form a coherent thought, she was powerless to utter a word, for she suddenly felt as giddy as a schoolgirl.

No, definitely not a schoolgirl. A girl would have blushed and fended him off, but she was a sophisticated woman, who craved his good favor. His grinning statement sounded improperly attractive. Returning his smile, she asked, "What *do* you care about?" her voice unusually soft and coy.

"You," he replied, holding his arms open.

The hope that he at last saw her as a desirable woman flared into life, and Adele came into his welcome embrace with a blissful sigh. As his arms folded around her, she gave up all her worries.

Dy cared for her, and for now, that was enough. She was glad to rest within the shelter of his arms, leaning her cheek against his smooth lapel.

It had been an eternity since they had held one another, she thought; even though less than a month had passed since they had shared two impulsive kisses, kisses that had led her to the mistaken conclusion that he loved her.

She would not be so naive again as to attribute feelings to another that she could scarce admit herself.

Priscilla was right about wearing one's feelings upon her sleeve. They were too easily snatched away and made a mockery, as schoolboys sometimes plucked little girls' hats from their heads. How much safer to guard one's tender feelings or share them among friends like chocolate cordials than pour them out lavishly on one person.

Wondering suddenly if she had perhaps been too forward even in this friendly show of affection, Adele disengaged herself and moved uneasily towards the mantelpiece mirror, just as a footman entered to close the shutters and light the candles.

Repulsing the second assault on their privacy, Dy considered Adele's anxious response to his embrace.

She had always been careful not to favor any gentleman over much, and he had taken pains to discipline the true nature of his feelings towards her so that she was content to consider him a very good friend. Except for those two foolish, delightful kisses, which he could still taste.

If she knew he was determined to make her his wife, he doubted she would ever allow him past her servile guards or that dragon of a companion, Miss Willoughby. But the golden lights that shone within Adele's eyes so encouraged him as he held her that he was on the verge of speaking his heart's desire.

Then, fearing the untimely entrance of another servant, she wriggled out of his embrace and scurried towards the safety of her mirror. He wondered if she had orchestrated the repeated interruptions.

Was she unwilling or afraid to reveal too much of herself to him? The perception aroused his protective instincts and he started to follow her. But that, he knew, would only stiffen her resistance. Immediately checking his advance, he enquired in an off hand manner that was born of long practice, "Did I loosen a curl or two?"

"No," she assured him with an over bright smile, though she placed a nervous hand to her head. "I, how forward you must think me to fall so dependently upon you." A tortoise shell hairpin fell from her hair to the floor, allowing a burnished curl to tumble down her shoulder.

Dy moved forward and retrieved the hairpin, placing it in Adele's hesitant fingers. Pressing them to her bosom, as if his brushing touch had burned her, she turned to the mirror at once and repaired her coiffure. Over her shoulder, she could see him watching her with a curious grin enlivening his handsome face.

Although she might have encouraged his appreciative appraisal a week ago and even prolonged it, now she was embarrassed by it. She made quick work of her repair, then turned to face him.

"Done so quickly, yet done so well," he said, admiration raising his brows and the corners of his lips. Then, he waved a dismissing hand as he commanded, "Forget my ward for now; Elvira will spoil her for our company while you drive with me."

Glancing at the ormulu clock on the mantle, Adele saw that it was just half past three. "But Dy," she said. "No one will be in the park."

"Hyde Park at four must be ever so much quieter than Hyde Park at five," he said reasonably.

"There is an explanation for that," she interjected. "No one is there except mushrooms."

Dysart smilingly considered her protest, then shrugged and said, "Haven't we long considered that wherever *we* are, that is the fashionable place?" His smile broadened as she nodded slowly in agreement. "Go, don something that will turn every budding mushroom's eye green with envy. I shall order my racing curricle brought round." Then, as if confident that his plans met with her approval, he strode towards the door.

Not long after, Dy was seemingly preoccupied in the task of keeping his fresh pair of chestnuts from bolting on the crowded street, when he was in fact absorbed by his quiet companion. Adele's pale complexion glowed with a becoming blush that he knew owed nothing to artifice. The unseasonably bright afternoon sun glinted with highlights of flame off hair that was piled in artful disarray beneath a pert bonnet. Her gown of white muslin clung like spun sugar to an under dress of apple green silk.

With an almost Herculean effort, he controlled the fancy to say she looked good enough to eat. Lord, he thought, mentally thumping his Windblown with the heel of his hand, what would she think if I uttered such flummery?

She seemed so completely oblivious to the almost painful effect she had upon him, that he wondered as he turned onto the Ring whether he had been mistaken about the spark of delight he had earlier detected in her eyes.

On the second circuit around the park, Adele wondered what had been the point of dressing expensively when the one person she most wished to notice her did not pay the least attention? Peering at him from under the shade of her fringed parasol, she teased, "You are uncommonly quiet, my lord. Parenthood must have affected your wit."

"Hardly, Adele," he growled, wishing he could confess his thoughts. Inwardly he allowed that something had affected his mind, for he could think of nothing to say she probably had not heard before. Not wishing to sound like a cub in the throes of calf love, he kept his tongue between his teeth, and drove on, staring ahead like the overbearing guardian she thought he was.

Adele, twirling her parasol in apparent indifference, lapsed into despondent silence, thinking it odd that he should be compelled to pay such close attention to the team when they were practically the only carriage making the tour of the Park. The others plodding around the ring were occupied by ancient dowagers who kept insisting their doddering coachmen slow down or soberly clad merchant wives calling at their children to be quiet. Surrounded by ravens and magpies, Adele began to suspect she looked ridiculous in what she had originally thought a very becoming ensemble.

Suddenly he drew his team up short to avoid a collision as a laundalet cut in front of them. Its elderly passenger leaned over the side and spat as her coachman inexpertly sawed at the mouths of his cattle.

Adele felt very much out of her element. By bringing her to the Park at a distinctly unfashionable hour, the Viscount Windhaven had impressed upon her that she was sadly outdated.

As soon as the danger of collision was

past, Dy drew his curricle off the path into the lacy shade of a budding elm. "Now, we can be comfortable," he said, tying off his pair, adding, "And talk," in a significant tone that impelled her to meet his warm gaze.

"We can talk at home," she reminded him.

"Very true," he replied. "Only there, we cannot be private."

"Oh," she said in a breathless little voice. "Oh, yes, I see. No servants underfoot, no companion, no ward. Quite private. And completely respectable, as we are friends."

Her assertion inexplicabl seemedy to harden his eyes. Knowing she had somehow said the wrong thing, she nervously removed her gaze from his, and began to inspect the appearance of the members of the ton who were already descending on the Park.

"Friends," he repeated dully. "Do you not wish for more?"

"Of course," she replied, trying to sound flippant, but failing. "What female does not? They say bachelor life is the envy of married men. But who envies the spinster? Rather, she is reviled as unnatural, cursed as selfish, and for her sin of remaining unwed, committed to special tortures in hell." As if enduring the special social hell reserved for unmarried females in this life were not enough, she thought, recalling aspersions which only recently had been directed at her.

He took her gloved hand in his, saying fervently, "You do not have to look forward to such treatment."

"No," she agreed. She squeezed his fingers. "I have reformed, Dy. No more selfish Adele causing Miss Willoughby endless megrims or filling abigails' heads with fashionable extravagance that can only get them in trouble. From now on, I shall live a sober life of good works. I shall be the perfect example for Priscilla."

"I have always thought you were near enough perfect," he said in lover-like tones that Adele failed to detect.

She was too caught up in her resolution. "I do not think so," she replied thoughtfully. "I can teach Priscilla how to get on so she will be a credit to you and her family."

"I never doubted your ability to do so," he grinned, "Until you gave my presents to her. And if that is what you mean by being unselfish, I won't have it." He shook his head ruefully, adding, "She's gone on long enough thinking she might have what she liked as she liked it."

Adele felt his hand tremble over hers, and replied in a soothing manner, "She cannot help it, Dy. She is pretty; people cannot help giving her things, and making allowances for her."

He nodded and exclaimed, "That is exactly what I mean. Pretty is as pretty does, and my ward fails to do the pretty. But I did not bring you here to discuss Priscilla. There is a matter on which I can no longer keep silent," he said, raising her fingers to his lips and pressing a fervent kiss on them.

"My lord!" she cried as she tried to free her imprisoned fingers. "This isn't the place."

Lowering her hand to his knee, he said, "I thought you would welcome my address. I mean, I had hoped—"

Immediately she ceased struggling and stared, not adoringly at him, but across the Park in dismay. "Dy, look!" she commanded. "Over there."

"Why?" he demanded, not wishing to be distracted.

"It's Priscilla," Adele said.

"Yes," he said, his gaze still fixed upon her. "Driving with Elvira."

"No," Adele said in urgent, but hushed tones. "She is not in my carriage." Leaning forward to get a better look without calling attention to herself, she added, "I see no crest, but the vehicle is of the first quality."

"Then, she is with one of Elvira's acquaintances," Windhaven said impatiently. "You need not fret over the girl, Adele."

"I suppose you are right," Adele sighed, subsiding against the cushion as he flicked the reins, setting his pair in motion. "Where are we going?" she asked.

"Home," Dy replied. "We may as well be interrupted there after all."

Recalling their earlier conversation which he must have considered important, Adele attempted to rein in her anxiety over Priscilla and said, "I beg your pardon, my lord. What were you saying?"

He grimaced, as if the memory cost him some pain, but only said, "Perhaps later." Nodding, as they passed a black lacquered town coach, he asked, "Is that the carriage?"

"Yes," Adele said. A beam of late afternoon sunshine seemed to illuminate Priscilla within the coach, but all else was in shadow. "I see her, Dy, but where is Elvira?"

Then, through the open window, she saw Priscilla lean towards her companion. To Adele's horror, a masculine chuckle erupted from within. She knew Dy had heard it, for he stiffened at her side, his tense grip communicating itself to his horses, which danced skittishly along the path until he managed to control his spasm.

"I don't know," he said through clenched

teeth as the coach rolled forward on the graveled lane, "But I intend to find out."

Dy was frustrated in his effort to move towards the shadowed coach by the crush of traffic which crowded the Park lanes. Just as he began to move forward, another coach would cut him off, merge into his lane, or stop so that its occupants might chat with an acquaintance. Indeed, Windhaven himself had thus blocked traffic countless times in the past without twinges of conscience, calling ridiculous those who insisted on keeping the flow clear. He wondered now whether they had been possessed of an almost desperate parental apprehension on behalf of a foolish daughter. If so, then he fully deserved the punishment of dealing with a rebellious chit, since he had formerly been one of those guilty of blocking traffic. But knowing he merited the penalty didn't make it easier to bear.

He also understood that voicing his concern would only make him seem ridiculous and shred Priscilla's reputation. So he attempted to guide his pair through the crush without seeming too intent on the act, greeting those who called out with a hard won cordiality when he would prefer snubbing everyone to get to his goal.

Adele smiled and nodded to various acquaintances as Dy maneuvered through traffic, endeavoring to listen patiently when they came to a dead halt, while keeping an eye on the town coach, which was just making its way through the gates marking Hyde Park Corner. Inhaling an anxious breath, she watched it roll down Park Lane, gathering speed, while they were still caught in the snare of traffic within the Ring. Losing sight of the black vehicle, she sighed a defeated, "She's gone, Dy."

"Only thing to do is take you home," he said, frowning as he drove around a carriage full of brightly dressed demi-mondes and rowdy young gentlemen. "And hope Elvira is there and our fears are the result of overactive imaginations."

"Oh, dear," Adele said, hoping rather that Elvira was with Priscilla.

When they arrived back at Number Thirty Green Street, only Miss Willoughby was at home. Taken aback by Windhaven's hasty accusation that she had left her chick in the care of a wily fox, Elvira retreated in tears to her room.

"I should have listened to Mrs. Beaton," he growled, "And applied a hand to the seat of knowledge."

"No," Adele cried, laying a restraining hand on his arm. "Pray do not beat the girl, or she will come to hate you, too."

"My dear, I have already had the misfortune to fall under Priscilla's bad graces."

"No, really?" Adele asked. "But she was desolate to leave you."

"She could scarcely wait to leave my care," Windhaven asserted. "Within an hour of leaving Osmotherly, she hated me. Nearly had me arrested for abduction in York, which everyone took as a grand joke when Mr. Reeves upheld my cause."

"Did you doubt he would?" Adele enquired.

"No," he replied, flashing a wry grin that raised the corners of Adele's lips. "I think he was glad to be rid of the girl. She has had her pretty nose out of joint more times than I care to count."

"It comes from thinking no one loves her," Adele mused, recalling her own unhappy reflections of recent and distant memory.

Casting an unconvinced look at her, he said, "Hard not to dislike her," adding, "I am merely being realistic," when Adele shook her head. He soothed a hand along her shoulder, when she buried her face in his shoulder.

"I am so frightened for her," she whispered. "If only I had been more watchful."

Holding her tightly against the storm of her recriminations, he said, "You are not to blame yourself for my ward's disappearance." Placing a kiss on her too-pale forehead, he held her for a moment longer, before moving toward the staircase.

Thirteen

"Where do you go?" she enquired, her voice tight and modulated rather higher than was her custom.

"To find her, of course," he replied, as if finding a lost girl in London was the simplest thing in the world to accomplish.

Adele hastened after him. "Then I shall go with you." Mrs. Murphy, as if having read her mistress' mind, was proffering an apple green pelisse, gloves and hat.

"No use in that," he protested, staying her from slipping her arms into her pelisse. "If you leave the house, Priscilla will waltz in a quarter hour later."

"And if she does not," Adele replied, tugging on her gloves. "I shall pace a hole in my carpet. I am going with you." Resolutely, she slipped her arms within the sleeves of her pelisse, and said, "Mrs. Murphy, kindly tell Simone I shall need her later than usual for dinner this evening."

The housekeeper's ruddy complexion

seemed of a sudden to pale as she said, "I had hoped to break it to you in another way, miss. But Simone never returned from Mass."

"What?" Adele gasped. "But that was early this morning. Where could she have gone."

The housekeeper handed Adele a note. "It came this afternoon when you were driving with Lord Windhaven. From the Bull and Mouth. I have already sent a man to enquire after the girl."

"And?" Windhaven asked, plucking the note from Adele's limp fingers.

"The footman said she boarded the stage to Coventry," replied Mrs. Murphy. "With a gentleman name of Avery Finch."

"Avery Finch," growled Windhaven. "Sounds like a hum to me."

"Do you think our Priscilla may have done the same thing?" Mrs. Murphy asked. "Run off, that is; not with Mr. Finch, o' course, but with someone else?"

Adele clutched a hand to her breast, hoping the outside pressure might relieve her inner anxieties.

But at that moment, her worry proved unnecessary, at least as it concerned Priscilla, for she blew in through the front door. Her cheeks were aglow, her eyes sparkling. As she passed her fuming guardian and apprehensive sponsor, she breathed a rapturous, "Isn't it a lovely evening?" and sailed toward the staircase.

Adele stared after her, her feelings a confusion of relief that the girl had returned, and fury that she had gone off with a stranger.

"Where do you think you are going?" Windhaven demanded.

"To my room," Priscilla replied, her progress arrested on the bottom step. Trailing her fingers around the gleaming newel post, she explained, "I must change for dinner."

"Your dinner must wait," the viscount replied, holding open the door to the book room. "Adele, will you kindly join us?"

At his request, she moved forward obediently, and stood beside him.

Priscilla glanced nervously between the adults. They presented an appearance of unshakable unity as they stood side by side at the door. She began to see the afternoon which had been tinged with the rainbow colors of a fairy tale fade into dingy storm clouds. But rather than cower before them, she squared her little shoulders and strutted past them into the dimly lighted room.

Windhaven and Adele exchanged glances before he followed her into the book room and joined her on the settee. Following their example, Priscilla sat on the edge of a chair facing them, her hands clasped tightly in her lap. She ran her tongue over dry lips then pressed them together.

As she witnessed Priscilla's guilty, nervous behavior, Adele regarded her with disappointment. The viscount frowned, then said, "Do you realize you have given Miss Fonteyne a fright?"

"I do not see why," Priscilla said in a high, defensive voice. "I was with a friend. Lady Mathilda wanted us to become better acquainted." She lowered her chin a little guiltily and stammered, "It was perfectly respectable; her maid went with me."

Dy raised an eyebrow. "The lady's maid may have accompanied you," he said, "But it remains to be seen whether it was a proper visit. A respectable young lady does not go riding with a gentleman until her guardian has been introduced to the young man."

"What?" she yelped. She raised herself off the chair, as if seeking escape, before seating herself again and remarking in an amazingly collected manner, "Well, there is nothing wrong in accompanying a friend around the Ring, is there?"

"Not if that friend was Lady Mathilda or Lady Katherine Bermondey," Dysart said mildly. "However, I have heard you are on the outs with that charming lady."

"Charming?" Priscilla laughed. "She has as much charm as an old horse."

"How unkind in you, Priscilla," Adele said. "Lady Katherine's manners are much nicer than yours; that is what makes her company sought after."

Priscilla tossed her glossy black curls and sniffed derisively. "From what she told me, she was a wallflower until you made her into your image."

"If that is true," Dy said ominously, "You would do well to imitate her."

"What, Lady Katherine?"

"No, your sponsor." Adele colored prettily under his warm, approving gaze. "Her only fault is in being too soft-hearted."

That appraisal was not one in which Priscilla indulged. "You are quite wrong. She has done nothing all week but prohibit and preach at me. You ought to see my newest dresses. They are beyond anything plain and all in black or gray. She did not once ask my opinion."

"She did well not to allow you to voice a preference," said the viscount. "Your opinion is like a nutmeg grater, meant to wear one down with to-ing and fro-ing." Drawing in angry breath, he collected himself before he pronounced words which might crush the girl's spirit. "Neither Lady Katherine nor Miss Adele is on trial, but you are.

"The world is judging you, and if you do not wish Society to pronounce from your behavior that you are bad ton, I would advise you to copy Lady Katherine's example and learn from your sponsor how to get on."

"But my friend says the world is an unfit judge," Priscilla interjected.

Hearing the frightening assertion, Adele placed a restraining hand upon Dy's shoulder. He looked capable at that moment of throttling his unthinking ward.

After a moment's reflection, the viscount was able to enquire, "Does your friend say who *is* fit to judge?"

Priscilla seemed at once less sure of her defense. "He says we must judge for ourselves."

"Who is this Radical?"

"Why, nobody," she replied anxiously.

Fists clenched in an effort not to do violence to the girl, he growled, "Does this nobody have a name, or are we to call him Beelzebub?"

"No, of course not. He is not wicked," Priscilla hastened to say. "I dare say he is the most fit to judge, for he is old and very respectable, only I think he is lonely and sad. I would be less than Christian if I did not stop to talk to him."

"There are any number of reasons why Society has nothing to do with someone," Windhaven said. "And I am a better judge than you who is fit company and who is not for—" He broke off in exasperation. "You have not answered my question," his voice increasing in volume as he stepped forward in a threatening manner.

Rising from the settee, Adele again placed her hand on his arm and softly spoke his name. This time her touch seemed not to check him as he demanded, "Who is this person?"

"You do not have to shout," Priscilla said, wrinkling the fabric of her lavender gown. "I can hear perfectly well. My friend is not a nobody. He is a nobleman."

"Do you think that stands him in good stead?" Windhaven demanded. "His name?"

"I don't know his name," Priscilla replied. Tears began to slide down her cheeks. "He said we shouldn't stand on ceremony; asked me to call him Brush, only I did not think it proper, since he was so old, and a peer."

Dysart was for a moment lost in thought as he went over in his mind the list of family names of the peerage. Brush sounded more like a rakish soubriquet than a respectable surname, and did nothing to decrease his rage. "Lord Brush," he repeated, as a sickening thought occurred to him. What if Brush was Adele's nemesis, Lord Peverley or someone like him? "Very foxy of the old man," he said. "Likely he thought we'd be thrown off the chase."

"He is not foxy," Priscilla defended. "He is old, said he regards me as a grand-daughter."

"Well, that is a relief," Windhaven said in mocking tones. "Likely he said that to win your trust."

"I do trust him," Priscilla said.

"And do you wish to discover what happens to girls who trust unwisely?" he demanded.

"Dy, I do not think . . . Priscilla, please," Adele said, passing appealing looks between the two. "We were just worried about you."

"But there was no need," Priscilla insisted, holding out her hands as if laying out the facts of her case. "I have gone driving with him several times in the past week."

At this revelation, Dy clenched a fist and announced, "I forbid you to see him again."

Immediately a veil seemed to descend over Priscilla's expressive features. Adele

recognized the signs of strengthening re-
bellion in the girl's straight lipped stared.
"You cannot stop me," she was saying as
tears poured down her red cheeks.

"Do not think I cannot," Dysart ground
out. "Your father trusted me to care for
you, and I'll be . . . dashed if I'll let you
ruin yourself within a month of coming to
town." He strode to a table and laid out
paper and the standish. "You will write a
note informing this . . . Lord Brush that
your guardian forbids you to meet him
again."

"I will not!" Priscilla retorted. "He is my
only friend."

Reaching forth a beseeching hand, Adele
began soothingly, "Pray calm yourself, my
dear." Priscilla recoiled from her gentle
touch. After a moment taken to compose
her own agitation, Adele continued, "Lord
Brush will understand how improper the
relationship you have struck up appears. If
he is any kind of friend, he will not question your guardian's wish to protect your
honor. He will gladly present himself."

"You don't understand," Priscilla wailed.

"I understand you very well," Dysart
said as he placed a chair firmly before the
writing tools. "You are in a pet because I
refused you. But I am not likely to change
my mind to suit your whims, when, the

one time your fancy was indulged, *I* suffered the consequences."

"I did not know the coach would fill up with water," Priscilla sniffed. "You are angry because you cannot control me."

"That is the first true thing you have said," Windhaven said. "However, I have no wish to exercise such ruthless power over you."

Priscilla did not seem convinced of his concern. "No? Then why do you persist in refusing everything I ask?"

"For your own good, my dear."

"Grown ups always spout that sorry excuse," she interjected, her lower lip protruding rebelliously. "Whenever their will has been crossed."

"Yes, and look what good it has done you," he said in a parental tone. "You have lost the privilege of visiting until I see an improvement in your manners."

With his threat, Adele was certain that the discussion must deteriorate into a full blown battle of wills. "Please, Dy; Priscilla. I think it might be better if we ask pardon for words uttered in haste."

"I have nothing to beg pardon for," Windhaven said. "However I will be happy to hear Priscilla's apology."

The girl's apple cheeks seemed of a sudden to puff out before she exclaimed tearfully, "You have ig-nored me all week while *she* has forced me to si-it through boring concerts. Did you think I could not hear the whispers behind my back?" Tears suddenly made it impossible for her to go on. She covered quivering lips until she was able to explain her feelings. "I felt as though I was being put on display and found wan . . . ting. I . . . think Bru-ush is the o-only person who lo-oves me." With that sobbed pronouncement, Priscilla sprang from her chair and fled the room.

Windhaven crumpled the sheet of foolscap and threw it at the door which she slammed closed. Understanding his frustration, Adele gazed at him in concern, hoping that her silent warning would keep him from pursuing Priscilla in his anger.

"So, she thinks this Brush loves her," he said after a long breath. He began to move towards the door. "Well, he had better if he knows what is good for him."

Hastening after him, she exclaimed her fears. "Dy, no! You cannot mean to call him out!"

He threw open the door and strode into the hallway. "I will if he refuses to do the honorable thing."

She cast about in her mind for a means of dissuading him from offering a challenge to protect his ward, other than the fact that dueling was illegal. "But Priscilla's reputation—"

"She does not regard it," he replied. "I hope we may convince her to take better care of it."

"Yes, I understand," Adele soothed. "But won't a duel rather appeal to her fondness for the romantic?"

"Lord, yes,". he agreed ruefully. Stroking his jaw, he regarded her thoughtfully as he said, "This Lord Brush will assume heroic proportions if I challenge him. But if I ignore the association, Priscilla will have no regard for my authority. What do you suggest I do?"

"It is a puzzle," she said, "Only, if one thinks, not as difficult as it seems. Invite Lord Brush to dinner."

"Dinner, Adele?" he snorted. "I hardly think. . . ."

"It is a perfectly polite way of discovering what manner of man he is," Adele reasoned. "If he declines, you will know he is not a proper friend."

But we do not know who Lord Brush is," he argued, unwilling to entertain someone he was determined to dislike.

Adele smiled. "Then we solicit Lady Mathilda. She, at least, will understand your concern. And I believe she will convince her mysterious friend of the importance in attending."

"And if he declines," Windhaven persisted. "I shall pay a call on him. A polite one, of course. No sense increasing Priscilla's sympathy for the old man."

"None at all," she said. "I appreciate your restraint, my lord."

He gave her a long, searching look that impelled her nearer, but she broke the gaze and tugged off the gloves she had forgotten to remove when Priscilla skipped into the foyer. He forced her to look up at him by asking, "Do you, Adele?"

"Yes, it is remarkable how well you deal with Priscilla, seeing that you have not grown into the responsibility, but had it thrust violently upon you."

"Violently," he agreed as he put on his great coat. "That is no excuse, however. Every parent is thrown violently into the role."

"Perhaps," Adele allowed smoothing his lapel unconsciously. "But an infant may be more biddable than your Priscilla."

"Only because one may turn him over to his nurse," he said. Looking tenderly down on her, he said, "I told you how it would be, Adele. I am not cut out to be a parent."

"Who is?" she enquired, gently running

her hand down his sleeve. "At any rate, I wish you will not tax yourself any more."

He caught her fingers and squeezed them in a convulsive grip, then let them go. "No, I won't," he assured her. "I know I can count on you."

Blushing, Adele agreed, "I promise we'll salvage your ward's good name. It is too bad we cannot invite Mr. Finch to our dinner as well. I should like to know what kind of man Simone would elope with."

"The kind who has no regard for her friends," Windhaven growled, handing Simone's farewell note to Adele. "Go ahead, invite them. Coventry is not so far away that Mr. and Mrs. Finch cannot travel back to London for to reassure her former mistress."

"I shall write to them immediately," she said, opening Simone's letter. Opening it, she discovered Mr. Finch lived near Southam. "In a week, we should know where everyone stands, whether honorably disposed or not." Laying her hand on his sleeve, she said, "Do you think she has trusted unwisely?"

"I shouldn't jump to conclusions just yet," he soothed, placing his arm around her shoulders.

"No, I won't," she said, depending on his strength to hold her fears for her maid in check. "Thank you, Dy. I don't know what I would do without you."

Burying his nose in her clean, fragrant hair, he could not reply, so glad was he to hear that she needed him. Hoping she would soon regard him as vital to her well-being as air or water, he contented himself with holding her a few moments longer, when he compelled himself to let her go.

Lady Mathilda's reply was everything Adele hoped it would be. The lack of a response to the invitation sent to the Finches in Southam, however, proved worrisome to Adele, so much that Windhaven sent his coachman to discover, if he could what had become of Mr. Avery Finch and Simone.

A week later, on the day set for the dinner, they still had heard nothing. The viscount arrived an hour early at Adele's home. He had come from a bout at Jackson's, but his heart had not been in sport. Jackson had slipped one around his guard, leaving him with a bruised cheekbone and battered pride.

"Are you all right?" Adele asked, coming forward.

"Yes," he said, gingerly touching his wound. Wincing, he said, "Remind me not to lower my guard in the ring. Jackson has a wicked left hook."

"Thank heavens," she sighed. "I feared you had—"

"Done something stupid like call Lord Brush to account?" he prompted. "Not likely, Adele. For all I know he outweighs me. But you look lovely, as always."

Wearing an antique gold silk gown that was embroidered with ivory roses, Adele did look radiant to him, but he recognized the signs of apprehension in her appearance. Though her chestnut colored hair had been brushed until it shone with highlights of golden fire, she had arranged it simply by drawing it within a gold and ivory clasp. Simone would have dressed it in a more elaborate style. Dy could not say he was sorry to see the braids and curls go. He liked the classic style.

Warm candlelight illuminated Adele's pale skin with a golden radiance that seemed more fragile for the almost liquid quality of her gaze. As she stood hesitantly on his arm, she looked like a gilded statue. Dy thought he had never seen her look more beautiful. Or more vulnerable.

Before he could say anything else, Adele said, "I am glad you've come early." Smiling up at him, she admitted, "Priscilla refuses to come down."

He returned his lady's worried smile, then raised a regretful eyebrow. "Somehow," he said, "I am not surprised." To Adele's pleasure, he did not go immediately to deal with Priscilla. Instead, he raised her bare hand to his lips and pressed a lingering kiss on her wrist, before adding, "You, however, never cease to amaze me."

Feeling of a sudden as giddy and insecure as a girl in the throes of first love, she prompted him for more compliments, "How is that?"

He tucked her arm within the crook of his elbow to keep her near him. "I always forget how lovely you are."

"That does not surprise me," she teased. "Men always have more important things to attend to, like right hooks and jabs."

"Obviously I wasn't attending," he replied, drawing a breath of her exquisite perfume of roses. "I was rather preoccupied when Jackson caught me. Thinking of you."

Feeling the warmth of a delighted blush steal over her features, she pressed close to him and said, "I shall have a miniature made."

Arching an eyebrow, he gazed hungrily upon her, saying, "Would you do that for me, Adele?"

"Yes, of course, so you won't have to

think so hard," she teased, smiling in delight as he inched nearer. Unconsciously, she sighed an invitation to a kiss.

"Pray forgive my tardiness," Elvira said, bustling into the salon. The pair of them started apart as she halted nervously on the threshold.

"Good evening Miss Willoughby. Pray excuse me, ladies while I persuade Priscilla to show herself."

Announcing himself at Priscilla's door, he strode in and said, "It's all the same to me what you do. But I don't believe you will meekly accept whatever fate Lord Brush and I decide you deserve."

Flung across her bed in a posture of abject misery, wearing her provincial dress of lilac, Priscilla challenged, "You wouldn't dare," through a mist of angry tears.

"Do you think we cannot decide your future without your interference?" he asked.

"But that is Gothic!" Priscilla said, sitting up and drying her tears with the palms of her hands.

"Yes," Windhaven agreed, amiably. "But so much easier than relying on you to make up your mind."

"I won't allow—"

No," he said, reaching within the inner pocket of his coat. "I know you won't force Lord Brush to do anything he doesn't like, so you will come down stairs to dinner with a smile and . . ." drawing out a black velvet case out of the pocket, "wearing these pearls."

Hugging herself defiantly, she said, "I won't take a present from you."

"They're not a gift, Goose," he said, opening the case to reveal a matched pearl necklace and eardrops.

"Where did you get my mother's pearls?" she demanded, leaping off her bed to snatch the set out of his hands. Clutching it to her bosom, she said, "I thought they'd gone to pay debts."

"Mr. Reeves was kind enough to save them," Windhaven replied.

"But—"

"I paid everything." The viscount shrugged, explaining his generosity, "I was also executor of your mother's estate."

"So now you own my vowels," Priscilla said, in theatrical tones. Holding out the parure, she said, "Here, take them back. I don't need them. I don't want them. Count them blood money."

"Oh, will you stop," he groaned, rubbing his hand over his head in frustration as he strode towards the window overlooking the awakening garden. "Must you attribute everything I do to evil motives?"

"Not you," Priscilla said. "Mama's family. They didn't want her or Papa, and they don't want me. Well," she defended, when Windhaven turned to glare at her, "What else am I to think when they left me with strangers?"

"Thank you," he said. "Will you accuse me to Lady Mathilda and Lord Brush of holding you prisoner the way you did to Mrs. Beaton?"

"No," Priscilla sniffed. "I promise I will be good."

"Hah!" laughed Windhaven. "Only promise to wear your mama's pearls, and I shall call your debt paid."

After Lady Mathilda and her frail gentleman friend arrived and were ushered into the gold salon, word came through a nervous housemaid that Priscilla wished to see Miss Adele upstairs. Windhaven started to move forward to intervene, but Adele smilingly excused him, saying she expected the girl needed help with a final adjustment to her ensemble.

She found Priscilla sitting dejectedly upon the window seat, wearing a new white muslin and her mother's pearls. Her hair, however, hung in glorious curls down her back, making her appear like a heroine in a gothic novel. "I don't know if I can go down," Priscilla said. "Lord Windhaven says I must, only . . ."

"You needn't be afraid, my dear," Adele said, sinking onto the cushion at Priscilla's side. "You are among friends."

"It's not that," Priscilla sighed. "It's Mama. She disappointed everyone's expectations," Priscilla said. An explosive sigh shook her shoulders. "And I have done the same."

"Not at all. And don't fret about your mother. She married for love," Adele amended gently, looking up as Elvira entered the room, before she asked, "You weren't thinking of marrying anyone, were you?"

"No," Priscilla said hopelessly.

Elvira took up the standard as if she had been listening at keyholes. "Too early for that, my dear," she assured the girl. Now, as for your dear mama, it was before my cousin's time," she said, sitting Priscilla down at her dressing table. Brushing her hair, she said, "But as *I* recall, your parents were quite happy."

"But her father rejected the marriage," Priscilla muttered, "Because she refused to marry a gentleman."

"Your father was a gentleman in all but name, Priscilla," Adele said, relying on Windhaven's knowledge.

"He had no money," Priscilla said mutinously as Elvira braided her hair.

"Money does not make a gentleman," Adele said, fearing some tattler had repeated the ancient complaint against Arthur Gaines, that aside from being a commoner, he had no property or funds. She felt it was imperative that she restore the memory of Priscilla's father's good name. "Do not think Arthur Gaines was a fortune hunter, child. Were he after your mother's dowry, he would have sold her pearls for a tidy sum."

"Mama wanted him to," Priscilla explained. Absently twisting the stuff of her gown around a finger in the manner of a nervous child, she added, "Said she had no use for fal lals, but he insisted she keep them with an eye towards the future. I thought he meant she could sell them later."

"It was fortunate for you that she did not," Elvira said reasonably as she tied off the braid and wound it into a knot. As she secured it with hair pins and a sprig of violets, Priscilla shrugged as if to say it did not matter.

Adele and her cousin exchanged thoughtful glances. When Adele nodded, Elvira said, "There is no shame in being Arthur Gaines's daughter. However, your fits of sullens and starts of temper lend fuel to Society's old claims that Lady Pamela married beneath herself."

Priscilla's eyes opening wide, she ignored the insult and exclaimed, "My mother was *Lady* Pamela?"

Given leave by Adele's silence, Elvira replied, "Yes, and if you will only come down stairs I believe you will discover all this fuss was for nothing."

"Do come, child," Adele agreed, adding as she came to her feet, "It is bad ton to hide from your guests."

Fourteen

While Adele and Elvira were thus engaged with Priscilla, Windhaven was able to enlarge his acquaintance with Lord Brush. He did not at first like what he saw as the elderly gentleman cut straight to the reason for the summons. "You must think me a complete hand," he said, "to have forgotten the conventions as I did with Priscilla. I assure you, I was rather surprised myself."

Windhaven glared at the elder man, wondering whether he ought to play the enraged guardian. Restraining himself he did allow, "Surprise was not my first reaction, my lord. Nor is it my present one."

"Indeed," Lord Brush replied in a more subdued tone. "Priscilla has been most kind in indulging an old man," he confessed.

The viscount came to his feet to renew his guest's glass, but paced around the room to control his temper before saying, "And you repay her kindness by taking advantage of her inexperience?"

"There's where you're out. I am every bit as concerned as you with Priscilla's welfare."

"Give me leave to doubt, sir," Windhaven said, his arms crossed negligently before him. "Priscilla is unfamiliar with town manners. I am sure you understand that I wish to protect her from . . . unscrupulous individuals."

"Meaning myself, I am to assume." Lord Brush glared until Dy confirmed the older man's suspicions with a slow nod. "Well, I have no one but myself to blame," said the lord. "Who could be expected to trust a nobleman who calls himself Brush?" He chuckled. "I see I must prove myself before I state my interest."

"I am inclined not to regard your interest in Priscilla," Dy protested. "It seems plain to me that you cannot have her interests at heart."

"I assure you she is never out of my thoughts," insisted Lord Brush as he straightened a leg and rubbed it as if it pained him.

Taking a turn about the room to give him space in which to form a civil reply, Dy was finally able to say, "Permit me to say, my lord, *that* is not a sentiment inclined to allay my suspicions. Priscilla is young enough to be your daughter."

The older gentleman smoothed the fabric of his well-cut coat before he accepted the claret. "You are too kind, sir, when it is quite obvious she could be my granddaughter."

"Precisely," Dy snapped. "Such disparity in age between the two of you makes an attachment completely uncreditable."

Lord Brush smiled enigmatically.

"Priscilla is by nature far too romantical, Dy posed. "I am surprised that she has developed a tendre for—"

"One of my ancient years?" chuckled the amused lord. "Well, you may rest easy, Windhaven. The wind does not blow from that quarter."

"I cannot say I share your confidence, my lord," Dy said. "She is too headstrong, and may see you as a means of kicking over the traces."

"Just like her mother," said Lady Mathilda.

The old man's face flushed, angrily it seemed to Dy, as he sipped his Madeira. But when he spoke, his tone was rather wistful. "And not likely to change, I warrant."

"If you knew the chit better," Windhaven said, "You would understand that what pleases her today will not appeal to her tomorrow. It is because she is so young," he explained.

Lord Brush regarded him silently for a long moment, then said, "I think it is because she always expects her hopes to be dashed."

"I don't intend to ruin her expectations," Windhaven said. "Do you?"

Rather than reply to the query, the elder man said, "It seems Priscilla's father chose the right man as her guardian."

"Arthur Gaines was my best friend. I would gladly have given my life in his stead."

"But it was to Arthur that lot fell," said his lordship.

"Yes, and I am determined that his daughter not throw hers away."

"Admirable." Brush sipped his wine before enquiring, "How do you propose to restore Priscilla to this stern grandparent of hers? He is not likely to embrace an unknown country girl without proof that she is in fact his grandchild."

"He will not be expected to," Dy said, whereupon the discussion was ended as Priscilla entered the room with Adele and Miss Willoughby. The girl seemed to light up as she saw that her guardian and friend had not come to blows, and after greeting Lady Mathilda, came to sit beside Lord Brush when Adele and Miss Willoughby sat with the lady.

"I hope my guardian has not been brow-beating you, my lord," she said, proffering a kiss upon the elder one's cheek. "Lord Windhaven is as stern as Cerebus."

"That he is," agreed Brush, patting her shoulder, "And as tenacious. You are a fortunate girl to have so many friends."

"You mean because so many people seem to know better than I how I should go on," Priscilla said, in a voice surprisingly without bitterness. "I own I am out of my element in town; I shouldn't wish anyone to think Mama failed to bring me up as the lady she was. Especially you," she said smiling up apologetically at her friend.

"No chance of that," Brush said. "Your mother has done an admirable work in you, Child. Too late for her to hear it from the family, but not, I hope, too late for you."

"I think it must be," Priscilla said sadly. Then in brighter tones, she said, "But if they care nothing for me I do have friends—Adele, you and Lady Mathilda—who do. *You* can be my family."

Lord Brush dropped his gaze and cleared his throat. When he replied, his voice was thick with emotion. "I accept your offer, child, and hope you will feel the same when you come to visit me."

"Of course I will," Priscilla replied. Then casting a nervous glance towards

Windhaven, she added, "That is, if my guardian allows it."

Lord Brush directed a considering look upon the viscount. At that moment Adele's butler announced dinner and the resolution of the conversation postponed.

Dinner was a cheerful meal. Priscilla was charming and the guest kept up a lively conversation. But after the ladies had withdrawn, Priscilla looked apprehensive.

"Have no fear they will come to blows," Lady Mathilda said, smiling over her cup of tea. "Brush has become sensible in his dotage. And we are both convinced your guardian has your good in mind."

"Oh thank you," Priscilla said. Then, accepting a cup of tea from Adele, she asked, "Do you think Lord Windhaven will let me visit Lord Brush?"

"We'll see," said Adele, pouring out tea for herself.

"How pretty you look," said Lady Mathilda. "Wearing your mother's pearls."

"Yes, she had them from her father," Priscilla said, sipping her tea.

"Who gave them to her, if I recall, on the eve of her wedding," said Lady Mathilda. "You may wonder at it child, since legend has it he was so hardened against the match; but when he came to see it was *a fait accompli*, he was not unwilling to accept it. Arthur was a gentleman in truth, if not in fact, and I think your grandfather lived to regret his early prejudice."

"It seems everyone knows my family but me," Priscilla said, uneasily fingering an eardrop. "But my experience leads me to doubt."

"It is a loss," Lady Mathilda said on an unconscious sigh. "We can none of us regain, child. But I hope you will forget the past and press on . . . with your friends."

A sudden hardening of Priscilla's expressive features depressed such hopes. "I will never forget. I can never forgive."

Placing a gentle hand upon Priscilla's sleeve, Adele said, "I don't wish to criticize, my dear. But it has been my experience that one may be forced to eat one's words when voicing such unalterable sentiments."

"No, it is of no use to prose at her," said Lady Mathilda, in choked tones. She appeared as one in the shock of grief. "I have heard it before, and know how. . . . Only I had hoped the parents' sins would not. . . . But I see it is hopeless. Would you be so kind, Miss Fonteyne, as to request my carriage? I am sorry, my dear," this to Priscilla, who came to her feet as the stricken lady arose. "And I pray you will not waste your life in bitterness."

Lady Mathilda's request being made known to a servant, the only thing left to do was pass the time remaining to them in inconsequential chit-chat. When the carriage arrived, she hugged Priscilla as one who did not wish to let go. Then as if she resigned herself with a regretful sigh, she mounted to her seat and said, "I will send the carriage back for my brother."

As the lady drove left, Priscilla puzzled, "That is odd. She called Brush her brother. Always before they were friends."

"And so they may be," Adele said.

"Well, I am glad she is not completely alone," Priscilla said. "But why did she feel compelled to leave so soon?"

"I cannot say," Adele said, pondering their conversation. Lady Mathilda seemed to know more about Priscilla's family history than was common knowledge. Certainly it had not been her purpose to perpetrate gossip. But Adele felt it was not her place to ask how the lady came by her understanding or that it would be proper to pose the question to Priscilla.

Her musings were interrupted when her butler informed her that Lord Windhaven's coachman had just presented himself at the kitchen door with an urgent message.

Fifteen

Dy was still occupied in her dining room with Lord Brush. Not wishing to intrude, yet needing to interrupt, she looked in and was welcomed with two masculine smiles. Bidding her come in and be seated, Windhaven announced, "Adele, we have been entertaining an angel without knowing it. Lord Brush is none other than Priscilla's grandfather, the Marquess Chaseldon."

"I beg your pardon," she said in surprise, accepting the elder gentleman's hand. "You have quite taken my breath away. Are you going to tell her?"

"Not yet I hope," Windhaven said.

"Now she has accepted me as a part of her chosen family," the marquess said in hushed but excited tones, "She may be more willing to accept our true family ties."

Recalling the girl's resentful outburst, Adele said, "I hope you may be right, my lord." Pressing his fingers, she added, "It may be shockingly rude of me, but I need to speak privately with Lord Windhaven. Priscilla is in the salon with my cousin. Lady Mathilda felt suddenly unwell, but said she would send the carriage for you."

"Good," Lord Chaseldon said, coming to his feet. "I had hoped to speak with my granddaughter before leaving. That is, provided you have no objection."

"There can be no objection now," Windhaven said. "Only I should exercise restraint with Priscilla for awhile. Her attitude has hardened over years. One cannot expect an immediate reconciliation."

Moving toward the door, his lordship admitted, "I know. She is very like her mother." Passing a trembling hand over his balding head, he paused long enough to regain some of his former confidence. "But Priscilla is my flesh and blood. She must reconcile herself to that fact." Then strode toward the gold salon.

Placing an anxious hand on Dy's sleeve, Adele asked, "Do you think she will?"

The viscount pressed her hand in a reassuring manner, before saying, "There is no way of predicting what Priscilla will do. But that is not what you wished to say."

"No," she said, looking away nervously. "It is Jackson; he has returned from Coventry. Gresham is taking care of your horses," she said. "And I suspect Mrs. Murphy is taking care of Jackson right now."

"No doubt," Windhaven said, smoothing a hand down Adele's sleeve. Her arm was stiff with tension, but under his gentle touch, the anxious knots slipped free. "Adele," he said. "You need someone to take care of you."

Blushing, she asked, "Do you have anyone besides Mrs. Murphy or Elvira in mind?"

"Yes," he said. He was determined that she should rely on him and only one state would give him the right to protect her and her people. "I know this is not the time, but before another crisis, another runaway," he stammered "I must speak."

Adele's heart was beating furiously in hope and fear of what he was about to say. She was afraid to say anything that might hint at an unladylike eagerness. So she gazed encouragement at him.

"We have been friends too long to beat around the bush," he said, "And don't have time for formalities . . ."

As if his declaration was a premonition, a disturbance erupted from the gold salon.

"I fear we shall never have time," Adele said on the end of a sigh. Breaking free of his embrace, she urged, "Come Dy; Priscilla is on her high ropes again."

"I suppose we'd best prevent her from flinging your Meissen figurines about the room," he agreed, catching her hand in his.

Entering the salon together, they quickly deduced the probable cause of the controversy. Lord Chaseldon was standing in the center of the room, arms flung out in arrested anticipation, his face a mask of disappointed hope. From Miss Willoughby's arms, Priscilla was crying loudly and calling him every bitter name she could think of. Each imprecation seemed to score lines deeper in the elderly gentleman's face.

Rolling his eyes toward the ceiling, Windhaven commanded his ward to be silent, then groaned, "Tell me you did not announce yourself to her."

"I could not help doing so," said the marquess, his shoulders slumping in bitter dejection.

"Just as you couldn't help abandoning my mother?" Priscilla said, shaking off Miss Willoughby's gentle restraints.

"You cannot believe that," Lord Chaseldon said.

"I did not want to believe it," Priscilla cried, "but experience does not lie, sir. I cannot set aside seventeen years in one afternoon."

"No, I don't expect you to," Chaseldon

said. "Only, I had hoped we were good enough friends—"

"That I would break faith with Mama?"

"Never," said the marquess, appealing to Lord Windhaven with a look.

"I believe we would all benefit from an intermission," Windhaven said. "Priscilla, you have suffered a shock this evening. Would you take her to her room, Miss Willoughby?"

"Come, my dear," said Elvira in cajoling tones.

When they had gone up stairs, Lord Chaseldon spoke in a broken voice. "I have been a foolish old man," he said.

"Don't lose heart, my lord," Dy volunteered. "You have been lonely and in a hurry to make your granddaughter love you."

Lord Chaseldon shook his head sadly and, in a halting manner which spoke eloquently of age and weariness, leaned his forehead on his palm and lamented, "So much time lost."

Adele hastened to console him. "It is natural to regret lost opportunities, my lord. But that will neither change nor retrieve the past. All it can do is rob us of hope for the future."

"My only future is the grave," Chaseldon said.

Adele met Dy's gaze over the despairing nobleman's head. Smiling, Windhaven said, "Rather than let that inevitability prey on your mind, I hope you would consider the good you can do."

Growling, "You preach like an infernal Methodist," Lord Chaseldon abandoned his melancholy preoccupation and glared at the viscount.

"Not I," Dy maintained in an amused style. Smoothing his neck cloth, although there was not the least need to do so, he added, "I am not religious, my lord, except in matters of taste. Moreover, I am such a selfish creature that I considered it dashed inconvenient to travel into Yorkshire to fetch your wretched relation."

With an arrogant raising of his steel grey eyebrows, Chaseldon said, "Won't have you regarding her a nuisance."

"Well, she is," Dy assured him steadily. "But I considered my duty to Arthur more important than pleasure."

"Duty!" exclaimed Lord Chaseldon. "Now, there's an emotion I *can* understand. Well, you've done admirably, Windhaven. I bow to your superior understanding."

"Not superior, sir. I defy anyone to understand Priscilla."

As he spoke, his smiling gaze encompassed Adele's. She could not bear to look away. His face, so familiar in its handsome arrogance, seemed to have undergone a subtle alteration that made its dear features more pleasing. For a moment she was at a loss to describe the quality that had transformed his expression, as there was no outward lowering of his customary dignity. Yet as he returned her regard, she recognized a tenderness therein that did not harden when he looked again toward the marquess. "But I do believe," he added, placing a fond arm about Adele's shoulder, "The girl needs her own family, no matter how much she protests against it."

"You are more optimistic than I," Chaseldon confessed.

"No, sir, rather more selfish. You may as well know that I am impatient to realize a personal ambition which compels me to discover a way to hasten your granddaughter's adjustment." He cut short the marquess's expression of gratitude by saying, "I have every intention of speeding that forward, unfortunately, I must attend to another matter now. Will you meet with me tomorrow?"

"You are welcome here," Adele said.

Dy pressed her to his side and said in a teasing manner, "Do you suggest we meet on neutral ground?"

"I think," amended Chaseldon, with a re-

newal of confidence. "She rather desires
your company and is willing to endure
mine. Very well, Windhaven," he agreed,
coming to his feet resolutely. "Tomorrow
we'll see if we can unravel this tangled cord.
Would you be good enough to send for a
chair."

Adele wished to have her own carriage
brought around but the marquess insisted
he would make his own way home and took
his leave.

Adele sent for Jackson. "I hope he has
good news."

"Are you up to hearing what Jackson has
to say?" Dy asked.

"Yes," Adele said. "He will not fly up
into the boughs."

"My concern is rather that he might not
upset you," Windhaven said.

Stiffening her spine in mock outrage, she
said, "Really, Windhaven. You make me out
to be the kind of female who suffers hysterics."

"Not you," he said fervently. "That is
one reason I like you so well. "Ah, Jackson," he added, as his coachman appeared
on the threshold of the gold salon. "Come
in and make yourself comfortable."

"Yes, will you have a chair?" Adele said,
indicating an armchair.

"No, thank ye, miss. I am still in my

dirt," Jackson said. "If ye don't mind, I'll stand."

Adele placed herself in the chair, and Windhaven positioned himself at her side, asking, "What did you discover?"

"Well, sir," Jackson began. "I went to Coventry like you told me. Only no one knew a Mr. Finch. Checked the taverns, and stables and even the churches, like you said. Nothing there." At his declaration, Adele could not help breathing a sigh of disappointment. "Sorry, miss," Jackson said. "What took me so long, was I checked at the towns nearby, too. Baginton, Kenilworth, Meriden. Nothing."

"You did as well as could be expected," Windhaven said. "But it all proves Simone trusted a rogue, like too many other gullible girls."

"That was my guess," Jackson said, turning his broad-brimmed hat around thoughtfully. "As I was travelling back down the Oxford-Coventry Road, until I stopped in Marton to water and feed the horses. Then, an ostler gave me to understand that Mr. Finch was known about those parts as a gentleman farmer. Pigs," he said, by way of explanation. " 'Lives down Southam way,' 'e told me."

Southam is less than fifty miles from Oxford," Windhaven said.

"Thirty-five, according to mileposts," Jackson said.

Impatient for news of her dresser, Adele asked, "What news had you in Southam, then?"

"Well, miss, in Southam Mr. Finch is known as a man of means and is considered honest as the day is long."

"I do not want his references," she said. "Where did he take Simone?"

"That I was coming to," Jackson said, imperturbably. "His house servants told me Mr. and Mrs. Finch embarked on a honeymoon trip along the Grand Union Canal three days ago."

Laying her hand on Windhaven's sleeve, Adele enquired, "Do you think it may have been Simone?"

Covering her hand with his, Dy said, "Patience, Adele. Jackson will reveal all in his own time."

Grinning in response to his employer's confidence, Jackson said, "Wish I could say for sure, but no one in town could describe the bride, and the Finch's people are close-mouthed. So, I went to the church and asked to see the parish registry."

Adele could not help but believe Jackson was finally going to impart news of a happy ending for Simone. But he shook his head, saying, "I wish I could say that

I found what you were looking for, but there was no listing for a wedding between Avery Finch and Simone . . ." Here, he consulted a notebook that he had drawn out of a pocket.

"Beaumaris," Adele sighed, arising in agitation from the chair. "Oh, dear, I am sorry. But you did try."

"Thank you, miss," Jackson said. "On a subsequent visit, his housekeeper did say they had not celebrated a wedding there. Could it be possible they married in London?"

"Why of course!" Adele said. "Simone is Roman Catholic. They must have spoken their vows in her church."

"I don't think so," Windhaven said. "By law, Catholics must be married in the English Church. But they may have tied the knot in town, if Finch was able to procure a special license. I'll ask of the bishop," he said negligently.

"If you'll give me the name of her church, I'll ask the priest," Jackson volunteered.

"St. Peter's," Adele said, arising to offer her hand to the coachman.

He gave it a gentle shake, then tugged on his forelock as if the courtesy had flustered him. "Well, I'll be off, if you've nothing else," he said.

"Thank you for all your trouble," Adele said.

"No trouble, miss," Jackson said, winking. " 'S doin' my job. Don't know many of the Quality as would care what happened to a runaway."

Shamed by the coachman's indictment of her class, Adele did not know what to say. But Windhaven was not so reticent. "I have always believed Miss Fonteyne was one of a kind."

"Yes, sir," Jackson agreed. "Your dresser was a lucky girl to have so caring a mistress."

"Thank you, Jackson," Adele said. "I can only hope she is more fortunate in her husband."

Dismissing his coachman with a generous vail discreetly pressed into his hand with a firm handshake, Windhaven turned toward Adele. Wrapping his arms around her so she could not slip out of his reach, he was pleased that she submitted without complaint to his embrace. Grinning, he teased, "Are you going to save all your thanks for Jackson?"

"No," Adele said breathlessly. "Thank you for sending him on the chase."

"Is that all?" he prompted. Leaning closer, he whispered, "I am going to a lot of trouble."

"Quite out of character," Adele said in mock seriousness.

But she was smiling up at him with a look akin to hero worship and he was emboldened to say, "I don't do this for just anyone."

"I know," she replied, still gazing on him with awe.

"Are you prepared to pay a price for my good work?"

Giggling, she said, "Yes, Dy," and rested her head on his shoulder.

"That was almost too quick," he said, "Perhaps you ought to reconsider."

Shaking her head, she said, "That you offer me the chance to change my mind proves your good intentions."

"Lord," he groaned, "You make me so noble, I scarcely know myself."

"I know you," she said, stroking his jaw in wonder, "Better than you know yourself."

"I think you will have me paying for my good deed," he said, pressing a kiss into her hand. "Forever."

"Oh, no," she said. "It is customary for the bride to pay the blacksmith."

"Are you asking me to marry you?" he asked.

Never taking her eyes from his, she nodded slowly. "I know it is unladylike, completely too forward, but I don't want to lose you."

"And you're willing to marry over the anvil?"

"Yes, Dy. Aren't you?"

"As much as I'd like to carry you off to Gretna, my dear, I must resist your too tempting offer," he said. "My team has just completed a journey to Coventry and back. And we can't very well leave Priscilla to tyrannize Elvira or Mrs. Murphy while we're gone. And think how disappointed both our houses would be if we eloped and didn't let them share our joy." As he spoke, he pressed feathery kisses along her brow. Then, covering her lips with his, he offered to relieve whatever disappointment she might feel in his refusal. It was a pleasant panacea for heartache, as he very readily admitted, adding as he ended the kiss, "Very likely the lot of them would give notice as soon as we came back."

"No one would believe it of us," she allowed breathlessly.

Grinning wider, he said, "I do not care what others think, as long as I can make you smile. That is the reason for every good work I attempt."

"No, Dy," Adele said, "You do it so you may look yourself in the mirror. And because you keep trying to repay Arthur Gaines for his sacrifice."

"You are quite right, my dear. I am ever in Arthur's debt. Perhaps that is why I have been so thoughtless lately."

"Perhaps." Then gazing adoringly upon him she said more thoughtfully, "I think it is because we feel guilty for having been spared. It is much easier to waste one's life than to give it up."

He smoothed a finger along her brow. "Is that what we have been doing, wasting our lives?"

"For the first time in my life, I feel truly alive, " she said. Closing her eyes against the thrill of his touch, she said, "For a long time neither of us regarded anything but fripperies." She gently caught his hand as it trailed across her cheek. Pressing a kiss into his palm, she sighed, "In thinking of ourselves, we could scarcely spare a thought for others."

"You have been constantly in mine," he said, tilting her face upwards to place a kiss on her lips. "And I would have you constantly at my side."

As his lips covered hers, she sighed, "There is no place I would rather be, Dy. Even if you won't elope with me." But as they gave themselves up to the pleasure of exploring their mutual desire, the opening of the door once more propelled them apart.

Adele moved to the mantel mirror to repair the minor damage their embrace had done to her hair while Windhaven called entry to the intruder. A footman bowed stiffly, saying, "Your curricle is arrived, your lordship."

"Ah yes, Jackson is doing his duty," Windhaven said. "I go to the bishop, Adele, to see whether he authorized a special license for Mr. Finch and Simone."

"We could go together," Adele said, turning to regard him hopefully.

"We could," he agreed. "But I can better attend to the business without you hanging on my arm."

"Are you calling me a distraction?" she asked.

"A very pretty one," he allowed. "Don't fret, Adele; we'll find Simone, and redeem Priscilla. And then we'll consider our future. Together."

Sixteen

When Windhaven arrived on the door-step of Number Thirty Green Street the next afternoon to tell Adele Mr. Finch had applied to the bishop for a special license, Priscilla intercepted him with a filial kiss and exclamations over the nosegay he was trying to hide behind his back. "Oh, violets! How sweet." She held out her hands beseechingly as he backed away.

"Do you think I mean these blossoms for you?" he enquired. When she nodded and reached for them greedily, he laughingly held them above her reach. "No, Priscilla, you do not suit them. Tell Adele I am here."

Having lost interest in a bouquet that was not for her, Priscilla said in an off-hand manner, "I doubt you will see her any time soon. When last I saw her, she was unable to decide which gown to wear."

Dy found it difficult to credit Adele with such indecision in matters of dress. She was used to knowing precisely which gown was most becoming. Wondering whether his caresses or his refusal to elope yesterday had left her wishing to avoid his company, he said, "Kindly inform my lady that I am desperate for a few moments with her."

Giving him and his floral tribute a look which seemed to say that a man desperate for the sight of his beloved ought to have brought a more lavish offering than a bunch of violets, Priscilla sauntered upstairs.

Absently tapping his hand against his immaculate buff-coloured breeches, Dy took a turn about the salon.

But before Adele managed to array herself to her satisfaction, Lord Chaseldon was ushered into the library. The two gentlemen bowed stiffly as if measuring the other's mettle, before Dy offered the marquess a chair. As the elder man lowered himself with the aid of his cane onto the cushion of a sturdy leather chair, Dy cast a regretful look at the open door and placed the violets on a commode. Removing the tail of his morning coat from danger, he took the companion chair, then silently regarded his visitor and pulled an oblong bundle from an inner pocket of his coat. "I believe the contents will prove beyond a doubt that Priscilla is indeed your granddaughter," he said, turning the package over in his hand before placing it in the marquess's outstretched fingers.

"*I* do not doubt it," he replied in a shaky tone of voice that gave Dy to understand that he rather feared the contents would further stiffen Priscilla's back against any overtures he might make to regain her trust and win her affection.

As the marquess still made no attempt to open the bundle, Dy said, "Perhaps you will discover something in it which will convince your granddaughter that you did not abandon her mother." He pushed to his feet, sweeping the violets in crushing grip from the commode, and moved towards the door. "I imagine you want to examine the bundle in private. I shall just see what is keeping Adele."

He discovered her on the landing above him. Unaware that she was being observed, she was fussing with a fall of lace at her wrist as if she was unsure whether she looked her best.

Her flutterings were not studied or meant to call attention to her beauty. It was evident in her nervous manner and the loose tumble of curls that fell over her shoulder, that she had finally thrown on the gown of pomona green with its modest lacy adornments. She was not dressed at all modishly, but in Windhaven's eyes, she could not have been more lovely. The simple frock enhanced the delicate bloom on her cheeks and gave her eyes the appearance of emeralds as her gaze danced around the hallway. In short, she was more desirable now than she had ever been at any rout or ball.

"Well," he said, stepping into her path. "I was wrong; you do surprise me."

He had not expected to startle her so, but she jumped and gasped. Hastily, he led her down the remainder of the steps and sat beside her on an Egyptian styled bench until she began to breathe in a more regular rhythm. "Excuse me," she said. "I did not expect you."

"No?" he said. "Did you forget our appointment?"

"No," she said. "I was on my way down to entertain Lord Chaseldon until you arrived."

"He is occupied for the time being. Would you like to entertain me?" he teased as he gave her the violets.

Unconsciously, she raised the flowers to her nose and bestowed a lingering gaze upon him that set his heart pounding. He felt he had just gone another round with the first gentleman of the ring.

"Are you comfortable?" she asked.

Unaccountably, he grinned foolishly and said, "Not at all."

"What a rude thing to say," she laughed. "But I do not regard it, for I am not at ease myself."

"Mr. Finch did apply for a license. Does that relieve your anxiety?" he asked, giving her a brief, but tender kiss.

"Yes, thank you," she said on the end of a sigh. A door at the far end of the hall opened and closed, reminding her they were not alone. "Are you certain Priscilla will forgive her grandfather?"

"Are you worried?" he asked, kissing the tip of her nose. Smoothing a hand down her spine, he called on every bit of his self control to keep from making love to her. "Go, fetch Priscilla down to the book room. We'll have an end to this now."

"I don't understand," she protested dizzily. "You will not throw her on the street?"

"I think I can assure you she will not suffer that indignity," he said. "Go now, my dearest."

The viscount discovered the marquess staring over a stack of letters. Holding two yellowed documents in a shaking hand, the elder gentleman seemed to have suffered a shock. Immediately, Dy poured out a glass of brandy and pressed it into the stricken man's unburdened hand. "Well, my lord," he said, "what have you learned?"

"Unopened," he wheezed, raising reddened eyes from the letters. "Every one of 'em unopened." He pressed the letters into Windhaven's unresisting fingers.

The viscount stared at the direction written on each letter. "To Lady Pamela Gaines," he read. The first letter, water stained and wrinkled, had been directed to Egypt and Malta; the second had been sent to Brussels. For fifteen years, perhaps more, the marquess had been seeking his daughter's forgiveness. In all that time, Lady Pamela had remained adamantly opposed to him. "Then why did she keep them?" he mused aloud.

"To throw them in my face," replied the marquess in shocked tones. "Don't regard it," he said when Dy clenched the letters in his fists. "She had every right to hate me. Not only did I oppose their marriage, but I bought Arthur's commission."

"At his request," Windhaven protested. "Told me you'd come through for him when his own family would not."

The marquess heaved a regretful sigh. "You, of all people ought to realize I did him no favor. Merely signed his death papers."

"What would you have had him do instead?"

"I could have welcomed him into the family; made him a gentleman. He'd have been the best of our world."

"Arthur cared nothing for our world, my lord. I think all he cared about was his duty to England."

"If he'd paid more attention to his family, I'd have seen my granddaughter grow up." A sob was torn from the marquess's throat. "Foolish old man," he wept.

The door to the salon opened, the rustle of silk skirts heralding the arrival of Priscilla. "Miss Fonteyne said you wished to see me, my lord."

Adele caught her from behind and propelled her into the room. "Please my dear. Windhaven wishes you to make peace with your grandfather."

"I have no grandfather," Priscilla maintained.

"I think you will reconsider when you have read these," Windhaven said, coming towards them and drawing Priscilla into a chair. She made an attempt to rise, but he lowered her forcefully onto the cushion. Dropping the sealed letters on her lap, he withdrew, leading Adele towards the marquess.

As he had hoped, Priscilla's hand

dropped to the older letter. With hesitant fingers, she picked apart the seal and unfolded the brittle parchment. She sat unmoving while she read the short letter, then, before refolding it, a hand fluttered to her cheek.

Adele made as if to go to her, but Dy restrained her with a hand on her sleeve. "But she is weeping."

"Let her be," he said tucking her arm around his and sitting them both on the settee near the older man.

After a moment, Priscilla plucked open the second letter. Several notes fluttered to the floor. She ignored them, choosing instead to read the words scrawled across the page. When she had done, she clutched the paper to her bosom and flew across the room. "Grandpa," she sobbed, falling at his feet. "I didn't know, I didn't know."

The marquess caught and lifted her from the floor. Embracing her as he would have when she had been a child, he soothed her tears, "There now, child. *I* know."

"But how could she have . . ."

"Not a word will I hear against your mother," he warned. "She did what she thought was best."

"But it was wrong!" Priscilla sobbed out her anguish. "I thought no one loved me.

Mama, always busy; Papa always away. That dismal school."

"We all loved you, child," the marquess assured her.

She looked incredulously at him. "Even you?"

"Especially me."

"But why did you never come to see me?"

"I did see you, child. Your father asked me to look after you, but I had to be . . . careful."

"Why did you not . . . ?"

Placing a finger over her lips, he replied, "I loved you, Priscilla. I loved your mother. I could not give up hoping some day she'd forgive me."

"Grandpa, I wish she had." Overcome by emotion, Priscilla buried her face in his shoulder and wept cleansing, forgiving, joyful tears.

The older man closed his eyes and leaned his head upwards as though praying. After a few moments of silence he pressed a wet cheek to Priscilla's dark head and said, "I think she did." Raising her face to his, he said, "Now will you come home with me, child? I've had at least one gentleman camping on my doorstep, and I want you to shoo him away."

Priscilla squeezed him, then enquired, "Who is it, Grandpa?"

"Told me he was Viscount Stanley."

"Well, why did you not send him here?" she pouted.

"What, and lose my ace? What do you take me for: a doddering old man?"

"No, of course not," she said, linking her arm within his and drawing him towards her guardian and sponsor. "But really, Grandfather, Viscount Stanley. He is the only gentleman who hasn't fallen under Lady Katherine's spell. That is too cruel."

"Forgive me?"

"Only if I can go home with you now."

Dy laughed and said, "Go with my blessings, Priscilla. I shall even pack your baggage if it means I shall be alone with Adele."

As Priscilla hastened to ready herself to leave with her grandfather, Adele gazed upon Dy lovingly. His arm slipped around her shoulder to draw her against him.

"Well she is coming home at last," said the marquess. "No doubt you are impatient to have me gone as well," he laughed as he started down the first flight of stairs. "Good bye, I am going; you may have your lady to yourselves. I need not worry that you will enjoy too much privacy in a house populated by women."

As if he had conjured up a duenna from his thoughts, Miss Willoughby met him at the half landing. "Ah, Miss Willoughby," he said bowing over her hand. "You will want to wish your Miss Fonteyne and her gentleman happy. I left them cooing in the book room."

In consequence of the marquess's attentions, Elvira's nervous twitterings and reassurances rose to the head of the first story. Adele bestowed a look upon Dy that conveyed her complete inability to weather her companion's effusive compliments, when he returned her to the library. Closing the door firmly in the face of the advancing companion, he turned to Adele and, gently grasping her arms at the elbows, compelled her to meet his fervent gaze. "Lord Chaseldon has the right of it. I shall never have five uninterrupted minutes with you as long as we are under this roof. Fly with me right now."

Nervously, she began to laugh. "But, Dy, where should we go? How could I abandon my household?"

Miss Willoughby set up a persistent tapping on the outside of the door. Exasperated, Dy threw up his hands and passed his fingers through his Windswept. "By all means, let your household rule you with their frights and starts. I count for nothing!"

Overset by his claim, Adele captured one of his hands between both of hers in an attempt to reassure him and cried, "That is unjust! And so unlike you," in a voice elevated over the sound of the rattling door.

Of a sudden, the persistent interruption ceased. Relieved that her companion had suddenly given over her attempt to force entry, Adele gazed earnestly at Dy and inquired, "What has cast you so suddenly into the dismals?"

"Nothing except that the World is conspiring against me," he declared, drawing her into his embrace. "All I desire is a few uninterrupted moments with you."

"All?" she inquired on a teasing note.

"Not quite," he allowed grinning. "But we'll have no more mistaken ideas as to what has been proposed and to whom the proposal was made." Dropping to one knee, he possessed himself of her hand. "I have long called you my friend, Adele, but friend does not adequately describe my true feelings for you. I admire you, and respect you, and will not indulge any talk that discredits you. Will you do me the honor of becoming my wife?"

Adele made an attempt to respond in kind to Windhaven's formal address, but could only giggle, "Maddening man. I will marry you, but not merely to silence gab-blemongers."

His calm confidence and affectionate gaze were unshakable. "My dear, do you think I offer for you to spike Elvira's guns, you are quite wide of the mark."

"Then why?" she asked, a provocative smile teasing the corners of her lips.

Drawing her into his arms as he swept to his feet, he brought her up against his full length in a dizzying arc that made her catch her breath. "I can think of only one rea-son," he said. "Perhaps you need a re-minder."

To regain her balance, Adele settled her arms about his neck. Her fingers curled into his hair to draw him nearer. "I think I do," she whispered. "Will you kiss me again, Dy?"

His mouth hung tantalizingly over hers so she could feel the seductive rhythm of his breath. Grinning, he said, "As often as you like," then placed a chaste peck on her lips.

Disappointed by the teasing, brotherly sa-lute, she nibbled the corner of his mouth and said, "No, a real kiss; a long one."

He chuckled against her protest, saying, "Do you mean to rule the roost?"

"No," she said, drawing a little apart to regard him. Her hand rested on his chest, his heart thudding powerfully beneath her fingers. Pleased by the throbbing rhythm that betrayed his attraction, she bestowed an alluring smile on him, then sighed, "If you do not *want* to kiss me, I shall understand."

"Understand this," he said, "I want to kiss you very much, so much that it's dangerous, Adele. I might not be able to stop with a kiss."

"Really?" she asked, fingering a button on his shirt. "Then we ought to marry, Dy, before we get into trouble."

"Oh, bother," he said, catching her lips against his.

At first the kiss was chaste, hesitant, almost respectable in its restraint. In the next moment, the kiss took on a life of its own. Their joined lips ignited a spark that melted two very separate people into one flesh.

Dy's kisses wandered from her lips to the swell of her breast. Caught up in the unfamiliar awakening, Adele was glad for his supporting arms. Without them, she was quite incapable of bearing up her own weight.

He seemed more than adequate for the charge, however, as he lifted her and settled them both more comfortably on the sofa to renew his loving attention. As she reclined trustingly before him, he skimmed his fingers over the thin fabric of her dress, outlining the globes of her breasts, the narrow span of her waist, the swell of her hips, as if by touching her he might memorize her form.

As his hands moved expertly over her body, awakening sensations she had not dreamed possible, Adele voiced a susurration of delight. "Why has no one told me making love was so wonderful?"

She did not know she had said the words aloud until she heard Dy chuckling in her ear. Gazing at him through a shimmer of desire, she blushed when he drew another kiss from her bruised lips and teased, "If I had suspected you were curious, my dear, I would have introduced you long before this."

She wanted to make him feel what he made her feel. But as she pressed her hands along his back, delighting in the feel of his muscles beneath the finely tailored coat of bath superfine, she knew a growing dissatisfaction. Frantic with wanting him, she peeled off his coat, sadly crumpled from their embrace, pulled his shirt from his waistband, and soothed her hand along his back.

Her touch startled him into drawing in a ragged breath, before he exhaled her name in what sounded like a pained plea.

"Now you understand, my love," he breathed into her ear. Then, leaning his forehead against hers, he said in a gentle command, "We must be married soon."

"Yes, Dy," she whispered, stealing a kiss. "Soon."

"I have in my coat the means . . ." he said breathlessly.

"A map to Gretna?" she asked.

"No, a special license," he replied, covering her mouth with his once more.

Adele felt they were celebrating a Jubilee. The spinning world seemed to be aglow with brilliantly exploding skyrockets.

But someone seemed determined to douse their celebration. A thin, whiny voice called out, "Adele? Are you still in here?" Miss Willoughby stuck her head in the door cautiously. "We have guests."

Startled by Elvira's intrusion, the couple slid to the floor with a thud. "Adele? Are you all right?" Elvira started to come forward, then stopped dead in her tracks as she saw her cousin sprawled in a tangle on the floor with the viscount. "Oh," she squeaked, turning an about face and closing the door with a click.

"What was that all about?" Windhaven growled, picking himself up off the floor and giving Adele a hand. Drawing her to her feet, he allowed her to shake her skirts into some semblance of order and smooth hair that had come free of confining pins.

"My cousin, doing her duty," she giggled. "Did she say we had guests?"

"I believe so." He frowned, asking, "Can't you let her make excuses for you?"

"I could, but Ellie is an abysmal liar," Adele said, straightening his cravat. "Everyone knows it, for she blushes and stammers until she finally blurts out whatever truth she is trying to evade. We had better go save our reputations from the effects of her hapless tongue."

Seventeen

Finding her cousin in the gold salon, Adele tugged Windhaven in behind her and said, "Here we are, Ellie."

"Oh," said Miss Willoughby, her cheeks aflame. "Yes, here you are."

"Since we have agreed where we are, will you introduce us to our visitors?" Adele said.

"Of course, look who has come," Elvira said, glancing nervously towards a couple seated on the sofa and indicating them with a flourish. "Simone and her new husband, Mr. Finch."

Mr. Finch looked like a man who spent every moment outdoors. Ruddy-complected, with a long, straight sunburned nose, he affected no gentlemanly airs or graces. Nor did he adopt a fashionable appearance. His rotund form was covered modestly in a drab colored coat and breeches that had been constructed with an eye to comfort rather than style. Bending from the waist, he swept an inelegant, but sincere bow and said, "Avery Finch at your service, my lord, Miss Fonteyne. May I present my wife, Mrs. Finch."

"Simone," Adele breathed. Relieved that her dresser had not come to a disgraceful end, she rushed forward to embrace the girl. "As you can see," indicating her wrinkled gown, "I miss you sadly. Why did you not invite me to the wedding?"

"Wouldn't be proper," said Mr. Finch. "Not a Society wedding, after all. No, Avery Finch don't put on airs or pretend to be what he ain't. I'm a farmer, plain and simple."

Simone wept on Adele's shoulder. "What's this?" Adele said, drawing her back to the sofa. Seating them both, she said, "I hope you don't think I hold your wedding against you, for I don't."

"No, miss," Simone said, sniffing into a lace handkerchief. "Can you believe I would marry a . . . farmer?"

"I own I am a little surprised," Adele said, patting her former dresser on the shoulder.

"I confess I was surprised when she accepted me," Mr. Finch interjected. "Oh, thank you, my lord," he added as Windhaven offered a chair. "I believe I will sit."

"Cupid pays no heed to such things

when he launches his arrow," Windhaven said, looking fondly upon Adele as he poured out two glasses of Madeira.

"Well, he ought to pay attention," Mr. Finch said sadly. Taking the glass the viscount held out to him, he said, "Didn't think when we tied the knot that we might not suit, but there it is."

"No, don't say so," Adele said, clasping Simone's hands. "Your farewell note was full of his kindness and your hopes for the future."

"He is kindness itself, all consideration . . ." Simone allowed. "But . . ."

"What can have marred your happiness so soon?"

"Pigs, Miss," Mr. Finch said. "I raise 'em."

"And they are so . . . *malodorant,* so *malsain.*"

"They do smell," Mr. Finch said. "But they ain't unhealthy, muh dearest."

"I have heard that swine are no dirtier than cattle," Adele said. "That they actually prefer clean pens."

"Well, it is the truth," Mr. Finch said. "Only you can't keep them in a grass pasture like sheep, miss, for they root up the plants, and they roll in the mud for protection from the sun and stinging insects."

"It is so inelegant," Simone sighed tragically.

"Dy, I am sure you would like to show Mr. Finch your cattle," Adele said, looking at him in hopes he would pick up on her hint that she would like a few moments alone with her maid.

"Yes," he said quickly. Coming to his feet, he said, "I have a fine stable, Mr. Finch," he said.

"Well, I'm not a horseman," Mr. Finch said, "But I'll come with you. Like to light up my pipe."

Simone shuddered at his declaration. Adele patted her soothingly, until the gentlemen took their leave, then said, "What has happened to you?"

"I am *tres miserable*," Simone sighed.

"Well, of course you are, if you married a pig farmer you do not love," Adele said firmly.

"But I *do* love him," Simone protested.

"Then you did not marry him?"

"*Non,* we did marry," Simone said. "By special license, we married at St. Michaels."

"I am confused," Adele said, passing a hand over her brow to clear her thoughts. "You married the man you love, and you are miserable? Does he beat you?"

"*Non,*" Simone confessed. "He treats me like a queen."

Staring incredulously at her maid, Adele demanded, "Then what is the problem?"

"Is it not plain as the nose on Mr. Finch's face?" Simone sniffed. "When he carried me over the threshold of his house, and I smelled the pigs, I knew I had mistaken my feelings. I cannot love a man who lives with pigs."

"He keeps pigs in his house?" Adele said, imagining the animals tearing up carpets and draperies.

"Non, just the babies," Simone replied. "The ones too weak to nurse. They are so dear, but they smell, too."

Adele wanted to shake her former maid, but restrained herself from doing violence to the girl. Breathing deeply to calm herself, she asked, "Does Mr. Finch live in a hovel?"

"Non," said Simone. "His 'ouse is every bit as nice as yours, except for the pigs in the kitchen."

"Simone," Adele said, "Will you listen to yourself? What does it say about you that you cannot love a man who lives with piglets who stay in the kitchen until they are old enough to survive in the pen? He raises the animals, to sell, to support his family—to support you in a grand style. Why did you not ask him what his circumstances were before you married him?"

"Non, how could I? I am French, and finances are not *romantique*," explained Simone. "I thought he was a *gentleman* farmer—a landowner who rode his fields while peasants did the work."

"Meaning an aristocrat," Adele sighed. Crossing her arms to keep her temper in check, she stared daggers at her maid. "I knew you aspired to greater things, but did not believe you could be such a snob. Mr. Finch is a good man, an honest man, and he loves you enough to give you up. But if you love him, you would be miserable without him."

"But the pigs," wailed Simone. Wringing the fabric of her made over gown, she cried, "What will people think?"

"They will think you are a good wife to take care of your husband and his livestock," Adele said sternly. "But if you abandon him and break his heart, they will think you are no better than you ought to be. And you will deserve to be miserable."

"*Non*," Simone sniffed. "I am a good girl, have always done my work, have I not given satisfaction?" Since Adele did not answer, Simone went on. "But I grew up on a farm in Provence, it was the meanest sort of existence. That is why I became a lady's dresser, so I would never have to live on another farm."

"It seems God has made other plans for you," Adele said in an attempt to lighten Simone's attitude.

"He is laughing in my face," Simone said.

"Very well, if that is what you wish to think, but how much better to believe He is laughing with you. Think, Simone," Adele pulled her onto the sofa. "You worked every bit as hard as my dresser. You were up early, mending or pressing my clothes, and were still up when I returned from a ball to undress me and put me to bed. You burned your fingers on hot irons, and curling irons, and pricked them with pins and needles."

"But that was genteel work," Simone maintained. "I lived in an elegant house, travelled frequently, and my nose was not offended by filthy animal smells."

Out of patience with Simone's foolish arguments, Adele sprang to her feet and began to pace. "Perhaps Mr. Finch would be better off without you."

"Then you will take me back?" Simone asked, folding her hands prayerfully.

Stopping before her, Adele said, "I will not take you back. It gives me pain to say it, but you are a selfish, stupid girl."

Tears slid down Simone's cheeks. "I know, miss. And I am ashamed. I love Mr.

Finch, but to go back to his farm is the end of my dreams."

"My dear, don't throw your love away for the sake of a foolish, unattainable dream," Adele said. "If you come back to the city, you might find someone willing to support you in the first style of elegance, take you to the Opera, drive with you in the Park."

"That is what I want," Simone said naively.

"No it is not," Adele said. "For the only way you could command such a life is if you become a nobleman's mistress."

Simone gazed at the floor, saying, "That would bring disgrace on Mr. Finch."

"He would live it down," Adele said, as if reputation was of no importance. "And pigs care nothing for consequence as long as they are fed."

"But his customers do," Simone said, for the first time sounding as if she was actually concerned about her behavior affecting others. "In Southam, Mr. Finch is highly regarded as a businessman and a stockman. It would ruin him."

"So," Adele shrugged. "You must decide which path you wish to travel. A life of gaiety in London as some gentleman's depraved darling, or a quiet life in Southam as a cherished, respected wife."

Sighing, Simone said, "I think I have already made my choice."

"That is too bad," Adele said. "You know what you have in hand with Mr. Finch. Why go chasing after birds in a bush?"

If Windhaven's grooms were surprised that he drove himself to the mews and brought a guest with him, they revealed no sign. Rather they went about their business with the confidence that their employer would find everything in its place and his cattle groomed and fed to his satisfaction.

After delivering a satisfying tour of the stables and hearing dutiful appreciation of his stock, Windhaven returned to the brick yard where Mr. Finch could light his pipe and blow a cloud. They sat on a bench that caught the late afternoon sunlight and enjoyed a companionable silence until Mr. Finch had satisfied his initial craving for the smoke. Then, settling the pipe between his teeth, Mr. Finch regarded his host and said, "I thought I was the right sort of man for Simone. She grew up on a farm, did you know?"

"No, I did not," Windhaven said, leaning against the stable wall. Stretching out his legs, he crossed his arms and thoughtfully considered the toes of his hessians.

"She was perfect for me," said Mr. Finch. "Not afraid of hard work, and elegant to boot. Who could fail to love her?"

"Not you," Windhaven said diplomatically.

"Fell in love with her on first sight, a month ago. Didn't think I stood a chance with her, she being so elegant, genteel and refined, and me . . . well a pig farmer ain't any of those things."

"I think you have finer qualities than you allow yourself," Windhaven said. "My coachman said you are known in your county as an honest, upstanding man."

Mr. Finch did not reply to the encomium, but puffed on his pipe to conceal a blush that betrayed his modesty.

"So, unaccountably Miss Simone fell in love with you," Windhaven mused. "And is having second thoughts because of the pigs."

"She is so nice," Mr. Finch allowed.

"If you say so." Windhaven stroked his jaw to discipline the urge to say more.

Drawing again on his pipe, Mr. Finch released a stream of fragrant smoke and watched it dissipate in the breeze. "I told her I would support her in town, but I cannot like her being here without me."

"Will you sell your farm to live in town then?" Windhaven asked.

"No sir." Mr. Finch slapped his thigh. "Pigs is my living. Were I to move to the city, I'd have nothing to do."

"Then you would be a gentleman," Windhaven suggested. "You could invest your funds, and enjoy the fruits of your labor."

"Simone would like that. But what kind of gentleman would I make, my lord? A miserable one, that's what. Don't know how to do nothing. Don't know the right people. Don't like gaming. Can't ride; don't shoot, except varmints. I'd be a laughingstock."

"But you enjoyed your visit to London," said the viscount.

"That's different. One cannot always be living in a hotel and seeing the sights."

"No. It does get tiresome."

"And I was paying court. That's not like real life, where the pigs must be fed and the pens mucked out."

"Real life can be messy," Windhaven allowed. "But surely, your wife understands that life is not all champagne and roses."

"Does she?" Mr. Finch wondered. He clenched the mouthpiece of his pipe between his teeth and drew a thoughtful breath. "In truth, she wishes it was. Thinks that's the way a lady must live."

"Romantic foolishness," Windhaven said. "Sounds like my ward. Trouble is, they've been too sheltered, and are gudgeons. Easy marks for rogues."

"True," said Mr. Finch. His pipe having gone out, he tapped the blackened tobacco out of the bowl and began to scrape the inside with a penknife. "I screwed my courage to the sticking place when a gent I knew for a Captain Sharp made advances on Simone. He'd have chewed her up and spit her out, and her never the wiser until it was too late."

"Your wife is fortunate to have you as her champion, sir."

"Thank you. But the reality of my country life has revealed me a bumpkin with manure on his boots."

"Well, I suppose you could save your wife anew every few weeks."

"I'd do it gladly every day, if I could," Mr. Finch said. "But there is a scarcity of rogues in Southam."

"In other words, you'd be tilting at windmills." Windhaven grinned as Mr. Finch nodded thoughtfully.

"I am not cut out to play knight errant," he said, scratching his jaw. "Rather not see my lady acting the part of a damsel in distress."

"You're a practical sort," Windhaven said. "And Mrs. Finch is of a romantic turn."

Mr. Finch nodded glumly. "Two more

unlike individuals the Good Lord never created."

Clapping him sympathetically on the back, Windhaven came to his feet. "Sounds desperate. What do you plan to do?"

"Only one thing *to* do," said the farmer, following Windhaven towards his vehicle. "Go back and have an end to it." Tucking his cold pipe within his vest pocket, he mounted into the curricle and rode silently back to Number Thirty Green Street.

Upon arriving at their destination, Windhaven let Mr. Finch into the library, believing he could better deal with his bride in the masculine setting, then dispatched a footman to fetch Mrs. Finch from the gold salon.

Without regard to consequence or courtesy, Mr. Finch lowered himself into an armchair. Leaning his chin on a ham-shaped fist, he continued his brooding silence.

A few moments passed with only the slow ticking of the grandfather clock to break the quiet. Rather than distract his companion with inconsequential chitchat, Windhaven took a turn about the room before settling in a chair near a window where he could peruse the Times. But aside from reports of the impending marriage between Princess Charlotte and her prince charming, Prince Leopold of Saxe-

Coburg-Saalfeld, the news was not good. Rising unemployment, Parliament's continued failure to enact pensions for War veterans, while establishing higher taxes to pay for the Regent's appalling extravagance, bread lines, rumors of riots in the Midlands. It all made him wonder how a man could fall in love, as if nothing else mattered in the world.

But when Simone came into the library, Windhaven ceased to wonder at it, for Mr. Finch came to his feet in an explosion of boyish energy that gave him the appearance of a knight rising to do battle for his lady. Glancing towards the viscount as if suddenly mindful of convention, he halted his headlong rush halfway across the room. Mrs. Finch gave no heed to the third party in the room, but ran into her husband's arms and burst into a flurry of apologetic tears. *"A'h mon* Avery," she sighed, stroking his vest. *"Pardones moi,* I have been so stupid. Will you take me 'ome now?"

"Whatever you like, my little bird," said Mr. Finch adoringly.

Sensing himself to be superfluous to the rapprochement, Windhaven let himself out of the library and returned to the gold salon and Adele. As he entered, she looked up from the embroidery she was considering in her lap. Smiling, she held out her hand and said, "I hope we may celebrate their happy ending."

Windhaven nodded as he strode to her side. Taking her fingers and drawing her to her feet, he said, "It seems more than likely." Then hearing the thump of a trunk being carried downstairs, he grinned wider. "And Priscilla is going at last."

"That will make you happy," Adele said.

"Only if it means we may now set the date for *our* happy beginning," Windhaven said, raising her fingers to kiss them before he drew her into a commanding embrace. "The sooner the better, I might add," he said, bestowing a reverent kiss on her lips.

Melting against him, Adele could only agree with his impatience. Her heart pounding against her ribs, she gave herself up to his loving. Her arms slipped around his shoulders to bring him nearer, to mold them into one being.

The flames of passion seemed to ignite in one breath. She felt him come alive as he pressed hot kisses on her mouth, his tongue dancing with hers in a feverish waltz that left her dizzy and anxious for more intimacies.

Of a sudden, he broke off the kiss. Cupping hands along either side of her face he gazed at her for what seemed like an eternity. She wondered whether she had repulsed him with her impatience and asked him so.

He chuckled low in his throat, shaking his head as he said, "No, my love. I am glad you like my kisses."

She stroked a fond hand over his lapel and smiled up at him. "I do like them; why did you stop?"

He dragged a long breath and pressed one lingering kiss on her parted lips. "This," he said, rubbing his thumb over them as if memorizing their soft, yielding nature, "is dangerous behavior for an engaged couple."

"I don't think you're dangerous," she said, smiling an enticement.

"Obviously," he said, grinning lasciviously, "you think me of very noble character. But you are wrong, my dear. You drive me to distraction. I want to kiss you again and often."

"Is that all?" she asked, pouting.

"No, that is not all," he vowed, soothing a hand over her curves. "Only good manners prevent me from telling you how I want to love you." He nuzzled her throat until she giggled and squirmed in his arms. Laughing in delight at her sensitivity, he said, "Perhaps I shall tell your household instead."

Giggling breathlessly, she shook her

head, saying, "No, Dy, pray do not shock them."

"I do not intend to shock anyone, my dear," he said, releasing her, yet keeping a gentle grip on her wrist. "They will want to wish us happy." Lowering his voice, he added in husky tones, "And I want to offer my own compliments."

Placing her on the sofa, he tugged hard on the bell pull so that the silken cord broke loose in his hand. "I beg your pardon," he said foolishly. "Well, a man can be forgiven a little enthusiasm, can't he?"

"Yes, Dy," Adele giggled.

At the clamor of the bells belowstairs, Mrs. Murphy came running. Adele heard her hastily worded command to the kitchen maid to fetch the chambermaids. Alerted by the flurry of activity in the house, Miss Willoughby scurried in on her heels, her lace cap askew betraying the nap she had been indulging. Even Priscilla came to see what was the matter.

When the household and Mr. and Mrs. Finch assembled in the salon, Windhaven moved behind his blushing *fiancée* and placed a tender hand upon her shoulder. Adele gazed upward and bestowed a hesitant, but adoring smile upon him. "Miss Fonteyne and I would like to announce," he said, returning Adele's wondering stare as he continued, "that we are to marry."

The respectful silence erupted in loud congratulations as the staff descended joyously upon their employer. "Dear Adele," cried Elvira, hugging her, "I knew, didn't I? How wonderful. Even when you had almost given up hope. I wish you will both be very happy."

Embracing her cousin, Adele replied, "Thank you cousin, and I hope you know you will always have a home with us."

"Oh, I wanted to speak to you about that," Priscilla said. "Grandfather so enjoys Miss Willoughby's company, I was hoping she might come live with me."

A becoming blush stole over Elvira's features as she said, "Oh, I couldn't, that is, I mustn't abandon—"

"Please convince her, Miss Fonteyne," Priscilla said, kneeling at her side. "I need her to teach me how to go on. But you," glancing between Adele and the viscount, "have each other."

"That is true," Elvira said. "I would forever be in your way, interrupting—"

"You have convinced me," Windhaven laughed. "Pray excuse your cousin, Adele, so we may have *some* privacy."

"Yes, very well, but you are not to think you are being banished," Adele said, urgently pressing her cousin's hand. "You are only on loan to Priscilla and her grandfather."

"Unless he has other plans," Priscilla said, winking at Elvira. "Oh, but don't fear, I shall act as your chaperone. You will be perfectly safe."

Giggling, Elvira said she doubted she would need a chaperone, but would allow herself to be guided by Lord Chaseldon's preference, when the gentleman himself strode into the salon.

"I suspected something was up, when I had to let myself in," he grinned. "What is it? A robbery?"

Bounding to her feet, Priscilla drew him into the family gathering. "No, Grandfather; Lord Windhaven and Miss Fonteyne are engaged."

"Of course they are," said Lord Chaseldon, petting her cheek. "And they will not want us underfoot any longer. Are you coming with us, Miss Willoughby?"

Elvira fluttered towards him, excusing herself profusely. "I could not abandon my cousin now," she said. "She will need me to—"

Laughing, Lord Chaseldon said, "Hush, Elvira. Your cousin needs you to go with Priscilla now. And I want you to come with us. I have missed a lady's conversation all these years."

"Oh, well, if you do not object," Elvira demurred, blushing again. "I will come with you . . . Priscilla."

Laughing to see her cousin so happily confused, Adele turned to gaze upon Windhaven. "There, my chaperone is going. We will need to marry quickly."

Mrs. Murphy wiped glad tears with her apron and commanded in grave tones, "No fear of that, miss. You take care of my lady, sir; or have me to contend with."

"Lord, what a threat," Dy said. Laughing, he offered the housekeeper a good natured hug. "I promise, I shall be good to *our* lady. Who wants to force down burned roasts and lumpy porridge?"

"Obviously you have been; you're much too thin," said Mrs. Murphy in a knowing manner. "But a happy marriage and a good cook will change you for the better."

Thanking everyone for their good wishes, Dy ordered a round of champagne. All drank a toast, offered by Mr. Finch with his arm about his bride, that the happy couple would live long and love forever, after which Windhaven dismissed everyone to attend their various duties. Wishing them well, Lord Chaseldon ushered his granddaughter and Elvira towards the door behind the happy Finches. Mumbling blissfully about the best of happy endings, Elvira closed the door on the couple.

As soon as they had gone, Windhaven took Adele's hand and knelt before her. Capturing her gaze in his steady one, he said, "Adele, I love you with all my heart, and have wanted to give you this for the longest time." Reaching within his vest pocket, he withdrew a small velvet box.

Taking it from him in shaking fingers, Adele opened it and removed the gold ring which rested therein. A diamond setting sparkled in the soft lamplight. "It's lovely," she said, holding it to the light.

Settling it on her finger, Windhaven looked reassuringly upon her as he said, "I know diamonds are not fashionable just now, but the stone has been in my family for generations. I wanted to give you a visible sign that my love will last forever."

Burying her face in the curve of his shoulder, Adele whispered, "Oh, Dy, it's perfect. I love you."

"Do you?" he asked, tucking a finger beneath her chin to lift her face so that her watery gaze met his. Unable to break the gaze, she nodded. His grin widened boyishly before he kissed her, tenderly, thoroughly and continuously. When she was completely persuaded of his devotion, he said, "Tell me again."

Always before, Adele had been compelled by the constraints of Society to hide her feelings beneath a veneer of haughty reserve. She was almost struck dumb by the astounding realization that she was now free to wear her feelings for Dy on her sleeve. Clinging to him, she gazed upon him like the woman in love that she was.

"I do love you," she said, each word reverberating from her heart to his. "I love you so much I want the whole world to know. Society will not credit it of us, but I still want to elope."

He kissed her once more. And she could not help bursting into delighted laughter when a teasing smile lighting his beloved golden features, he said, "But my dear; that is so unfashionable."

ELEGANT LOVE STILL FLOURISHES —
Wrap yourself in a Zebra Regency Romance.

A MATCHMAKER'S MATCH   (3783, $3.50/$4.50)
by Nina Porter
To save herself from a loveless marriage, Lady Psyche Veringham pretends to be a bluestocking. Resigned to spinsterhood at twenty-three, Psyche sets her keen mind to snaring a husband for her young charge, Amanda. She sets her cap for long-time bachelor, Justin St. James. This man of the world has had his fill of frothy-headed debutantes and turns the tables on Psyche. Can a bluestocking and a man about town find true love?

FIRES IN THE SNOW   (3809, $3.99/$4.99)
by Janis Laden
Because of an unhappy occurrence, Diana Ruskin knew that a secure marriage was not in her future. She was content to assist her physician father and follow in his footsteps . . . until now. After meeting Adam, Duke of Marchmaine, Diana's precise world is shattered. She would simply have to avoid the temptation of his gentle touch and stunning physique — and by doing so break her own heart!

FIRST SEASON   (3810, $3.50/$4.50)
by Anne Baldwin
When country heiress Laetitia Biddle arrives in London for the Season, she harbors dreams of triumph and applause. Instead, she becomes the laughingstock of drawing rooms and ballrooms, alike. This headstrong miss blames the rakish Lord Wakeford for her miserable debut, and she vows to rise above her many faux pas. Vowing to become an Original, Letty proves that she's more than a match for this eligible, seasoned Lord.

AN UNCOMMON INTRIGUE   (3701, $3.99/$4.99)
by Georgina Devon
Miss Mary Elizabeth Sinclair was rather startled when the British Home Office employed her as a spy. Posing as "Tasha," an exotic fortune-teller, she expected to encounter unforeseen dangers. However, nothing could have prepared her for Lord Eric Stewart, her dashing and infuriating partner. Giving her heart to this haughty rogue would be the most reckless hazard of all.

A MADDENING MINX   (3702, $3.50/$4.50)
by Mary Kingsley
After a curricle accident, Miss Sarah Chadwick is literally thrust into the arms of Philip Thornton. While other women shy away from Thornton's eyepatch and aloof exterior, Sarah finds herself drawn to discover why this man is physically and emotionally scarred.

Available wherever paperbacks are sold, or order direct from the Publisher. Send cover price plus 50¢ per copy for mailing and handling to Penguin USA, P.O. Box 999, c/o Dept. 17109, Bergenfield, NJ 07621. Residents of New York and Tennessee must include sales tax. DO NOT SEND CASH.